PORTLAND NOIR

PORTLAND NOIR

EDITED BY KEVIN SAMPSELL

AKASHIC BOOKS
NEW YORK

Published by Akashic Books
©2009 Akashic Books

Series concept by Tim McLoughlin and Johnny Temple
Portland map by Sohrab Habibion

ISBN-13: 978-1-933354-79-8
Library of Congress Control Number: 2008937354

First printing

Akashic Books
PO Box 1456
New York, NY 10009
info@akashicbooks.com
www.akashicbooks.com

Also in the Akashic Noir Series:

Forthcoming:

St. Johns

Willamette River

Highway 30

Montgomery
Park

Pearl
District

Legacy Good
Samaritan Hospital

Powell's
City of Books

Old To

5

26

5

PORTLAND

urnside
atepark

Sandy
Boulevard

84

S.E. 82nd
Avenue

S.E. 28th
Avenue

Mount
Tabor

205

Seven
Corners

Clinton

Powell
Boulevard

Oaks
Bottom

TABLE OF CONTENTS

PART III: DESOLATION CITY

INTRODUCTION
Crime and Unrest in Utopia

I wonder how people think of Portland from the outside. Is it a hippie haven where everyone reads Ken Kesey and hangs out at open mike night? Is it the gray, grungy, junkie-riddled streets of early Gus Van Sant movies? A cheap, trendy town full of myopic record labels and zinesters? Sex worker paradise? Bookstore heaven? A place where New Yorkers come to feel important and/or relaxed? Some wet old logging town that somehow became "one of the best cities in America"?

Yeah, it's all that and a fancy coffee spilled on your Gore-Tex jacket (the same one you soiled with microbrew last night).

People who live in Portland love being here, despite its imperfections. We tend to love our mayors (even the currently scandalous Sam Adams) despite the sketchy police force, and we cherish the great public transportation even when every other neighborhood is being torn up for renovation. The restaurants are amazing and the music scene seems like it's in a perpetual heyday. If Portland was Seattle's kid nephew in the past, these days it's more like Seattle is our creepy old uncle. (Sorry, I didn't mean to get off track.)

I moved here in summer of 1992. I grew up in Eastern Washington and lived in a few places before this (even Seattle). I'm not ashamed to admit that I moved here partly because of Powell's, the giant bookstore, where I eventually started working. I wanted to live in a city that valued reading and geeked out on books.

I quickly found out that Portland is a city of stories and uncertain history. I've decided that the shady history lessons ("people were kidnapped in the Shanghai Tunnels"), perverse sightseeing tours ("this is where Elliott Smith first shot up"), and cultish rituals ("you can get married at the twenty-four-hour Church of Elvis") that make up the town's mythology are more interesting if you don't take them too seriously. Local fiction writers like Katherine Dunn and Chuck Palahniuk have obviously been inspired by this place's blurry yin and yang as well.

Settled in 1843 and named by a coin flip (we were almost named Boston), Portland had troubles from the start. The first sheriff, William Johnson, was busted for selling "ardent spirits." He had been "reduced by an evil heart," said the indictment. The first couple of decades were probably pretty rough, what with the constant flooding and muddy streets making all the citizens cranky. In the 1870s, a couple of laws were created in an attempt to tame this wild west. You couldn't fire a pistol downtown and the speed limit for your carriage was six miles per hour.

Later, in the 1940s and '50s, the city practically thrived on criminal activity. Speakeasies, brothels, and gambling dens popped up across the downtown area. The police, the district attorney, and local Teamsters were all in bed with local vice pushers. Portland became known as quite the decadent town, even prompting Bobby Kennedy to wrangle up its main bad guys for a televised Racketeering Committee meeting in 1957. One senator said at the hearings, "If I lived there, I would suggest they pull the flags down to half-mast in public shame."

A lot of these places of "shame" remain standing, and while many are occupied now by salons and offices, some of them are probably still home to gambling and stripping. (Portland does, after all, have more strip clubs per capita than any other city in America—and yep, they take it *all* off here.)

Our history of bad behavior just doesn't go away.

In putting together this collection, I was thrilled to see the contributors capture fascinating details from the various neighborhoods and settings, including the aforementioned Shanghai Tunnels and familiar locales on Burnside Avenue and in the posh Northwest part of town. We also got the depressing warehouse area that borders Highway 30 and the old Americana vibe of St. Johns. On the other side of the Willamette River, you get wild skateboarders, anarchists, lesbian damsels in distress, and a junkie breaking into a house in the Mount Tabor neighborhood. (Note to outsiders: Mount Tabor is our very own volcano!) And because Portland is essentially a small city, you may notice some intentional déjà vu, some bleeding together of stories and places. Like pieces of a puzzle that snap together to show a colorful map.

When I first moved here, I thought the statue of that guy in Pioneer Courthouse Square, the bronze man with the umbrella (on the cover of this book), had a panicked look about him. Like he was hailing a cab to get the heck out of here. But now I see his dapper suit, his forward-moving pose, and his confident hand gesture as a comforting symbol of strength.

Portland continues to update its own version of a contemporary utopian society as more and more people flock here. But even in utopia, crime and unrest are always bubbling right under the surface.

Kevin Sampsell
Portland, OR
March 2009

PART I

Bloodlines

THE CLOWN AND BARD

BY KAREN KARBO

S.E. Twenty-Eighth Avenue

Charlotte is sprawled on the bathroom floor of my apartment on Southeast Ankeny, the one I rented because I thought she'd like it. Rundown but arty, with forced-air heat and bad plumbing. High ceilings, creaking stairs, walls plastered in thick, sharp stucco. The lobby smells like mold and cantaloupe two days past its prime. The couple downstairs has a pirate flag tacked over their front window, and the landlord is twenty-three and walks around her apartment in a red thong and T-shirt. The building is shaped like a V, so I can easily see into her windows. She has a small wrought-iron balcony where she grows orange flowers in green plastic pots.

Since Charlotte deceived me with the film critic, I've done pretty much whatever I've wanted to do. Free rein is what I've got. She bombed the country and I'm just looting the shops. She would say I mixed my metaphors right there. That's what being married to Charlotte got me. Now I know about mixed metaphors, and how it really is possible to feel someone pull your heart straight out of your chest like in *Indiana Jones and the Temple of Doom*, then stomp on it.

I drop the toilet lid—*bang!*—and sit down. It's possible Charlotte's not dead. This is just the sort of thing she would do to make me feel bad. Like all chicks, she's a drama queen. I stare down at her head, angled like she's trying to lay her ear on her shoulder. Blood trickles out of one perfectly round nostril. There's no blood coming out of her ears that I can see. Most likely she's just conked out.

Charlotte thought she had the right to have an affair with the film critic because I occasionally found myself associating with Lorna, my ex-wife, the mother of my son. Once in a blue moon, after I'd taken Ray Jr. to the zoo or Malibu Grand Prix, I'd return him to Lorna's apartment and we'd knock one out for old time's sake. It was like looking through a photo album. Associating with someone after you've been married is not the same as meeting a film critic at the bar in Esparza's, where you share a plastic wooden bowl of chips and hot sauce and listen to Patsy Cline and comment on the stuffed armadillos hanging on the ceiling and then share an order of ostrich tacos, all the while talking arty crap.

The film critic has more hair than I do.

Once, when Charlotte refused to show me respect by answering whether she was in love with the film critic, I was forced to shove her into a bookcase, so she knew we weren't just having one of our usual arguments. I meant business.

I said, "This thing with the film critic is a dalliance, right? There's nothing to it, right? Answer me. Yes or no."

She said, "He's actually more of a film *reviewer*."

She bruised her back on the edge of the shelf. It wasn't that bad. What's a little bruise? She's hardy. Skis and ride horses and takes kick-boxing classes. Most of the top row of books rained down upon her head and neck. They were only paperbacks. Still, she bitched to anyone who would listen, her herd of sympathetic friends, her therapist, her divorce lawyer, and of course the ostrich taco–loving film critic. Charlotte wouldn't touch an ostrich taco when she was with me. Now it's the new white meat.

Now Charlotte's lying on my bathroom floor, wedged between the hot water pipe and the toilet. Is it laying or lying? Charlotte would know. She has a master's degree and a daily subscription to the *New York Times*. The hot water pipe serves the whole building, and why it goes through my apartment I don't know. At night it's hot enough to leave a blister. Charlotte hit it on the way down, which caused her to twist her body, which caused her to lose her balance and hit her head on the edge of the tub. I stare at her head. Her curly hair is coming out of its scrunchie. She doesn't look like she's breathing. I stare at her tits. I wonder if she still wears an underwire.

It's possible she's holding her breath just to piss me off, to punish me for going to Prague.

She acted like I planned this. That's what Charlotte never *got*. I'm a simple guy. I take life as it comes. When I mentioned going to Prague I was just talking, just filling the air with my words. She should know how it is. She's fucking a film critic.

It was the last week in August. The leaves hung exhausted on the trees. I was still living over on Northeast Sandy. We met for dinner at the Kennedy School. The film critic was at the Sundance Film Festival. I told her the next time we met he had to be in town, for her to prove to me there was still hope for us.

"I don't think there's any real hope for us," she said.

"Then why are you here?" I asked.

"I wonder that myself," she said. She ordered a gin and tonic.

"That's what he drinks, gin and tonic? *Tanqueray* and tonic?"

"Sometimes in the summer I've been known to order a gin and tonic," she said. "Jesus."

She lied. She was a liar.

She used to love me. Now she picked fights. Like about the gin and tonic. I buttered a piece of bread and put it in front of her. She folded her arms and looked out the window at the parking lot. A guy wearing a red plaid skirt pushed a shopping cart full of empty bottles. I could tell she was itching to get out of there. The back of my neck got hot, the way it did when she was pissing me off.

Suddenly, I said I had something to tell her. She looked back at me, but it was polite. She was so polite. I'd been fired from the pest control company out on Foster Road and was now working at a place that made clamps, couplings, screws, and knobs. They also made a really nice brass drawer pull. The week before, in the break room, one of the machinists was talking about quitting and moving to Prague, and then the HR chick, who'd never looked at this guy once, was practically in his lap. She said she'd always wanted to go to Prague.

"I'm going to Prague," I said.

"Prague? What's in Prague?"

"It's something I've always wanted to do."

"You have?" Her green eyes were on me. She leaned forward on her pale forearms. I could smell her grapefruity perfume, something called Happy I'd given her one Christmas. This was where she should have said, *Ray, you are so full of shit*. This is where her master's degree failed her, where all her books and snooty left-wing websites let her down.

Did I say she worked in R&D at Intel, designing stuff she wasn't allowed to talk about? Something to do with microchips and biology. When I met her I didn't know what R&D was. She used words like *ebullient* just to make me feel stupid. Who was the stupid one now? Yeah, I'm off to Prague. The only foreign place I'd ever been before was Ensenada.

"Is this work-related? Like when they sent you to Chely-abinsk?"

"Sure," I said. "A business trip."

I'd forgotten I told Charlotte I'd done a business trip to Chelyabinsk.

Last year Donnie, a guy at the knob company, had found a terrific and extremely hot Russian wife on the Internet. Her name was Olga but she liked to be called Bootsie. She was a great gal. Once Donnie surprised Tootsie with a subscription to *Self* and she fell to her knees and sobbed with gratitude. She wrapped her hands around his heels and laid her forehead on his shoes. She then gave him the best blowjob he'd ever had, after which she went into the kitchen and whipped up a roast.

Donnie had given me the name of the website where he got his wife and I thought, *Why not?* Charlotte didn't love me anymore. She was off drinking gin and tonics with the film critic. So one night after work, after I'd had a few beers, I typed in Charlotte's height, weight, hair, and eye color, and out came Agnessa Fedoseeva.

She was studying to be something called an esthetician, but was hoping to find a big strong man she could love and kiss with enthusiasm. She was anxious to inquire if I was a big strong man. She was curious how many flat-screen TVs I had. She sent me a videotape of herself dressed in a red, white, and blue teddy and high heels, dancing around her living room with a sparkler sizzling in each hand.

I put the trip to Chelyabinsk on a credit card, and told Charlotte I was being sent there by the knob company, to set up a new factory.

"But why are they sending *you?*" Charlotte had wanted to know. "I think it's great. Really exciting, and really good for you. You need to have the dust of the world on your feet. But you don't speak Russian."

"They're impressed with my work ethic."

"You do work hard," said Charlotte. "When you have a job."

I'm tired of staring at Charlotte laying or lying on the bathroom floor, playing passed out, milking the situation, doing her best to make me look like the bad guy.

I walk back down the long hallway to the kitchen. I sit in the dark at my kitchen table. Outside, the streetlights shine on the snow, filling my front rooms with that weird aquarium light. I look out the window at the Laurelhurst Theater marquee. They're showing *Alien* and *Meatballs*. Charlotte would think that was funny. Agnessa spoke no English, but she'd laugh anyway.

Charlotte will come out of the bathroom eventually. For being so smart, she is so predictable. That's how she works. If I stand over her and wonder whether she's dead, she'll act dead on purpose, just to piss me off. But if I turn my back on her, leave the room, she'll come marching out and wonder what's going on.

The back of my neck feels hot. None of this would have happened if she had let the Prague business go. It was just something I'd said to get her attention. Then I found myself saying I was moving in September, just after Labor Day, and would be there for at least six months.

"Six months?" she said, eyes big.

"Maybe a year."

I thought she'd forget about it. She'd go home to the film critic and they'd open a bottle of merlot and discuss the early films of Martin Scorsese.

Charlotte started e-mailing me. Where would I be living in Prague? Did I know Prague was settled in the fourth century? Prague Castle was the largest castle in the world. There was also an entire wall of graffiti dedicated to John Lennon. I should definitely check out the museum of the Heydrich assassination. She sent me links to websites, and guidebooks she'd ordered on Amazon. She gave me books by Czechoslovakian writers. Who the fuck is Kafka? She signed the e-mails with *xo*.

Agnessa read romance novels. She loved stuffed animals. She was thirty-one and still lived with her mother, who needed new teeth and an operation. I'd sent her an international calling card and she rang me every evening. She confessed she had two other men who wanted to marry her, one who lived in Indiana and had four flat-screen TVs, and one who lived in Florida and had three flat-screen TVs. Did I know how dear I was to her, that she was still interested in me even though I only had one TV?

Charlotte and I started meeting on Wednesdays for coffee at a place that served stale pastries and had too many free newspapers. Every so often I'd take Ray Jr. out of school for the morning and bring him along, just to remind Charlotte what a good dad I could be. Being a good single dad is better than having a pit bull puppy when it comes to attracting women. I made Ray drink his orange juice and study his spelling words. Charlotte said she was really going to miss me.

One day I got her to go with me to Hawthorne to shop for presents to give to the family who would be putting me up in Prague, before I had my own apartment.

"Who exactly are we shopping for?" she asked. We nosed around a crowded shop that sold expensive journals, massage oil, and funny greeting cards. The rain had started. The shop smelled like wet dog and patchouli.

"There's a thirty-one-year-old living at home, a girl who loves stuffed animals."

"Is she . . ." Charlotte looked at me, narrowed one eye a little like she does. I could feel my pulse in my forehead. She was going to ask me if there was something going on with this girl, if somehow I was going to Prague to see her. It was all over her face. Behind her a woman was trying to get at the wire card rack. I just looked at her. *Go ahead, ask me.* I waited. ". . . mentally disabled or something?"

I thought of Agnessa and her living room sparkler dance.

"It's possible," I said.

Charlotte picked out a hand lotion that smelled like apple pie and a stuffed panda.

I sent them to Agnessa, who loved the gifts. I loved Agnessa, for being so easy to please. I spent entire paychecks sending her shampoo, socks, Levi's and one of those mesh bags girls stick their underwear in before it goes in the washing machine. I sent her some Happy too. Fuck Charlotte.

I gave notice on the apartment I was living in off Northeast Sandy. I told the landlady I was moving to Prague. Elaine was a chick with cats who worked in a bookstore and had a stack of books on Wicca beside her bed. She believed in the power of crystals and Match.com. I struck up an association with Elaine. It was an association of convenience. She was lonely. She liked helping me define just how evil Charlotte was, how slutty and duplicitous. Elaine volunteered to put a spell on Charlotte. I told her to stop; I wasn't looking for a commitment. When I told Elaine I was moving to Prague she smirked, "Prague, Minnesota?"

"Uh, no," I said.

"Where are you really going?"

"I got a new place on Southeast Ankeny, across from that yuppie wine bar."

"Noble Rot, where wine is a meal."

When Charlotte kicked me out she said I could take anything I wanted, so I did. The heavy stainless steel pots and pans we got as a wedding present. All the DVDs we'd watched together, and what the hell, the DVD player. The books she told people were her favorites. The flannel duvet cover with the roses. A black sweater that smelled of Happy, and a few pairs of her underpants, fished out of the dirty clothes hamper. Our wedding album, and from the freezer, the top layer of our wedding cake. It looked like a hat wrapped in waxed paper.

Elaine showed up on a Saturday afternoon to help me pack my stuff. She'd brought some empty boxes from the bookstore and started on the kitchen. The only things in the freezer were a few blue plastic ice cube trays, a pair of chilled beer glasses—a trick Charlotte taught me—and that damn frozen wedding cake. Elaine said I should toss it, didn't know why I was holding onto it. I said, "I'm a good guy, I got a sentimental streak a mile wide, so sue me."

Charlotte took me out for American food the day before I left. Before meeting her I had a sighting of Extreme the Clown's art car, parked near the Starbucks on Burnside. The art car looks like a Mayan temple on wheels with hundreds of heads sculpted into the sides and a pyramid-altar thing rising from the roof. It's well known that an art car sighting means good luck. I'm luckier than most people, but as I passed by I touched one of the open-mouthed heads on the trunk. The leaves on the maples were red and gold. I found myself wondering what the weather would be like in Prague, even though I wasn't going to Prague.

Charlotte took me to Esparza's. I'm sure she enjoyed the

irony, bringing her ex to the same restaurant where she betrayed him with another, but I was having my own private last laugh—my new place was just across the parking lot. I could see into my new kitchen on the second floor. I could see my box of pots and pans sitting on the kitchen table.

I could be in R&D too. I could have my own secret projects.

After we ordered margaritas she pulled out a red suede pouch. Her hands shook as she unsnapped it. She pulled out her engagement ring, the one we'd bought together, the one she'd paid for, technically, since at the time I was between jobs. I'd said anything less than a single karat was hardly worth the effort and she'd agreed, and there it was and she was giving it to me, saying she wanted me to have it, to take it to Prague, to keep it in a safe place, and to think of her.

"I'm just really proud of you, taking this big step. I'm sorry we didn't work out. I really am. But this is better. You're going to really see the world."

She cried. Her mascara ran. I made an old joke, about how she needed to get another brand of mascara, one that didn't run every time she cried. Every T-shirt I owned had a smudgy black stain on the shoulder. I could have definitely gotten some that night, but there was nowhere to take her. My flight was leaving in the morning, and I'd told her that I was sleeping on Elaine's fold-out couch. I liked to drop Elaine's name now and then, just to make sure she was paying attention.

A week passed, then two. I went to work at the knob factory, where my job was quality control. I sat on a tall stool in a room with no windows, making sure our wall brackets had the right amount of screw holes. At night I drank Czechvar beer and played World of Warcraft and kept an eye on the parking lot of Esparza's Tex-Mex to see if Charlotte and the film critic ever showed up.

I didn't tell Agnessa I'd moved to Prague, though I did give her my new address and phone number at Southeast Ankeny. Agnessa was getting impatient. Her other suitors were starting to tug at her heart ropes. She was running out of Happy.

One cold night the server crashed and I couldn't get back onto WoW, so I called up Agnessa and told her she should apply for a fiancée visa. What the hell. I'd spied Extremo the Clown's art car again that day, parked in the lot at Wild Oats. Lucky me, and lucky Agnessa. I figured at least I could get her to Portland. Get her out of Chelyabinsk, where her family thought nothing of eating moldy bread spread with rancid butter. I liked this idea, saving Agnessa from her difficult life. A fiancée visa lasted for ninety days. I figured then I could decide whether to ship her back or not.

"Oh, Ray!" she breathed. "Thank you, I love you, thank you."

"We'll get the fiancée visa and then let's give it a shot. Let's send the engagement up the flagpole and see who salutes. Let's take the idea of us out for a test drive."

"Ray? Ray—I—uh—I . . ." I could hear her moist gasps of confusion.

"We'll give it the ol' college try," I said.

Smoke and mirrors, smoke and mirrors. I admit I misled Agnessa, but she'd get over it. And I'm actually a good guy. To make things right I bought a black velvet box at Fred Meyer's, and sent her Charlotte's diamond, Federal Express. Agnessa called when she received the ring and wept. I should hope so. That ring cost Charlotte four grand. She sent me another sparkler video and some Russian chocolate. In the video, she showed off the ring and threw kisses into the camera.

* * *

Prague is eight hours ahead of Portland, or maybe it's nine. I e-mailed Charlotte at 1 a.m. so she would think I was writing to her first thing in the morning, when I arrived at the knob factory. The factory was in a suburb of Prague. I told her I had to take a bus to get there, along with the other workers. I even had a lunch pail, filled with sandwiches made with dark bread. In the evenings I strolled along the Charles Bridge. I saw the world famous astronomical clock (Wikipedia has a good picture) and discovered a great bar called the Clown and Bard, where the barmaid admired my tattoo and served me some dill soup, on the house.

Charlotte started writing, *Love,* C, at the bottom of her e-mails.

One rainy night after work I went to Holman's, around the corner from my apartment. The storm drains were clogged with soggy Cornflake-looking leaves. My Vans got soaked. I ordered a patty melt and a Bud Light. A woman a few tables over was wearing Happy. I smelled it over the cheap disinfectant and grilled onions. Ah hell. I used my calling card to call Charlotte from the pay phone.

She answered on the first ring. I told her I was calling from the Clown and Bard.

"Ray, are you all right?"

I loved that concern in her voice. I said I was fine, while making sure I didn't sound fine at all. I wanted her to think that maybe I'd had some food poisoning. Maybe a worker on the bus beat me up for being an American. Maybe I was dying of loneliness. Anything could happen in Prague.

"It's 3:30 in the morning. I thought you didn't have a phone in your flat."

"You were being missed," I said. A roar went up from the

bar. Monday Night Football on the TV. "I'm at the Clown and Bard. They're watching football. You know, soccer."

She didn't understand what I was doing at a bar at 3:30 a.m. I told her I couldn't sleep.

"So, what, you've just been out walking the streets?"

"I was hungry."

There was a long pause, as if she'd never heard anything so ridiculous in her life. I covered my mouth so I wouldn't laugh. Then it all went bad. It was the beginning of how I find myself at this moment, with her laying unconscious on my bathroom floor.

"Is it that woman?" she asked. "The one with the learning disability? Is that why you're out so late? You've been out with her?"

"What are you talking about?" What was she talking about?

"The one you sent the hand lotion to?"

I forgot I'd told her Agnessa lived in Prague.

The more I denied seeing Agnessa while I was in Prague, the more Charlotte believed I was lying. I said, "I haven't seen her. And anyway, we're non-touching friends." Charlotte went bat-shit crazy when I said that. It was true. I'm a good man. I don't lie unless I have to. When I was in Chelyabinsk, Agnessa let me hold her elbow when we crossed the street. Donnie said that's how these Russian women are. Until they receive a victory rock, there's no hope of any action.

"I haven't seen Ag in months," I said. "She's a friend. She reminds me of you. She's got that sense of humor, but not so cutting. And answer me this, why are Slavic women either as short as they are wide, or super models?"

"She's a super model?"

"It's usually the really old ones who are short and fat. The ladies who sweep the streets."

"Ray, just tell me. Is there anything going on with this woman or not?"

"Did you know they serve patty melts at the Clown and Bard? Bizarre, huh?"

Charlotte hung up on me. I paid for my half-eaten melt and walked home. If I left the lights off I could sit in the living room and drink a beer and watch my landlady paint her nails in her thong and T-shirt. Charlotte had given me an idea. As soon as Agnessa's fiancée visa came through I'd tell Charlotte my work in Prague was finished. I'd tell her I was coming home with my friend Agnessa, who wanted to start a new life in the States. Of course, she would stay with me until she found a place of her own. Charlotte would lose her mind. Maybe Agnessa and I could double date with Charlotte and the film critic. It would be fun.

My calls to Charlotte started going to voice mail, my e-mails went unanswered. My landlady got curtains. I took Ray Jr. to IMAX to see a movie about coral reefs. He vomited into my lap. I was counting on associating with Lorna a little, but she clapped her hand over her nose and told me to go home. There was a message on my voice mail from Agnessa, wondering whether I'd made her airplane reservations. Nothing from Charlotte after two full weeks.

I decided it was time to come home.

The forced-air heat comes on. Outside, big messy snowflakes blow out of the sky. From my window I can see across the snowy street into the Noble Rot, where wine is a meal. Once Charlotte stops playing possum and gets up off the bathroom floor I can take her right over there. Show there are no hard feelings. She thinks I am a vengeful type, controlling, but she has me all wrong.

Playing possum. I have to laugh. It is how we met, how she fell for me. I was still at the pest control company out on Foster Road. One spring morning she'd called up fairly hysterical. There was a dead possum in her tulips. A few of us were in the break room, shaking the snack machine to see if we could free a half-released bag of Doritos. The supervisor came in and thought we might want to draw straws. Charlotte lived in Lake Oswego, where the ladies tend to have nothing better to do than go to yoga, get their nails done, and flirt with the hired hands. Sometimes you can even get lucky.

Charlotte came to the door wearing baggy shorts and a University of Michigan T-shirt. Reading glasses on her head and a pen and sheaf of papers in one hand. Mint-green toenail polish. She held the backdoor open for me.

"I would have just tossed him in the trash but the garbage isn't until next Wednesday. That didn't seem very, I don't know, hygienic."

But when we got to the side yard where the tulips grew there were only a few flattened stalks, a petal or two strewn about.

"He was just here," she said, then whirled on her heel and startled me by punching me in the arm. She had a great loud laugh. "He was playing possum. Oh my God."

She offered me a beer for my trouble, and I told her that possums don't actually play dead, that they're so frightened they fall into a real coma. Then, after a few hours, they rouse themselves and go on their way. Charlotte thought that was fascinating. She made me sit down at her kitchen table and tell her more.

Not many women have ever looked at me that way.

Tonight she came over to my apartment uninvited. I'd sent her an e-mail two days ago telling her I was home from Prague, in case she cared. I didn't tell her where I live. I figured I'd let it slip next week, after Agnessa arrives from Chelyabinsk.

"Hello!" she said, stomping the snow off her red cowboy boots before coming right on in. She walked around my front room. Touched the DVDs stacked on top of the TV, picked up the empty Czechvar bottle on the desk beside the computer. Flipped through a stack of mail on the end table beside the couch.

"You settled right in here, didn't you?"

"It's good to see you," I said. It was good to see her. She wasn't wearing any perfume.

"I got your new address from Elaine," she said. "How's the jet lag?"

"Who?" I knew who. Elaine was the only person who was aware I'd moved to Southeast Ankeny.

"I had a dream about you last night." I didn't know where I was going with this, but chicks always liked to hear that you had a dream about them.

"I came to get my ring back," she said. She was in one of those moods. Fine.

"Why don't you sit down and I'll get it."

She pulled her hair out of its scrunchie and pulled it back up on top of her head. She didn't sit down.

I took my time. I walked down the long hallway to my bedroom. I sat on the bed in the dark. It occurred to me that Agnessa was going to need someplace to put her clothes. I didn't have a bureau, but instead used the top two shelves in the closet. I walked back down the hallway. Charlotte wasn't there. From the kitchen I could hear the freezer door open, then Charlotte's loud laugh. *Ha!*

I stood in the middle of my front room, stared at a

poster I'd taken from our old house, black-and-white, a young couple kissing on a Paris street. It had some name in French.

"This wasn't something I wanted to tell you over the phone, but one night someone broke into my flat in Prague and stole your ring," I called into the kitchen. I was glad not to have to look her in the eye. "They took my wallet too. And my passport."

She came back into the living room holding the frozen top layer of our wedding cake. "I can't believe this."

"It's our wedding cake," I said.

"Yeah, I know what it is. How is it you still have it?"

"You said I could take anything I wanted."

"What did you do with it for the two months you were in Prague?"

"I got a sentimental streak a mile wide, so sue me."

She started shaking her head. She shook her head and laughed. Laughing and crying, mascara running. "At first I thought Elaine was the nut job, but it's you! I didn't believe her when she said you didn't even go to Prague. It was impossible. No one is that crazy. She said if I didn't believe her to check the freezer."

"Elaine is a nut job," I said. "She thinks she's a witch."

"Stop, Ray, just stop."

"She wanted to put a spell on you but I wouldn't let her."

"You're out of your mind."

"The guys broke into my flat when I was out one night with Agnessa," I said. "You wanted the truth and this is the truth. I'm in love with Agnessa."

"The girl who lives with her parents and likes stuffed animals?" She put the wedding cake on the table so she could cross her hands over her chest like she does and throw her head back, the better to laugh her guts out. She was lucky I didn't throttle her right there and then.

I said that I strolled across the Charles Bridge with Agnessa, and admired the astronomical clock with Agnessa, and that Agnessa's family actually owned the Clown and Bard.

She said, "God, Ray, could you be a bigger loser?"

I stared at her. She wasn't supposed to say that.

"That's a rhetorical question, by the way."

She stalked down the hall to the bathroom to find some tissue to wipe her eyes. I followed her, and when she turned around I grabbed her by the neck and gave her a good shake. Grabbing a woman by the arm is a loser's game. They throw your hand off and shriek, "Don't touch me!" and act as if you're some low-life abuser. I just needed her to shut her up, and the neck is the pipeline to the mouth. I will admit that after she got quiet, I tossed her against that scalding-hot water pipe just to get my point across. So sue me.

Back in the kitchen, I put the frozen wedding cake back into the freezer. I looked out the window. Down on the street a girl rode past on her bike, the flakes setting on her hot-pink bike helmet. Portland is cold enough to invite snow but too warm to keep it. It has something to do with the Japanese current. Charlotte could tell you, but she isn't coming out of the bathroom anytime soon.

The snow stops like I said it would. I put on my Vans and locate my passport in the top drawer of my desk. Outside, the air feels good on my arms. The back of my neck is nice and cool. The forced-air heat was way too much in that place. In the parking lot I pull the plates off my truck, crunch across the snow, and stuff them into the dumpster behind Esparza's. Just as I'm closing the lid, I hear the slow koosh-koosh of bald tires on snow and look up to see the art car rolling down the street. I tell you, I've always been lucky.

At PDX I call the phone company to turn off my service. I'm doing Agnessa a favor. I only want the best for her and it's best for her to go with the guy with the multiple TVs. Then I call 911 and report an intruder. I give my address and tell them its right across the street from Noble Rot, where wine is a meal. Then I buy a ticket for the next plane out. Like I said before, I'm a simple guy. I take life as it comes.

JULIA NOW

BY LUCIANA LOPEZ

St. Johns

There was a photo pasted under the wallpaper, next to a note written on the wall. *Dear Julia, We both know the truth. RIP. Henry.*

"What's that?" Josh asked.

"I don't know," I said. Josh was wearing his painter's pants, even though we weren't planning to start painting for a while yet. There was no furniture in the dining room either, just the two of us, peeling off the old, faded wallpaper, a sort of peach brocade. We'd only just moved into the blue bungalow a week ago, in St. Johns, the only Portland neighborhood left where we could afford a house that wasn't already occupied by wildlife.

Josh read the note aloud, then whistled through his front teeth. He took the photo from my hands to inspect it. A woman, a little plain but not actually ugly, glared back at us, standing at a kitchen sink—our kitchen sink—in a blue housedress, a cigarette dangling between her lips. She'd turned her head to look at the picture taker, and except for those fierce dark eyes, her face showed no expression.

"Guess they lived here before us, huh?"

I rolled my eyes. "Thank you, Captain Obvious."

He shrugged, then kissed my nose. We'd been together five years. My mother was dying for him to propose; somehow marriage never seemed to come up between us. Buying the house together had been his idea.

"RIP. So she's dead," I said.

Josh laughed. "That's usually what it means, yeah."

"There's a date on the back of the photo. August 8, 1957," I read. Josh had already turned back to the wall, tearing off wide strips of the paper. Small frayed fragments dusted his brown hair, like bits of lace floating down. One landed in his eye, and he wiped his face with an impatient motion. Peach dust turned his brown hair pale.

I like to go running at night, after dark. Josh had joked once that I'd make a great mugger, the way I like to stay quiet and jog past at night. This was my first run in St. Johns. We lived a few blocks off the neighborhood's main drag, so we hadn't seen much else of the area. The sun had just set awhile ago, and the orange light was fading, streaking into dark blue out in the west. I set off with no particular direction in mind, just turning and turning and running down whatever street caught my eye. Some of the houses here were quite nice, big and roomy and expensive-looking. Many were like ours: tidy, modest, with well-kept lawns and painted trim, sometimes with roses or other flowers growing in the garden. Up-to-date. Important enough for someone to care about. They were small, but there was pride of ownership. I liked to see those houses.

Some were small and unkempt; dirty or peeling paint, weed-choked yards, fences missing slats. These houses looked old, and tired. Longtime residents, probably. People who'd lived here since it had been a working-class neighborhood, blue collar, the kind who lived paycheck to paycheck.

Portlanders have fuzzy bunny reputations as liberals, knee-jerk tree-huggers, and soft touches. But now that Josh and I owned our place, our house, I found myself looking at the rundown buildings with a more critical eye. How easy it would be to, say, mow that lawn, or to tear out that tacky fence. The fake tiki torches, or the sagging porch. Why don't these people do something about this? I was breathing easily now, in the middle of my run, the place where I feel I can go forever, until suddenly I can't. I passed a couple arguing in the street, the woman leaning out of a rusted car with plastic over where the rear passenger window should be. Then a woman pushing a baby stroller. Kids riding their bikes in the street. On my left was a store selling tobacco products; on my right, across the street, a small Thai restaurant with a buzzing neon sign.

This neighborhood could be so great, I thought, with just a few fixes. Once it had been considered too far from downtown for people like Josh and me to consider living here. But it was only about seven or eight miles—not so far, after all, as people discovered when the real estate boom meant a starter home in close-in neighborhoods went as high as $300,000 or $350,000. In the 1800s, St. Johns had been a separate city, but got absorbed into Portland in 1915. In many ways it still felt like a separate place, tucked into an odd triangular corner of the city's north end. It was awkward to get here, either through an ugly industrial area on the Southwest side, or through a stretch of commercial road and trucking companies on the opposite. The lack of scenery made it feel a bit cut off in some ways.

It could all be so great here, I thought. We can make this place really special. It could always have been special, but maybe now was its time.

I felt the pounding rhythm in my knees. A big black dog barked from a yard, behind a chain-link fence. I smelled roses from a nearby garden. Another batch of kids on bikes waved to me. "Hey, runner," they called out. "Hey," I called back, puffing just a little.

* * *

The next day I woke up with their names on my mind, where they stayed as I brushed my teeth and took my shower and combed my hair and got dressed. At our breakfast table, still the same beat-up oak hand-me-down from our apartment, I looked over at Josh as he read the paper. I could see the headline; a new Starbucks had gotten its windows smashed in, way over in Southeast. St. Johns had a Starbucks too, but it was hard to imagine anyone caring enough to vandalize it. "Henry and Julia," I said aloud, "Who do you think they were?"

He looked at me for a second around the Metro section. He was already wearing a suit and tie, his white shirt crisp and starched. I wore faded jeans and a puffy white peasant shirt. He was an accountant; I was a bike repairwoman. That's how we'd met—I'd stopped to help him fix his bike on the side of the road one day, got it patched up after he got run off by an SUV. Even in Portland, probably as close to American bike nirvana as there is, that sort of thing happens.

"Probably just people who lived here before," he said. "It was fifty years ago; they're probably dead by now." He gave me a wry smile to take the edge off his words and went back to his paper. I grabbed the front section of the paper and read it as I ate my cereal. It had taken us months of living together before we could simply be silent in each other's presence, and now I relished the velvety quiet between us. Josh was thirty-two and I was twenty-seven. I was 5'2", he 6'2", so much taller than me that his big toe was the same length as my pinkie finger. At night he liked to smell my hair, inhaling deep into his lungs, before falling asleep. It made me feel like he wanted all of me, even my scent, loved every bit about me.

I rose from the table first and kissed him goodbye. We used to live downtown, where our commutes were each less than a mile. Now we were more like seven or eight miles from our jobs. Josh drove, so it wasn't long for him, but I biked, riding south along the Willamette River until I crossed the water into the Southwest side. It was beautiful now that it was the summer, crisp, humidity-free weather with a vault of clear blue sky above. In the winter, in the rainy season, well, I'd probably bike then too. I was stubborn that way.

Henry and Julia. Henry and Julia.

I was early at the bike shop. Truth be told, I'd known I was setting out too early from home. This way I could kill some time at the library.

The downtown library branch was only a few blocks away. I locked up my bike and strolled over. The building was imposing, stone and red brick, tall and grand. I'd always been proud of Portland for having a place like this, even if I didn't use it a lot myself. It made me feel like we were a real city, a real, important place.

The reference librarians sat behind a massive desk on the first floor. There were three people there now: an older woman, a middle-aged woman, and a cute guy with red hair and gold wire-rimmed glasses. I walked up to the desk, but before I could get the cute guy's attention, the middle-aged lady glanced up at me.

"I'm looking for information on some people," I blurted out. I was cracking my knuckles now, an old nervous habit, and the pops sounded crass to me in the silence of the room.

"Which people?" she asked. I realized how stupid my answer—*Henry and Julia*—would sound.

"Well, maybe a place would be better to start," I said. "My house. I mean, the house I just bought, but the people who owned it before me. Us. Who used to live there."

Maybe I should have told Josh what I was doing. Maybe he already knew. When I was a kid I'd been the one to touch the poison oak to see if it was really that bad; it was, but the physical itching still burned less than my curiosity had.

The woman took down my address and suggested a few places to start—county property and tax records, some property websites, even, she suggested, the *Oregonian* archives, our daily paper. "How far back do you want to go?" she asked.

"August 8, 1957," I replied.

She nodded, as if unsurprised. "This could be tough. Those kinds of records can wind up all over the place."

I thanked her, said goodbye, and headed off to work. Josh would already be in the city by now, I thought to myself. Josh and Allison. Not quite the same ring as Henry and Julia, but nice in its own way, I thought.

Over dinner that night, I told Josh what I'd done. "She said it might be hard, but possible. But that maybe I'd have to do some digging."

Josh put down his fork with a sigh. He'd made apple-stuffed pork chops and baked potatoes; I usually dated guys who liked to cook, since, left to myself, I'd have peanut butter and jelly sandwiches for dinner every night. "Allison, we just got here. Can we maybe work on the house a bit first, maybe do some of the renovations and changes we talked about before you go flitting off into something else?"

I could feel my brow furrowing, and I tried to smooth it out. I know he hates it when I get, as he puts it, pouty; I wanted to make him happy. "But don't you want to know who these people are? What the truth is? All that? I mean, maybe there's Spanish doubloons buried in the backyard! How cool would that be?"

"Honey, we just got here, we have so much to do. Why waste your energy on this?" He was in sweats by now, though

I still wore the same jeans and blouse as earlier in the day. Across his sweatshirt was written, in gold, *Minnesota*. My mom loved that he was a Midwest boy. I didn't care either way. He grinned, his perfect teeth lined up like a picket fence. "And anyway, maybe Julia's the one buried in the backyard."

"My point exactly. Wouldn't you want to know that?" I asked, pointing my fork at him. A tiny sliver of apple fell off the tines onto my plate. Josh reached out with his own fork, speared the apple slice, and popped it into his mouth. He didn't speak until he'd swallowed it.

"No," he answered. "I really wouldn't." He went back to his pork chop, and the sound of his chewing filled our small kitchen. Beneath the table, though, I felt his foot slide across to mine and rub the inside of my arch. His bare foot was warmer than my own, and I rubbed his foot back.

It took me three weeks of running back and forth among county agencies. One place had ownership records, but not on computer, so I had to go request the file in person. Henry Lewis, it turns out. The house was in his name alone, so I tried tracking down a marriage certificate for him—Julia Crosby, Julia Lewis after 1951. Henry had owned the house until only ten years ago, when someone had bought the place and moved in. Then it had been sold again, a year ago, renovated, and sold to us. So few people separated us from Henry and Julia.

There wasn't much other information about them in the county files, no matter where I looked. Maybe they had simply led quiet, unassuming lives, I thought. Then I remembered what the librarian said, and checked the newspaper archives. The electronic records didn't go back to the '50s, only the '80s, so I had to go to the paper in person. The *Oregonian's* building sits at the south end of downtown. It looks like a holdover from the '70s, from that moment in American architecture when all taste seemed to have left us as a nation. Plain and squat and industrial looking, and no better inside, where nothing seemed to be of any particular color.

But I found Henry Lewis in the records stored there. And I found Julia Lewis. She'd been killed by a burglar, the newspaper said at first, coshed on the head. She'd bled to death on her kitchen floor. My kitchen floor. Then: Husband arrested for murder of wife. Then, a few days later, a brief, brief story: Henry Lewis had been released. Police had nothing to say; they let him go. And Julia Lewis's name disappeared from history. If they had known back then who killed her, the newspaper never mentioned it. If Henry Lewis had been guilty or innocent, they never said. Only that she was dead, and he was released.

"Let it go!" Josh yelled at me from the bathroom. "Just let it go! She's dead fifty years, he's probably dead somewhere too. Just let it go and forget about it!"

I'd been talking about Julia and Henry for the past month now, since I'd discovered her murder. She stayed on my mind. I'd put her photo on my nightstand. Every day, her face looked up at me when I groped for my glasses.

"You're not Nancy Drew," he said. He was in socks and pajama bottoms, standing in the hall outside our door, kitty-corner to the bathroom door. There was only one bathroom in the house so far, but we planned to change that, to put in a half bath, maybe a full bath. Our contractor said that would increase the house's resale value.

"I'm not trying to be Nancy Drew," I answered. I was in bed, sitting up, with the newspaper on my lap. We never had time to read the paper in the morning, when it was delivered.

Who does these days, anyway? "I just want to know more about them."

"You just think you can fix this," he said. "Baby, it's been fifty years. She's so dead she's not even a person anymore, just bones buried somewhere. And he's probably dead or senile or moved on. Why can't you just let it go?"

"Because!" I answered. "Because . . . I don't know why. Except that I can't. They lived in this house, in our house, and they did all the things we do, and Julia's dead and Henry knows the truth. And I want to know the truth too."

Josh ducked back into the bathroom. I heard him spitting out toothpaste, running the faucet. I turned off my bedside lamp and snuggled under the covers, closing my eyes. I was facing the wall. Maybe he would take the hint.

When he returned to the bedroom, he turned off the light and got into bed next to me. He reached over to hug me, and I felt the slight dampness on his face. He had strong arms. That was something I'd always liked about him, and I could feel his strength now when he put his arms around me. After the brief embrace, he reached over me, to my nightstand. He picked up the picture of Julia, brought it over to his side of the bed, and put it into a drawer in his nightstand. I heard him close the drawer. Then he turned back to me, buried his face in my hair, and took the night's deep breath. I pressed my back into him, to feel him next to me. The way we curved together, like two cats asleep together.

"Let's just sleep, okay?" he whispered. "We'll wake up tomorrow and forget all this."

Obviously I couldn't tell Josh anything more, I decided. I left Julia's picture in his nightstand. I didn't even try to sneak it out when Josh wasn't home, just in case he'd somehow know.

That was all right, though; I'd looked at the picture enough to have it practically memorized. And now I knew they were Henry and Julia Lewis, I didn't need the photo anyway. There were other ways to find Henry. Julia I didn't need to find; I already knew where she was. The newspaper obit had been brief and to the point. Donations, please, to the ASPCA; service at St. George's; buried in a cemetery not far from here. I kept meaning to go to her grave, but somehow I never found the time.

Henry, though, Henry was harder. He hadn't owned a house in Portland, that I could tell, for at least a decade. He didn't have a hunting or fishing or pilot's license. He didn't have any court records. He hadn't gotten sued or tried to sue anyone. Not even a parking ticket! The librarians and court clerks were tired of me; I'd visited the *Oregonian* twice more; and I'd called the *St. Johns Sentinel*, as well as some of the other neighborhood papers. I was starting to think he was dead.

I was running almost every night now. I looked at each house I passed, wondering if he lived in any of them. I puffed schoolyard chants under my breath, with his name: *Henry and Julia, sitting in a tree . . . Mr. Henry had a steamboat . . .* Sometimes I chanted aloud, softly. The people I passed by looked at me oddly, but the chants helped me stay focused, helped me keep my pace up. At night I thought I saw her form standing at our kitchen counter, or ducking into the bathroom. Stupid, of course. The house had been renovated since she'd lived in it; the rooms probably weren't even arranged in the same way as they were back then. My kitchen wasn't her kitchen; it was and wasn't the same house.

Sometimes, when I got very tired, I just used their names as a cadence, over and over. *Henry and Julia, Henry and Julia, Henry and Julia.* They had shared something, some burden.

I wanted to be the one to lift it from them, to take it for them.

"I found a Henry Lewis," Josh said one night at the dinner table. It was dark out, far darker than where we'd lived downtown, where the streetlights fuzzed out the stars. We were eating spaghetti with meatballs, one of the few recipes I could make well. Josh held a forkful of pasta up to his mouth, examined it for a second, and ate it.

"What?" I said. I almost spilled my wine on my T-shirt. "You found Henry? My Henry?"

Josh shook his head. He was wearing a T-Shirt emblazoned with *The Shins*, one of Portland's favorite indie-rock bands. Personally, I hated them, but that's not the kind of thing you could really say in Portland, where indie musicians who manage to chart are the closest thing to gods. I'd never told Josh how I felt about them.

Josh shrugged, chewing. After he swallowed, he spoke again. "I don't know if it's *your* Henry Lewis, but it's a Henry Lewis. He's about the right age, and he lives in St. Johns, so maybe it's your guy."

My eyes welled with tears. "How did you find him? I didn't even know you were looking." I felt overwhelmed to think we'd been searching for the same thing after all. It made me immensely grateful.

A shrug. "I didn't so much find him as he fell into my lap," Josh replied. "When I was at Roosevelt High this week."

I nodded. We'd both approved of his volunteer activities; it was like giving back—and coincidentally, I told myself, if it helped raised the high school's test scores, it would also raise our property values.

"Well, one of the volunteer clubs there helped out Meals

on Wheels for a few weeks. Some kind of senior project or something. And one of the guys getting delivered to is this Henry Lewis guy. Kid says he's short, a little fat, definitely old. Never tips or makes cookies for the kids or anything. It's just him, alone. So I got the kid to give me the address. They're not supposed to, but I made up some bullshit story about reconciling the group's gas expenditures and their status as a school group. Easy."

Josh took a folded piece of paper out of his pocket and slid it across the table to me. *Henry Lewis, 9911 N. Central*, in some kid's messy blue-inked scrawl. It had been two months since we'd found the photograph and the note.

I got up from my chair and circled around the table to hug Josh. "Thank you," I whispered into his ear. A strand of his hair got into my mouth, laying the taste of shampoo onto my tongue.

Henry Lewis lived alone, in a white bungalow less than a mile away. From the outside the houses looked similar; a lot of houses in St. Johns had been built off the same or only slightly modified plans. It had been the kind of neighborhood where people just wanted to own a house of their own, whether or not five others on their block were identical.

I felt like I was ten again, knocking on his door. I'd sold Girl Scout cookies back then, back when we still went door-to-door, our moms in the cars behind us. I knocked once and got no answer, so I knocked again, harder this time. "Mr. Lewis?" I called out. I was wearing gray slacks and a light sweater, pale pink, with short sleeves. Nice, nonthreatening, neutral.

Shuffling noises inside. The door opened with a creak, and he stood in the doorway. So this was Henry Lewis. He looked his age; his skin was lined and saggy, the wrinkles especially deep around his mouth. Most of his hair was gone, except for fringes of gray around the bottom of his head. He wore jeans and a faded red T-shirt and bright white sneakers, the kind that people who think walking in the mall is exercise wear.

I waited for him to say something. Nothing came.

"Mr. Lewis," I started. "My name is Allison Priest, and my husband and I just moved into 9535 North Leonard."

Nothing.

"Your old house?" I hated myself for making that a question, but it skipped out before I could stop it. "It was yours, right?"

He nodded.

"Well, I'm hoping I can ask you a few questions about Julia." I pulled the photo out of my purse. "We found this in the walls. It's Julia, isn't it?"

No nod this time, he just motioned me in. The living room was in shade. Not dark, exactly, but with a certain yellow light, a bit dim. Henry Lewis sat down in a brown easy chair; the velour on the arms was faded. The way he sat, his gut protruded forward. I saw a cane in the corner, though he hadn't carried it to the door. I stood for a moment, trying to adjust to the light. I sat down on a blue sofa, across from him. The cushions were firmer than I'd expected.

"I'm here about Julia," I said.

"Julia's dead," he replied. He made a noise, half clicking and half sucking, with his cheek.

"I know," I said. "And I know you were involved."

He snorted. "Involved all right."

"What does that mean? What happened?"

He glared at me. "You a reporter? Cop? Lawyer?"

I had been leaning toward him, but now sat back in surprise. "No, of course not. I fix bikes."

He shook his head, a slight sneer on his lips. "Women shouldn't do that sort of thing. Can't fix anything worth a damn."

I felt the old defensiveness rise in my throat. *Steady, he's old. Steady.* "How were you involved in her death?"

Was he falling asleep? His eyes were closed, and his head seemed to nod forward.

I raised my voice: "How did she die? What happened?"

His head was still down, and now he seemed to be wheezing. *Unreal.* I wanted to poke him with something, but the room was bare. "Hey, you!" I spoke as loudly as I could, to try to wake him. "What do you mean, involved? What does involved mean?" I was shouting by the end of the sentence, I knew. I could feel my muscles tighten up all over.

His head snapped up. "I killed her, you fool. You stupid woman, I killed her."

When I tried to speak, my throat was so dry the words got stuck. I tried again. "You did kill her? You did it?"

He nodded. "Yep."

"But—the note? And the photo, under the wallpaper?" I heard the wail in my own voice. "I found them. The truth, you said. You both knew the truth."

Henry Lewis chuckled, a wheezy sound, reedy and almost boyish. "That was just my little joke," he said. "Julia and I were the only ones who knew. Everyone else thought they knew—but they never knew why, or how. And they never knew what I knew: she deserved it. She knew it too, knew I was gonna do it and knew she deserved it."

He shifted, settled back into his chair.

"I'd been seeing this little yellow-haired gal on the side.

Sally or Sara or something. Anyway, she'd been good to me, real good. Better'n Julia ever was. Me and Julia were high school sweethearts, got married, I went to work. Dumb kids. We didn't know nothing. After we got married, well, Julia just about froze up. In bed she was nothing, just laid there, and she kept a terrible house. She hated it here, y'see. She hated the rain in the winter, hated the dampness. I told her we'd leave, but after we got married I started working for the railroad, and the money was too good to give up. I told her we were staying put. She didn't like that, and she just froze up on me then. When she wasn't froze, she was crying. When she wasn't crying, she was screaming. Man has a right to his house, to some peace and quiet. And Sally moved in a few doors down, and she was three years younger than Julia, still in high school. Pretty, sweet. Sally liked a man with some spending money. Julia found out. I told her I had a right to a girl who wanted me. She said she'd divorce me, take all my money, get me fired. All this crap."

He paused. I couldn't say anything. There was no sound from outside, either.

A cough, and he began again. "One day I came home from work and killed her. Hit her on the head with a frying pan." That wheezy dry chuckle. "She went down in a heap. I remember the blood came from her head here"—he pointed to a spot above his left ear—"like it was a drinking fountain. I wiped off my fingerprints and dropped the frying pan and ran outta there to pick up Sally for a movie. When I came home, I called the police and said I'd just found her like that, and that I hadn't been home at all that day cause I'd been out with my girlfriend. Sally backed me up—pretty girl, but dumb as dumb—and they could never prove a thing."

"So the truth was that . . . ?"

"The truth was that I killed her. She knew I was gonna do it, right up until I did it. And then she was dead and by God she really knew it. She wouldn't ever cross me no more." The chuckle again, and now its thinness sounded like wires rubbing against each other, scraping and raw. "Some people thought it was me, sure enough, but couldn't no one ever prove it. And no one ever knew how much that bitch needed killing."

I could feel the tears begin in me, the pressure building in my eyes and my sinuses. I swallowed, and my spit seemed to grate along my throat.

"What's so funny about that?" I asked. "How is that a joke?"

He just wheezed and shook his head some more. I felt the hair on my arms stand up, but I forced my face into impassivity.

"None of my other girlfriends or wives ever tried any of that shit with me again," he said at last. "Expect they heard about Julia and knew they'd have to shape up. Buried two wives, had girlfriends the whole time. They knew how to keep quiet."

"You kept cheating?" I asked. I took pride in my voice's evenness.

"Hell, I'm a man, ain't I? All men cheat."

"Mine doesn't," I said.

Henry Lewis laughed out loud, a choking sound that brought up something from deep in his lungs. "He cheats," Henry Lewis said. "You ain't caught him, but he cheats."

"No, he doesn't."

The wheezing chuckle now, with a shake of the head. "Little girl, you ain't know shit about men. You and Julia, thinking you can tell a man what to do, how to act. No one can! That's what makes us men."

"Why are you telling me this? If they never caught you, why are you telling me this now?"

"Maybe just cause I feel like." He gave me a hard look. "You come in here with your little purse and your expensive haircut and the way you pretend you belong here. You ain't here. None of you are here. It's like a play for you folks. And maybe I just feel like reminding you it ain't. Now get out. I've got better things to do than teach you how the world is."

I stood up, smoothing my pants with my left hand. I gave him a hard, long look; he returned part of it, then turned away. Not scared. Bored. He had killed her, and he didn't even try to deny it. I suppose no one could touch him now, more than fifty years later. Who would believe me, anyway? He started reading a *TV Guide* as I stood there. He was old now, a lifetime older. I was fit, twenty-seven, healthy.

I watched him for a moment.

"You're Julia now," I hissed. He looked up, turning a page. I walked over to him, ripped the magazine from his hands, and tore it in half. The paper was all twisted in my hands.

He didn't move, not even his face. That same bored look. He wheezed when he breathed, and his knuckles seemed too big for his hands. The whites of his eyes looked dull, like overcooked eggs. I was panting, my breath like sandpaper in my throat. He gave me another second of that vacancy, then closed his eyes and folded his hands on his chest, as if he were going to sleep. I dropped the mangled magazine, turned, and walked stiffly out of the house, banging the screen door behind me. I could still hear him wheeze.

Josh was sitting at the dining room table at home, going over swatches of paint. I saw shades of eggplant spread out before him. Very tasteful, all of them. They were for the living room;

we were hoping to paint next week. He looked up at me. He was wearing his oldest jeans, the ones all torn up at the hem that my mother thinks make him look like a tightwad. A piece of a leaf perched on top of his brown hair.

"How'd it go?" he asked me, his hands flat on the table now.

"He did it," I answered. I took the seat opposite Josh. "He admits it, doesn't even care anymore. We bought a fucking murderer's house. One who lives all of fourteen blocks away." I could feel the heat in my eyes, the quiver trying to move my chin.

Josh shrugged. "We bought the house, we bought the house," he said. "Anyway, Lewis is an old coot now. He can't do anything to us. And if he tried, I'd fix him." Josh grinned at me. His teeth were so white, so very white, that I thought I could see my reflection in their gleam. Like a dog's teeth, constantly wet and shining. He stood up, walked over to me, and gave me a quick one-armed hug.

Then Josh swept out of the dining room; I heard him rooting around the fridge, pulling something out. A pop, a fizz. A can of beer, then. The drink gurgled going down his throat. I heard the backdoor open, then close. Maybe he was sitting on the back porch. Maybe he was just standing in the kitchen.

Henry Lewis was within a few hundred meters of us, somewhere, maybe a kilometer or so at most. He too could be on his porch this night, drinking a beer and thinking of nothing.

The backdoor banged open, then slammed shut. I couldn't hear Josh anymore. I didn't know where he was. The dining room was almost all dark now. My hands began to shake. I couldn't stop them.

WATER UNDER THE BRIDGE

BY ARIEL GORE

Clinton

The kids lined the wall outside the Clinton Street Theater in the sepia-lit mist, waiting to see *The Rocky Horror Picture Show*. The girls with their big purple hair and skimpy dresses; the boys in tight black bodices or boxy leather jackets. Cold November night. They clutched their rolled-up newspapers and cups of rice, hid water guns in their pockets. I squinted at them through the drizzle—a time warp to the '90s, to the '80s, to the '70s. Bygone eras. I ducked into the dim red of Dots Café, slipped into a soft gold booth. The waitress had a tattoo of a hamburger on her shoulder. She nodded at me. "The usual?"

I winked up at her. Absolute martini. And spicy fries with tofu sauce.

As she walked away from me, I tried to recall when it was that I'd gone from being a housewife who'd occasionally sneak out for a midnight drink to a regular with a "usual." I glanced around the joint. Marie Claire, the sexy Midwesterner who ran the Italian restaurant on the corner, sipped a Rumba with one of her young dishwashers. Wilhelm, the frumpy commercial landlord from down on Powell Boulevard, sat alone, adjusted his Coke-bottle glasses as he studied the menu. Nameless hipsters huddled at their smoky tables, too cool with their bleached fashion mullets and pegged pants. I once read in *Nylon* magazine that you can't get away with retro fashion if you're old enough to have worn it the first time. Puts me out of the running for skinny jeans and dangling earrings, I guess. I looked down at my boot-cut cords, fingered the oversized holes in my lobes. For all appearances, a washed-up '90s girl. I'd recently signed up for NiftyWebFlicks, so I averted my eyes when the bearded guy from Clinton Street Video walked in. He sauntered up to the bar to drown his sorrows. A bygone business, video rental.

I got up to use the bathroom. No *Ladies* and *Gents* at Dots Café. Just *It*, *Doesn't*, and *Matter*. I walked into *Matter*. The tan and white tiles on the walls gave me a weird sense of vertigo. On my way back to my booth, I passed Wilhelm. He muttered something unintelligible, adjusted those ridiculous glasses.

A couple of drinks and a pile of spicy fries later, I was back outside, feeling too sober for the cold. Some nights after drinks at Dots, I ambled down to my secret spot on the river, sat there watching the flow of things. But that night I headed home. Little fliers picturing some missing woman were stapled to the telephone poles that marked my path. *Catherine Smith*, in bold letters. Grown people were always going missing in this town. A fire glowed from inside an old Victorian, the smell of smoke in the damp night. I zigzagged home through the rain, cut across the rail yard south of Powell, my shoulders hunched. I held my hood tight over my head; a feeble attempt to stay dry. As I rounded the last corner, a shadowy figure flickered into my field of vision. She was so thin, I didn't recognize her at first, but she said my name in a whisper loud and urgent: "Ruby—"

I was startled, took a minute to take her in. She looked like a wet Chihuahua after a flood, that cute little buzz cut I remembered all grown out now. Still, I'd have known her face anywhere. "Mustang?" I felt my chest tighten. She'd been a lover of mine back before I married Spider, but she ran off to Chicago amid a whirlwind of rumors. "My God, Mustang. What are you doing here?"

How long has it been? Seven years? I couldn't tell if she'd been crying or if it was just the rain on her pale face, but her mascara trailed down her cheeks like mud. She'd never worn makeup when we were together. Soft butch. I opened my mouth to speak, but I felt something hot in my throat.

Mustang cocked her head to the side, tried to give me a meaningful look, but it was like she was staring through me, at something on the other side. "I need a place to stay. Just tonight." Her whisper was gravel and whiskey. She moved closer, gripped my arm. Even through my hoodie, her short fingernails felt like little claws in my skin.

I thought about Spider asleep inside. He was prone to silent jealous rages when it came to ex-lovers—and he didn't much like unexpected guests. Anyway, I hoped he'd slept through my midnight escape. "Did you already knock on my door?" I asked Mustang.

She shook her head, narrowed her eyes. Her thin lips quivered a little. "C'mon, Ruby. We're family, aren't we? Even after all these years?"

I remembered that accusatory pout. I sighed, already defeated, and I wished I'd had another drink back at Dots. "Let me go inside first; give me ten minutes, then knock, all right?"

When I heard her at the door a few minutes later, I pretended to be awakened from deep sleep, I pretended to be groggy, I crawled out of bed real slow, but my charade was all for the night. Spider snored like an emphysemic sailor after a night at port.

As I led Mustang through the dark of the living room, floor boards creaking, she breathed hard. I pointed her down to the guest bed in the half-finished basement. "It's all yours, babe."

She squeezed my hand, whispered, "Thank you." I felt that tightening across my chest again, shook it off.

Spider got up at the crack of dawn, a perverse rod of morning energy even on Sundays. He took his cold shower, headed off to work in his new Prius, none the wiser. Or so I thought.

I lay in bed, just looking at the ceiling. I wondered, fleetingly, if Mustang's appearance in the night had been a dream.

When she staggered upstairs a few hours later, I was making coffee in my pajamas. I offered her a hot cup.

She still looked bedraggled. "It's fuckin' cold in your basement," she mumbled. "Where's Spider?"

"Are you gonna tell me what all the drama's about?"

She sipped her Stumptown brew, took a crumpled pack of American Spirit yellows from her hoodie pocket, lit one up. She held the pack in my direction. *How long has it been since I've had a cigarette?* I remembered the hot pulse of the nicotine patches I wore for a year. *But what the hell?* I reached out.

Mustang looked down at her scuffed Converse. "I need to talk to Spider," she said.

"Spider?" The round of the cigarette felt strangely familiar in my mouth.

Mustang offered me a flame.

I leaned in, inhaled.

Her big brown eyes brimmed with tears again as she dragged on her cigarette. The smoke she exhaled looked musty and brown. "I need a lawyer, Ruby. I might be in pretty big trouble."

"What kind of trouble?" Spider was a weed lawyer. And

somehow I couldn't quite picture it—Mustang in trouble for weed? Booze had always been our drug of choice. The smoke from my cigarette burned my throat. I pretended not to feel light-headed. "You been running pot?" I raised an eyebrow. It had been itching since I'd gotten it repierced.

Mustang gave me that accusatory pout again. "I don't want to talk about it." She hunched her shoulders a little. "A lawyer's a lawyer. You can get Spider to help me. We're *family*, Ruby. Aren't we?"

It grated on my last nerve that she kept saying that—*family*. But she didn't want to talk to Spider. He's a *weed* lawyer. And I knew he'd never take her on—not even for weed. My cell phone beeped from the counter. A text message from Spider: *get that bitch out of my basement by the time i get home.* I flashed Mustang the screen, shrugged. "Sorry, babe, you better go."

"Ruby—" she pleaded with me now.

I kept smoking, silent.

"I'll go," she finally said, shaking her head like she had any right to be disappointed in *me*. "But meet me later? When does Spider get home, anyway? Why's he working on a Sunday?"

He worked every day. "No telling when he'll be back," I admitted. "Probably not before 8."

"Meet me at that Italian place kitty-corner from Clinton Theater at 6," Mustang said, straightening her back and running her fingers through her hair, gathering some of her arrogance. "I'll explain."

I frowned, crushed my cigarette on a plate. Maybe I still had a soft spot for her—or maybe I was just bored—but even as I told her I wasn't sure about my plans for the evening, I knew I'd meet her.

I headed down to the basement to change the sheets on

the guest bed. I vacuumed the carpet remnant that covered the cement floor. I spent the rest of the morning and a tip of the afternoon doing laundry, sweeping the linoleum of the kitchen, mopping it, washing dishes. When the house was clean, I scanned the fridge for dinner prospects. Spider liked to have his food ready when he got home—whether it was 7 or midnight. I usually made a lentil loaf or a tofu-spinach lasagna—something I could reheat. I tossed a salad and left it undressed.

Early afternoon and I was already tired. I slipped an old movie into the DVD player, eased into the couch. This was how days passed now. Ever since Spider made partner at the weed firm and I decided to quit my job at the New Season's cheese counter to focus on my artwork, I'd fallen into this dull routine. See, I couldn't paint until the house was clean. It just didn't feel right. But once I'd spent the morning cleaning, I hardly had the energy to mix paints or stretch canvases. By the time my movie ended, it was getting dusky outside. I clicked the remote. Sports and travel shows, mostly. Sunday-afternoon network TV.

No art today? Spider would say when he got home. He always kind of smirked when he said that.

No. Not today, I'd sigh.

And then he'd check out his dinner and nod approvingly.

When we first met, Spider seemed so dark and complicated. I'd been an out lesbian since Hosford Middle School, but Spider wooed me with shots of brandy and a penchant for poker; that long, lanky body that signaled both strength and vulnerability to me. He wore high heels on our second date. I liked the way he wasn't afraid of his feminine side. But the truth, it turned out, was that Spider just needed someone to control.

It had even dawned on me recently that maybe Spider didn't much mind that I wasn't doing my art. For all I knew, he'd set this whole scene up on purpose. He had control issues. Ask anyone. Now he had me right where he wanted. Like a fly in a web. I wasn't making two dimes of my own money—I couldn't leave if I'd wanted to. I mean, sure, a girl can always leave a place, but it's different when you're broke and you're not twenty anymore. It's different when you've made this big deal to everyone about true love and then about quitting cheese for art. It's not like he was abusing me.

"No art today?" Spider had asked me one night when he got home, particularly late.

I'd been nursing a pricey bottle of vodka. "Fuck you, Spider," is all I said.

He just shook his head—that same self-satisfied smirk. "Anger is the enemy of art," he clucked. And then we just sat down to our lentil loaf and side salad.

I clicked off the television now, threw on some makeup, grabbed my Queen Bee bag, headed up to Clinton Street.

Marie Claire poured me a glass of Chianti.

I looked up into her dark eyes. "What happens under the rose?" I asked her softly.

She winked. "Stays under the rose," she promised me.

"Well, you remember Mustang?"

But Mustang never showed up.

I had my Tuscan bean soup, my penne with pesto. I ordered a Northwest by Southeast pizza to go, downed another glass of Chianti, checked the time on my cell phone, paid my bill.

Outside, it was cold and clear. I wanted a cigarette. I squinted at the flier of the missing girl on the telephone pole on the corner. *Catherine Smith*. I hadn't recognized her straight name, but now I saw the face. Birdie. A young artist. Successful in a local kind of a way—First Thursdays and Last Fridays and whatnot. Birdie. It surprised me that anyone paid enough attention to her daily life to make a flier. If you want to know the truth, Mustang cheated on me with Birdie back in the day. But to think of it now didn't make my chest tighten and ache the way it once did. It was water under the bridge. I nodded slowly at the color Xerox, breathed in her straight name. *Catherine Smith*. Last seen seven days ago exactly.

"You know her?" Marie Claire's voice startled me. She'd stepped out the backdoor of her restaurant into the dark.

"Acquaintance," I said. The moon hung in the night sky like a bad piece of art.

"I hear that investigation's getting intense." Marie Claire hugged herself against the cold, her voice low and steady. "The police questioned Wilhelm, the landlord who owns all those buildings down on Powell. People are saying she was last seen at Edelweiss Sausages. Talking to him."

Wilhelm. I nodded. Wilhelm had actually been a client of Spider's once. Tricky case. Mostly because he'd been so desperate to keep his name out of the press. It was one thing to get busted for running a few pounds of weed up from Humbolt, after all, but quite another to have all those businesses on Powell Boulevard implicated in the whole fiasco.

"Well," I shrugged, "I hope she's all right."

Marie Claire just squinted at me, didn't say a word before she slipped back into her restaurant.

I eased across the street and into Dots Café.

The waitress with the hamburger tattoo sat at a corner table, smoking American Spirit blues.

"Hey," I approached her real slow. "Can I borrow a cigarette?"

She exhaled a plume into the dark, handed me one.

I tried to sound casual: "You don't happen to remember a girl named Mustang who usta live around here?"

The waitress nodded. "Sure. She was just in here—I don't know—maybe three hours ago? Looked like hell. She had these dark bruises on her upper arms. I asked if she was all right, but she seemed pretty spooked. Ran outta here."

I nodded my thanks, ordered an Absolute martini at the bar, threw my debit card down. The owner shook her head at me. After all these years, I still forget. Only cash or checks at Dots. I got a twenty out of the ATM. Bastards at the bank get me with their little fee every time. I headed home with my pizza. I knew Spider wouldn't be thrilled to see takeout, but what was he gonna say?

How about: "Why'd you let that bitch into my basement?"

That's what he said when he finally walked in, loosening his batik neck tie. I'd always hated that tie.

"Jesus, Spider. She's not a bitch. She's an old friend. She just needed a place to crash."

"Well," he shrugged, softening a little. He grabbed his glass pipe from the mantle, took a hit, and closed his eyes. "I just don't like the way she treated you—that's all. Anyway," he sighed, "did you borrow my car the other day?"

I didn't see Mustang again that night. Or the next. I tried to put the whole thing out of my mind, best I could. I had a lot going on, personally. A lot of changes I could feel bubbling up inside of me. A lot that I felt *on the brink of*. I snuck out to Dots at midnight, sometimes made my way down to the river. Then Thursday around noon I was clicking the remote. Brenda Braxton on KGW news: a body had surfaced in the Willamette. Just downstream from Ross Island. *Catherine Smith*. They showed her face, that same picture from the flier. The police believed she was strangled, but they were waiting for autopsy results. They talked about her art. She'd always thought she was so special with her swift birds paintings and her ravens—like an artist named Birdie painting birds was avant-garde rather than straight-up cheesy. And now here she had to be dead to even get on the local news. Brenda Braxton said she'd gone to Evergreen.

Brenda Braxton looked a little sad.

I watched the story, surprised by my own lack of emotion. Lack of connection, really.

And then just this morning I get the news about Mustang. From the cops. A detective shows up at my door, plain-clothed and questioning. "Did Mustang have something to do with that Catherine Smith thing?" I ask, feigning cluelessness. The officer shakes his head. "Her body was found this morning."

"Mustang's?"

He nods real slow.

I invite the detective in, but he declines my invitation. He wants to stand on my doorstep. The incessant drip-drips from my eaves land right in the middle of his bald spot, but he doesn't move. I lean into my doorframe as I tell him my story—everything I've just told you. Well, almost everything.

He takes his notes, sniffles, finally slaps his little book shut, caps his pen, thanks me. As he turns, I think I hear him sigh—like he already feels defeated.

I slink back inside, clean the house. When it starts to get dark outside, I turn the news on again. The second body in the Willamette in as many days. Just downstream from Ross Island.

* * *

Spider comes in real late. We eat zucchini casserole by candlelight.

"No art today?" Spider asks.

And I shake my head. "Not today."

"Did you borrow the Prius yesterday?"

"When would I borrow the Prius?" He always had that damn car with him at work. I don't tell him about the detective or about Mustang. I just eat with him, silent. I wash the dishes while he showers. I climb into bed next to him and wait. As soon as he starts snoring, I'm out. I pull on my cords and my black hoodie, tiptoe across the living room and out the front door. I cut through the rail yard, cross Powell. Birdie's picture still clings to the telephone poles that mark my path.

As I step inside Dots, I take a look around the joint. The dark red feels like home. All the regulars sipping their usuals. I head to the bathroom, go into Matter. The tan and white check of the tiles doesn't make me feel so unsteady tonight. I apply some lipstick in the mirror. Back out at the bar, all the hipsters and the business owners are huddled closer together than most nights—abuzz with the news. One of the kids with a bleached mullet thinks it's a serial killer targeting lesbians. He seems impressed with his own theory, ashes his cigarette in a glass tray.

Marie Claire shakes her head, sips her Rumba. "The two women used to be an item," she says gravely. "It's not *random* lesbians. It was either murder-suicide or a Romeo and Juliet kind of a thing."

The bleach boy snickers. "You mean Juliet and Juliet?"

No one acknowledges him.

His hipster girlfriend breathes in my ear all sultry, "I heard they both recently joined NiftyWebFlicks." She glares at the guy from Clinton Street Video.

The waitress with the hamburger tattoo nods. "He's a loose cannon, that one."

I can't tell if she's talking about the guy from Clinton Street Video or about Wilhelm, who plays pool by himself, refusing to make contact with anyone.

The waitress shrugs, looks down at me. "Absolute martini?" She asks it like it's a rhetorical question, but I'm ready not to have a usual anymore. "Bombay," I tell her. "Bombay martini."

I tap the table as I wait, consider the theories.

As soon as the gin hits my throat, I feel strangely distracted, inspired. My mind bends and wanders.

Pretty soon, the regulars have changed the subject. They're on to a new mystery: someone has stolen the little picture of Marie Claire from the bathroom in her restaurant. That picture was so cute—Marie Claire at age six or seven, her geeky cat eye glasses, her hair askew, hardly a hint of the beauty she would become. I down my last drink. *Was that three? Four?* I don't even feel the cold outside as I float home, cut across the rail yard, slither in the front door and across the living room, floor boards creaking.

In the light from the neighbor's back porch through our bedroom window, I watch Spider as he sleeps. I don't know if you'll understand me when I tell you this, but there are people in this world who'll do you wrong. No matter what Oprah says, there are people in this world you can't forgive. There are people who, just the sight of them makes your chest go tight, your throat hot. Even when they're sleeping, the rise and fall of their chests just fills you with this sudden panic and you think: *No one will ever love me.* And you think: *You tricked me.* And you're right. And then that panic morphs into a quiet kind of a rage that radiates from the center of you and tingles down your arms and into your fingers. It used to frighten me, that feeling. I didn't know what to do with it. I didn't know how to make it go away.

I watch the vein on Spider's neck as it pulses life now. He shifts a little, snores, then shifts again, goes silent, that pale neck at once vulnerable and inviting.

Anger is the enemy of art. Spider said it himself. Smirked when he said it. But there was a lot Spider didn't know. He tried to make me believe that the anger lived inside of me—like it was something intrinsic I couldn't exterminate even if I wanted to. He thought he had me, like a fly in a web. Just like Mustang once thought she could pull the wool over my eyes. Just like Birdie. I chuckle, only a little, when I think of Birdie's stupid face. Did they really think I'd just let it go? *Family,* I laugh, sigh. I study Spider's neck and smile. Did he really think I was so stupid? That I'd never figure out how to handle an enemy of art? I feel those Bombay martinis in my very blood now, making things clear. As I reach for Spider's neck, for that stupid vein, I'm filled with a perfect sense of calm. I think about all the paintings I'll soon make—all the shows I'll have at First Thursday and Last Friday and whatnot. I glance up at the picture of Marie Claire on my nightstand and I think: *You'll still feed me, won't you?*

ALZHEIMER'S NOIR

BY FLOYD SKLOOT

Oaks Bottom

I t was about 10 at night when I saw her walk out the door. Now they're telling me, No, that's not what happened, she wasn't even there.

I don't buy it. The room was dark, the night was darker, but Dorothy was there. We were in bed and her curved back was against my chest. She wore the pale yellow nightgown I love, with its thin straps loose against the skin of her shoulders. My arm was around her, my hand cupped her breast, we were breathing to the same rhythm. Then she slipped from my grasp and I felt a chill where she'd left the sheets folded back. She drifted like a ghost over the floor, down the hall, and out the front door that's always supposed to be locked. I saw her fade into the foggy night.

They tell me I'm confused. What else is new? I'm also tired. And I have a nasty cough from forty-six years of Chesterfields, even after two decades without them. And I don't sleep worth a damn. That's how I know what I saw in the night. Confused, maybe, but the fact is that Dorothy is gone.

For three, four years now, Dorothy is the one who's been confused. That's what we're doing in this place, this "home." She has Alzheimer's. We had to move out of the place where we'd lived together around sixty years.

"Jimmy," she'd say to me, "you look so much like Charles."

Well, I am Charles. Jimmy's our son, gone now forty-two years since he went missing over Cambodia, where he wasn't even supposed to be.

It broke my heart. Filled me with despair, all of it: Jimmy gone too soon, then Dorothy slowing leaving me, now Jimmy somehow back because of her confusion so I have to lose them both again, night after night.

I miss her. Where is my Dorothy? I saw her walk out the door that's supposed to be locked. Because Alzheimer's people wander. They try to get out of the prison they're in, who can blame them? I feel the same way, myself.

But at eighty-two I still have all my marbles. Thank God for that. Memory? Bush Jr., Clinton, Bush Sr., Reagan, Carter, then what's-his-name, then Nixon, Jackson, no, Johnson, Kennedy, and I can go all the way back to Coolidge but I don't want to show off. Or I could do 100, 93, 86, 79, 72, 65, and so on.

I saw her fade into the foggy night. The staff here can't remember to lock the front door, and I'm supposed to believe them when they say what I saw with my own eyes didn't happen? It's a crime, what they did. What they're doing. Negligence. It's like they're accomplices to a kidnapping. Anything happens to Dorothy, I hold them accountable.

Truth is, I'm not sure how long she's been gone. I thought it was only a few hours, but then I look outside and see the day's getting away from me. Dark, light, dark again. Makes me weary.

"Let me use the phone," I say to Milly, the big one, works day shift.

"Sorry, Mr. Wade. I'm not authorized to do that."

Always the same thing. "Look, Dorothy wandered away! No one here's doing it, so I need to call the police and file a missing-persons report."

"What you need is a rest."

"What I need is a detective."

Milly shakes her head. "We've been through this ten times today." The phone is in a locked closet. She tests the door on her way to the kitchen.

I saw Dorothy fade into the foggy night. They tell me that's not what happened, she wasn't there, but I don't buy it. Her curved back against my chest, the chill, her long white hair fading as she drifted like a ghost over the floor, down the hall, and out.

Well, okay then, it's up to me. I'll have to find her myself. Be the detective myself.

Why not? I'm used to hunting around, discovering lost old things. Forgotten old things. For fifty-plus years, I had my own antiques business here in Southeast Portland, just a short walk from Oaks Bottom. Sellwood, the neighborhood's called, and that's just what I did: sold wood. Found my niche with bookcases—Italian walnut, mahogany, inlaid stuff with wavy glass doors—and then with other library furnishings, and rare books eventually. Always liked antiques. I just never planned on turning into one.

Wait a little while longer till it gets dark, till the other residents are in bed and the night staff is "resting" like they do. No doubt with a rum, a beer, whatever they drink. What I'll do is sit here in the old rocker, a perfect reading chair I found at an estate sale in Estacada, must have been '48. Dorothy wouldn't hear of me trying to sell this thing. Nursed Jimmy in it.

* * *

I find her at the Dance Pavilion. I knew she'd be there. With her long lean body and long blond hair, she's easy to spot. Lights reflect off the polished wood floor that's marred by years of dancing feet. The low ceiling makes for good acoustics, and in the temporary silence I hear Dorothy laugh. I walk right over to her and take her hand.

No, that was 1945, just after the war. I'd met her two weeks before, and she told me where I could find her if I wanted to. Oaks Park, the Dance Pavilion, not far from the railroad tracks and the totem pole. I'm nineteen and it feels like it's happening right now. Like I'm at the Dance Pavilion with her hand in mine.

I wake up in the rocker, still eighty-two. Stiff in every joint, I creak louder than the old oak itself. What I need is a shot of good Scotch. The kind that's been aged twelve years, the last two years in port barrels, say, with a hint of chocolate and mint. Nothing peppery. Even when she was going away into Alzheimer's, Dorothy remembered her stuff about Scotch. I enjoyed kidding her about it. The old dame knew her booze. How I'd love to toast her at this moment, to look across the room and see her gorgeous back exposed by one of those bold dresses she wore in the heyday, see her head turn so those green eyes twinkle at me, her hand rising to return my gesture, the amber liquid in her glass filled with light.

I find her tucked against the bluff in Oaks Bottom, looking up at wildly whirling lights. Discs, that's what they are, silvery and thin as nickels, and they're maybe forty or fifty feet above the ground, spinning in circles, blazing with cold fire. Mesmerized, Dorothy doesn't see me yet. She can't take her eyes off them, these flying saucers. But I dare not risk calling out and alerting the figures moving toward her in the mist. Any luck, I'll get to her before they do. Before they can kidnap her and whisk her onto their ship.

No, that was 1947, when she was pregnant with Jimmy. Dozens of people down there in Oaks Bottom screaming, pointing toward the heavens, saying the aliens were landing. All over Portland they saw these things. Cops, World War II vets, pilots, everybody saw them.

I find her sitting with a half-dozen women on the bluff over-looking Oaks Bottom. All their chaise longues face north, up-river, with a clear view of Mount St. Helens. It's twilight, but steam plumes are clearly visible and what feels like soft rain is really ash. Mount St. Helens has been fixing to erupt for months now.

Dorothy waves me over. She spreads her legs, flexes her knees, smoothing her flowered dress down between them, making room for me to join her on the chaise. I sit there on the cotton material she's offered to me and it's still warm from her body. I lean back against her, waiting for the mountain to blow.

No, that was 1980, when she was thinking the world might come to an end. Hoping it would, I believe. We were tired of it then, so you can imagine how we feel now.

No, we're not watching the mountain. We're watching Fourth of July fireworks from Oaks Park like we do every year. Surrounded by kids, happy kids, full of life.

Ah, Jesus.

It's time to go find her. At least there's no rain. Always rains around here, often deep into June, and that would make it harder to track her. Not that a little rain would stop me. I have a warm jacket, a Seattle Mariners baseball cap, a flashlight. Nothing will stop me because I think this is it, the last chance. Because I don't know how long Dorothy's been gone. Floating down the hall. The dark. The night.

The only thing that makes sense is that she's lost somewhere in the woods again over in Oaks Bottom. That's her place, all right. One of the big reasons I decided to move into this "home" instead of some of the others we looked at was because it was in Sellwood and close to the bluff above Oaks Bottom. Clear days and nights, we can see across the wetlands and the little lake to the Ferris wheel and the roller coaster and the Dance Pavilion there at Oaks Park. Jimmy called it the musement center. Loved to ride the merry-go-round, spend a whole afternoon at the roller-skating rink. Sometimes now we hear the kids screaming as they spin or plunge on the rides. We hear the thunder of wheels on tracks. Lights flicker. I think Dorothy thinks it's him calling. Jimmy.

Even after Jimmy was gone, she liked to walk in Oaks Bottom. Not go over to the musement center, of course, but wander along the trails now that the city has turned all that land into a refuge. She'd stroll along the trail and name the trees: maple, cedar, fir, wild cherry, black cottonwood. I think maybe she was pretending to teach young Jimmy. Breaks my heart. She'd stroll along and smell the swampy odor, stumps sticking out of the shallow water, ducks with their ducklings. She'd—

Then she started to get lost in there. One time I found her walking past the huge sandy-hued wall of the mausoleum and crematorium, up at the edge of the bluff. How she managed to climb there from the trail I never understood. She was silhouetted against the building, eight stories high, its wings spread like a giant vulture. Or like the great blue heron painted against a field of darker blue on the building's center wall. She was drifting vaguely north, and I hated to see her there, of all places. I had nightmares about that for months afterwards. Another time I found her ankle-deep in water at the lake's edge, swirling her left hand through algae then looking at it as though she hoped her fingers had turned green. There were three little black snakes slithering around and over her right hand where it braced her body on the bank. One time I found her on the railroad tracks at the western end of the wetland. Just standing there like she was waiting for the 4:15 to Seattle.

Dorothy has stamina. I can't be sure where she might have gotten to this time. Or who might have found her and done something awful to her. Those neighborhood kids in their souped-up cars she always used to annoy, telling them she'd call the cops.

I'm quiet leaving my room, quiet going down the hall, with its threadbare carpet, its dim lighting, quiet opening and closing the unlocked front door. But I don't have to be. No one is watching. I head off down the street like I'm going to buy a carton of milk, don't turn to look at any cars hissing by, just make my slow way toward the river and Oaks Bottom. It's not far.

On television, detectives always begin their investigations by going door-to-door, asking the neighbors if they've seen anything. But I can't risk that. Start ringing doorbells around here, people will just call the "home" and say another old loony is on the loose. Turn me in. I'd be finished before I got started. Maybe when I get closer to Oaks Bottom itself I can find someplace to ask questions.

But after a few blocks, I have to stop and rest. The weariness just keeps getting worse. I think my only energy for the last few years has come from caring for Dorothy. It's what's kept me going. Without that, I'd probably be in the crypt by now, dead of exhaustion, locked away in the big mausoleum there overlooking the musement park. Or I'd be technically still alive but sitting in a chair all day while time comes and goes, comes and goes.

Now it's a few minutes later, I think. Could be more than a few. Truth is, I'm not sure exactly where I am. But that's because my eyes aren't any good in the dark, not because I'm lost. I'm right above Oaks Bottom, somewhere. It's just that the landmarks are hard to make out. But there's a tavern here. I don't remember seeing it before. But it's so old, I must have seen it without noticing. Or noticed without remembering. That's what getting old is, I tell you, nothing but solitary seconds adding up to nothing.

I don't know how long I've been standing here. Or why I'm in front of this new old building. Squat little windowless place looks like it's made out of tin, painted white and red, with a tall sign in the parking lot: *Riverside Corral.* Then I remember: I should drop in for a quick minute and find out if anyone's seen Dorothy. Could have happened. The old dame knew her booze. Maybe she dropped in to the Corral for a quick Scotch on her last rambling.

I take a deep breath. Which at my age is something of a miracle right there. And figure I have maybe another couple of hours before I'll need to head back to the "home," before they might start to miss me. So this can't take long.

I walk in, planning to sidle up to the bar and question the keeper. But the music, if that's what it is, is loud, and what I see stops me dead: two stages—one dark, one light—and on the stage lit in flashing colors a naked woman with long light hair swirling as she gyrates above the money-filled hands of two men who look like twins.

Is that . . . ? It's Dorothy! I'd know those broad shoulders anywhere. How could . . . no, wait, I blink and see now it's not her. Of course it's not. I'm confused. What else is new? But for a moment there . . .

I would give anything to see her again. To touch her again. To stand here near her again.

"What can I get you, old-timer?" the bartender asks. He's twelve. Well, probably mid-twenties, pointy blond hair and a hopeful scrub of mustache.

I forget where I am, forget why I'm here. Looking around, seeing the dancer again, I say, "My wife."

He smiles. "I don't think so."

Then I'm walking through the parking lot, using my flashlight so I can access the trailhead and make my way down the steep bluff toward the trail. I'm too old for this, I know it. All the walking could kill me, even though I'm in pretty good shape. But I can feel through the soles of my feet that Dorothy has been here, and if it kills me I'm still going to find her.

A series of switchbacks gets me to the bottom, though I'm so turned around I'm not sure which way to walk. Time comes and goes like the wind, and I see the moon blown free of clouds as though God himself has turned a light on for me. It shines across the lake. Looking up through a lacing of treetops, I see the now-moonlit mausoleum. So that's where Dorothy must be.

I begin walking north. Maple, cedar, fir, wild cherry, black cottonwood. The water makes a lapping noise just to my left. It sounds spent. Stumps sticking out of the shallows create eerie shadows that seem to reach for my ankles.

Rising out of the water, just beyond a jagged limb, I see a figure stretch and begin to move toward me. From the way it strides, I know it's my son, it's Jimmy. He's wearing some kind of harness that weighs him down, but still he seems to glide on the lake's surface, so light, so graceful.

Jimmy was never trouble, even when he got in trouble. That time, when the cops came to our door, it was only because he'd gone to protect his best friend, Frank. Johnny Frank. Or maybe Frankie John. I don't remember. A wonderful boy, just like my Jimmy, but a scrapper, and that one time he was surrounded by thugs and Jimmy went in there and—

Oh, Dorothy was so good with our son, all that time they spent at the musement park, and Jimmy lost all fear of the things he'd been so afraid of. Came to love the rides, the scarier the better. Of course, that's why he went into the service, why he ended up in flight school, why he ended up in a plane over Cambodia, shot down where he wasn't even supposed to be. Dorothy told me once it was all her fault. I took her in my arms, told her all that was her fault was how wonderful our son turned out to be. And now look, here he is, still wearing his parachute harness, coming home to us at last.

"Come on, Jimmy. Help me find your mother."

"Where is she this time?"

I point toward the mausoleum. He follows my finger and nods, and just then the clouds return, and the mausoleum fades into the night, its sandy face turning dark before my eyes.

Jimmy can see anyway. He leads me and I follow. The trail rises and dips, follows the contour of the bluff. I think I'm doing well with the tricky footing for an old man. Then I realize Jimmy is carrying me.

No, he's stopped walking and now he's the one who's pointing. We're very close to the mausoleum. Up ahead, standing against the building where Jimmy's ashes are stored, where my ashes will be stored, where—I remember now—Dorothy's ashes are stored, I see my wife smiling. She is leaning back against the wall just under the legs of that giant painted-blue heron.

The wind rises. The clouds unveil the moon again and the building lights up. But no one is there after all. No one and nothing but a wall on which a hundred-foot-tall heron is preparing to fly toward heaven.

THE SLEEPER

BY DAN DeWEESE

Highway 30

1

At 2 a.m. I woke up and drove to the distribution station, a humid concrete bunker behind a rolling metal door, just off a street of coffeehouses and boutiques in Northwest Portland which stood dark and empty at that hour. A thin layer of greasy newsprint ink covered every surface inside the station: it varnished the old wooden worktables to a dark sheen, fell in a sticky gauze over the obsolete headlines on the leftover papers stacked in the corners, and became waffle-shaped prints left by the deliverers' shoes and boots on the wooden stairs that rose to the loft level, where the manager sat behind a plywood desk with an old black phone. The ink also stained the deliverers' fingers, and showed as dark smudges on their faces where they wiped their foreheads or scratched their chins or cheeks, and it especially streaked the sink beneath the cracked and spattered mirror in the little bathroom, where a roll of paper towels lay on the floor in place of toilet paper.

2

The manager—wincing, pale, middle-aged, with tightly curled hair that rose into a ragged afro—looked down over the deliverers as they inserted ads, folded and slipped the papers into plastic bags, and stacked the bagged papers in shopping carts. He introduced himself as Carl, and pressed a piece of worn cardstock paper grimed with newsprint into my hand. Smeared fingerprints laced the edges of the card, surrounding the handwritten directions to my route. The delivery addresses were written in large block letters, and between the addresses were smaller printed directives that mentioned which streets to turn on and how far to go until the next capital letters. Below us, deliverers pushed their loaded carts out the garage door to dump their papers into their sagging backseats or rusted truck beds, while others returning pushed their carts back into place so they could fill them again.

"You understand this is a seven-day-a-week job?" Carl asked. I said yes, I was fine with it. "I'm strapped tonight," he said. "Think you can try it on your own right off the bat?" I said I didn't see why not.

And so the first night was a disaster of missed addresses, cursing, and driving in circles.

3

Things got better after that, though. With every newspaper I threw those first weeks, I improved my accuracy and efficiency as I drove the deserted industrial streets of my route, slinging papers in a high arc over the roof of the car or flipping them backhand away from the driver's side. I watched the papers slap against the scratched aluminum garage doors or bent black metal stairs at the backs of warehouses, watched papers skid across empty parking lots to hit curbs near walkways, sometimes tumbling to perfect stops against glass doors on which an all-caps OFFICE was stenciled in white. Once, after rocketing a paper up against the garage door of an auto parts warehouse and listening with satisfaction to the sharp report of news against metal, I made a tight turn and nearly ran over the body of a huge deer that lay motionless in the middle of the empty lot. As I drove carefully around it, I saw that there was no head—the neck ended in a meaty stump, from which a thick black stream of blood ran downhill. Misting rain had collected on the deer's fur in pinpoint droplets that shone silver in the night, and I drove away thinking I should call someone to report it. I didn't, though, and when I returned to the warehouse the next night, the body was gone.

4

Two weeks later, at 3:30 in the morning, I saw the boy. It was only for a moment, through a screen door, from a distance. I was moving; he was in shadow. He looked three or four, but he was wearing a one-piece sleeper, the kind that zips from a toddler's ankle to his chin, so he was possibly younger. He stood behind the sagging mesh of the front screen door and looked out—at that time of night, he could only have been looking at his small dark lawn, and beyond the lawn my car, and within that car myself, throwing a newspaper toward his house. Beyond my car was only the summer night, humid and pointless: a rusted freight train went about its rumbling business; a million insects hissed their muted roar. Beyond that, there was nothing.

5

A young woman doctor at a local clinic diagnosed my injury. Her high cheekbones, green eyes, and long strawberry-blond hair were pleasant distractions as I sat shirtless on the paper-covered vinyl table, regretting my pale body. I recognized the woman—she'd treated my daughter Olivia just a year previously, after a bright red rash had blossomed across Olivia's face and her eyelids began to swell shut while my wife Sara and I played with her in the park. Unaware of the grotesque change in her appearance, Olivia had smiled when the doctor ruffled her wispy, translucent hair that day, and giggled as the woman laid her fingertips against Olivia's chubby cheeks and smooth forehead. The doctor had proclaimed Olivia cute, told us the rash was a reaction to sunscreen, and prescribed a bath.

When I sat before the same woman a year later, Sara and Olivia were with Sara's parents in Seattle, and the doctor told me it was the first time she'd seen a repetitive motion injury from throwing papers. I received the news with a measure of pride. "You'll want to take a few days off," she said, "the joint needs rest." I explained the seven-day-a-week nature of my job, and she frowned at the wall behind me for a moment, then delivered a short lecture on the mechanics of throwing motions, followed by some demonstrations of stretches to do before and after delivering. "You should treat the job as if it's an athletic event, or things will just get worse," she said, and when she bent to write on her prescription pad, I imagined trailing my fingers down the curve of her lower back, imagined her skin soft and smooth and warm beneath her white medical coat and green blouse. She tore the sheet from her pad and handed it to me. "Talk to the other deliverers," she said. "See what kind of motion they use. If you don't change anything, you'll just be back here in two weeks."

6

I got the prescription filled at a grocery store and took one of the cylindrical blue pills with some water as soon as I got home. Then I walked around the house, awaiting dramatic effects. If I didn't go into my daughter's room and didn't open my wife's closet or any of her drawers in the bedroom, it was almost as if there had never been anyone else there. The dirty dishes in the sink were my dirty dishes. The clothes in the hamper were my clothes. The conceit dissolved in the basement, though, where there were other reminders. The dusty wind-up swing Olivia had fallen asleep in as a newborn lay abandoned in the corner next to her first playpen, with the fabric toys that dangled down: a felt star, a plastic ball, and a plush purple octopus the size of my palm. Occasionally I would catch the toys swaying a bit—a response to some phantom draft, I suppose. Or maybe the toys had their own vague, blunted intentions.

Other things that belonged to my daughter had disappeared: the plastic blocks she liked to scatter across the carpet, for instance, and her empty bottles on the kitchen counter, waiting to be cleaned of their formula slick. I thought about her little fists, the way she clung to my shirt when I picked her up, or how she bounced her palm against my cheek and then waved her arms and gave a surprised peal of laughter when I tossed her in the air. The nights were oddly still without the sound of her crying, that persistent, desperate wail of hunger, fear, or confusion. Sometimes, when I used to go in and pick her up in the night, she would shove her hand in my mouth, and I could feel her relax as the sharp nails of her chubby little fingers picked their way along the contours of my teeth.

After half an hour of pacing the rooms, I raised my arm experimentally—though the shoulder still ached, the shooting, knifelike pain was gone. The simple fact that the medication had done what it was supposed to do cheered me, and I slept soundly for the first time in weeks.

7

I was already particularly aware of that house, because the people there were always awake. When I reached it each night at 3:30, braked to a slow roll, and prepared to throw their paper, I often saw a male silhouette standing on the warped boards of the small wooden porch, shoulders hunched, moodily sucking a cigarette. When the figure was absent from the porch, he was certainly one of the people I saw through the front screen door, one of three or four men and women who sat on a low couch in a narrow room, their faces lit by an unseen television whose shifting blue light illuminated a haze of cigarette smoke. I didn't have many residential deliveries, and the ones I had were to properly dark, quiet houses. It bothered me not only that the people in that house saw me deliver their paper, but that I found myself unable to avoid looking in as I drove past. I wondered why they weren't asleep. What they did. Why they couldn't at least close the door.

8

I decided the distribution station was like hell: everyone was there for a reason, and most wanted to talk about it. A man in his forties told jokes about prostitutes and animals between explaining the complexities of paying child support for four children among three ex-wives. A doughy woman who sweated through the same purple sweatsuit every night and smelled of sour milk had three children in private school, though she cheerfully claimed to earn nearly as much delivering newspapers as her husband did selling men's ties. A man with wavy auburn hair and no teeth loaded his papers into a cardboard television box on a dolly tied to the back of his bicycle—as he pedaled off into the mist, the dolly's small black wheels bounced and rattled, and the bicycle's rear tire sent up a rooster tail of spray that glistened orange beneath the streetlights, then disappeared. An aging Deadhead with sunken cheeks, a voice like loose gravel, and spider web tattoos covering his elbows alluded to massive debt from years of substance abuse.

His dog barked angrily from the back of his truck at anyone who walked past, and its snarls were the last thing I heard before I drove off to handle my own route.

9

I took my painkillers with my coffee as I drove to the station, but the toughest part was when I first arrived and had to assemble two hundred papers before the meds kicked in. Bagging papers was dull, mindless work, made even more difficult by the Deadhead's preference for tuning the small radio on his worktable to a station whose playlist seemed to have been culled exclusively from the soft-rock soundtrack of my childhood: Cat Stevens continued exhorting people to board the peace train, Streisand and Gibb continued declaring they had nothing to be guilty of, and Joni Mitchell still wanted us to help her, she thought she was falling in love again. The deejay bragged about broadcasting these laments commercial free between midnight and 3, and the Deadhead would play with the reception until he got it just right, and then tap his foot and nod his head while he hummed along. The love songs and the sentimental childhood memories they evoked in me, juxtaposed with the thuds of stacked papers and grunts of the straining workers, made me feel my life had become the punch line of some arcane conceptual joke. After the Deadhead left to deliver, the remaining employees would talk about how much they disliked his music, but no one ever said anything to him. One night, after listening to Michael McDonald claim he kept forgetting we're not in love anymore, I decided somebody had to make a stand for sanity, and I asked if there was another station we could tune the radio to.

"You don't like this song?" the Deadhead asked, incredulous. "That's the Doobie Brothers, man."

"I've heard this song five hundred times."

"It's the only station that comes in good," he said. "The others are fuzzed out because of all the metal in here, but I guess I can try—I don't want to annoy anyone." He started messing with the tuning, and for the next minute we heard nothing but static and garbled, distorted voices, until I had to tell him to forget it and just put it back where it was.

"Sorry, man," he said. "I didn't know it was a problem."

"Because you never asked," I replied.

"Shit," he said. "You've been here for a month? I've been here for three years. Just relax."

"How am I supposed to relax when I'm constantly hearing all those shitty songs?"

"So I'll just turn it off."

No one said anything else. In the silence that followed, the sounds of everyone working were distracting and over-loud. Even though I'd only said what everyone else was thinking, the silence felt like judgment. They considered me the bad guy, and I ended up wishing I'd never said anything in the first place.

10

Before she left, my wife claimed that she and I were driving each other crazy trapped in the house together all the time, and that with herself and the baby out of the way for a bit, I could apply all of my energy to my job search. Besides, she said, her parents would love to spend some time with their granddaughter. That I agreed with her when she said these things is not in dispute.

Olivia was starting to string together her first speculative, surreal statements at this time. *Daddy make a red roof house for Livvy*, she informed me on the telephone shortly after they left, and then repeated the phrase multiple times, as if it held crucial information. Her sentences seemed crafted of some cryptic, dreamlike symbolism that begged analysis, and I turned the red roof house sentence over in my mind for three days until, out of sheer desperation one night, I asked the Deadhead what he thought of it. All he could tell me was that it was pentameter, which I thought would be interesting, until he explained what that meant. I told him I thought maybe Olivia had snatched the red roof house from some song on the radio, but when he started listing old songs with the word "house" in them, I knew we weren't going to solve it. And we didn't.

11

When my refills ran out, I decided to find a place where I could get some more. I chose a walk-in clinic in an old hospital in the rougher part of town, and waited my turn on the hard plastic lobby chair, while next to me an old Asian man sat with his head bowed and his eyes shut tight, absorbed by some internal difficulty. Across from me, a stocky man in overalls pressed a thick wad of blood-soaked paper towels to his forearm while he explained in detail what was unsafe about the motion he'd used with a box cutter. At the climax of his description, he lifted the paper towels to reveal the awful result. And there were at least three different exhausted mothers with small children who clung to their legs or lay on the thinly carpeted floors. The children whimpered quietly while streams of gray snot ran down over their bright red lips, and one stared at me suspiciously for upwards of ten minutes. Her eyes were dark, her lashes incredibly long, and I smiled at her once, toward the beginning of the staring, but she didn't acknowledge it, and never changed her expression.

When I was called in to talk to the pimply young doctor, I complained of back pain—too many hours in the car, I said. I also mentioned neck pain, from craning my head out the window. I felt these were plausible injuries, and found I could speak confidently when I concentrated on the part that was true. When I wanted to demonstrate my pain, I just tensed the muscles in my shoulder, which sent pain rocketing through the joint—pain I ascribed to my back and neck, areas I knew were difficult to diagnose with accuracy. The doctor absently picked at a pimple on his chin and asked me to rate my pain on a scale of one to ten. I decided my pain was an eight, a nine being burning to death, a ten, crucifixion. The doctor looked me over, shrugged, patted me on the back, and wrote me a prescription.

12

I kept pills in a vial in the console of my car as I drove past the warehouses and factories and stevedoring businesses that populated my route. I also drove a stretch of undivided highway, two lanes each way, and delivered papers on all of the narrow residential roads that branched off and weaved their way up into the hills outside the city proper. Whole strings of large homes hid within the dense green foliage of those hills, though all a person could see from the road were the rundown little houses on truncated dirt or gravel drives that branched from the side of the highway at random intervals. Those little houses with their peeling paint and rusted motorcycles and long, dirty weeds depressed me, especially when the car's headlights illuminated a small bicycle, soccer ball, or other toy abandoned in the weeds.

The house with the boy in the sleeper was one of those houses.

13

During the occasional phone calls I received from her, Sara updated me on the places she had taken Olivia: Pike Place market one day, the aquarium another, and always the park. She claimed Olivia enjoyed Seattle, which annoyed me, because how can a two-year-old even know the difference between one city and another? And there were things I wanted to show Olivia too—it's not as if I didn't see my share of animals or greenery. Hanging branches whipped past the windows of the car as I drove up a winding road to throw papers at the houses hidden in the hills. I watched opossums scurry along the roadside ahead of the car, and when they turned to stare into the headlights, their eyes flashed like metal discs. Jogging through an industrial park one night as I delivered papers to multiple businesses while the car idled in the lot, I stumbled upon two raccoons ransacking a garbage can. They spun to face me, annoyed by the interruption, and then scampered grudgingly into the darkness, trading outraged bits of chatter. I saw plenty of squirrels and owls as well, and once even saw a wildcat dash into the roadside undergrowth. I thought Olivia would like to have heard about the animals, even if she wouldn't actually have been able to picture most of them, since the only animals she really knew were cats and dogs. But it wasn't something I would have been able to make her understand over the telephone.

14

What I thought would be Sara and Olivia's two-week holiday had quickly become four, and then four became eight. On the telephone, Sara and I took turns telling each other the story of our life together. It turned out that though we were

DAN DEWEESE // 89

using the same characters, we were each telling a different story, and between our competing installments, we offered each other updates on events in the present. In Sara's story, for instance, I'd said I would do many things that I actually hadn't, so I seemed either deceitful, hapless, or both—and also, she and Olivia had found a playgroup right in Sara's parents' neighborhood. In my story, I was working like hell to pull through a tough time, but I was finding a conspicuous lack of support—I had also shaved five minutes off my record delivering time the previous night. In her story, there was an entire thread devoted to thoughts on what love was and what it looked like and how it was demonstrated, and her parents had fixed up a room for her and Olivia to stay in. In my story, the characters had definite goals, and it was important to establish what they each respectively and realistically wanted to get out of life, and then to analyze whether the current situation was really going to help them achieve those goals, and also the last week had been so hot that I was sleeping in the basement. One thing our stories had in common were monologues devoted to doubts about whether the stories we were telling even raised the most important issues, and if not, what the most important issues might be, and if we couldn't figure out what the most important issues were, if it was possible that the important issues weren't even definable, that they were intangible and invisible but had real effects, like changes in atmospheric pressure, or the erosion of stone. At the end of one particularly confusing evening of competing stories and traded theories, Sara said, "Well, at least Olivia's having a nice summer vacation."

15

A hazy, half-realized scene of my wife and daughter backing

out of the drive in the car began repeating on a short loop in my memory. I couldn't even remember if I'd kissed Olivia before they left—I could just see her strapped securely in her car seat, looking at me as I waved to her through the side window. What remained clearest, the thing my memory rendered with the finest, most delicate detail, was the confused expression on Olivia's face. The memory didn't include the expression on my own face, of course—how could I see my own face?—but since children are such skilled mimics, maybe my daughter wasn't actually confused, but was simply mirroring what she saw in my own expression. Or maybe both of our expressions were authentic, and the same. It's a tough thing to unravel, the origin of an expression.

16

The next time I saw the boy, I was glancing through the screen door as I always did, my eye scanning the bright rectangle of light. The adults were there as usual, smoking cigarettes and watching television, but standing at the door was the child in his sleeper, looking back at me.

After I drove away from the house and accelerated back onto the highway, I found myself so angry that I had to pull the car to the side of the road to try and compose myself. I stood on the gravel-covered shoulder and watched a freight train roll past until its whistle pierced the air for no apparent reason, and then I climbed back into the car and waited for a logging truck to go by. Its trailer was filled with the trunks of felled trees stacked eight or ten high—strings of wet, pendulous moss hung from the trunks, swaying heavily in the breeze as the truck roared away down the road. I pulled back onto the highway to resume my route, but the image of the boy in the doorway stayed with me. The night was one of the warmest of the summer, and though I was sweating profusely, I also felt chilled. I opened the vial in my console to retrieve another pill, but my fingertips found nothing, and I became confused, unable to decide whether the vial had simply gotten low without my noticing, or if I'd lost track and had accidentally taken too many pills. I felt jittery and anxious, and almost started laughing as I watched my hand shake when I reached to turn on the car's heater. By the time I threw my last paper, a bitter nausea had risen in my stomach, as if my intestines had become entangled within some slowly winding gear.

17

I made it back to the station and into the bathroom in time to disgorge the contents of my stomach into the dirty toilet. After spitting the last of the humid brown stew from my mouth, I sat on the bathroom floor, my back against the wall. When I looked up a few minutes later, the Deadhead was standing in the doorway. "Your car's running," he said.

"I'll be out in a minute."

"You need anything?"

"I'm just a little sick," I said. "If you could just leave me alone for a few minutes . . ."

I closed my eyes, but I could sense him standing there, studying me. "What's your problem?" he said.

"For Christ's sake," I said.

"What's going on, Dale?" I heard Carl ask, and when I looked up he was standing next to the Deadhead, looking at me like I was an animal that had wandered into the station.

"He's sick."

"Is his route done?"

"It's done," I said.

"You can't spend the night here."

"I don't want to," I said. "I just need a minute."

Carl disappeared from the doorway, but the Deadhead, whose name was apparently Dale, remained. "Why are you even doing this?" he asked.

"Why are you bothering me now?" I said. "Why at this moment?"

"Because this is a shitty job I do because my life is fucked up. You walk around here like you're better than us, which makes you an asshole. But you're probably right. So what are you trying to prove?"

I hoped that if I ignored him, he would go away, but he didn't.

"You should at least take better care of yourself," he said. "Especially since you have a kid."

"How do you know I have a kid?"

"You were just talking about her last night. Or can't you remember last night?"

"Listen," I said as carefully as possible, "I don't need your help right now."

"You just puked into that shitty little toilet and now you're laying on the floor, but you don't need help. I used to say shit like that too."

"So then you probably know how much I wish you would leave."

"Have a nice day," he said.

I heard his footsteps recede, and I was alone again.

18

Later, I stood up, splashed some water on my face, and walked out into the empty station. An oscillating fan on a stand had been left on, and it nodded back and forth, as if speaking to someone it was unaware had left the room. When I stepped outside, my car was still sitting exactly where I'd left it, the radio on and the engine running. It was the only car in the lot.

19

The next time I talked to my daughter on the phone, she informed me that *Doggy make a walk with a flower sky flower.* When the phone was transferred to my wife, I asked if they'd gotten a dog now too. "No, but we did buy flowers," she said. She was focused on her new job as a receptionist in a real estate office, and I was the only one of us, it seemed, who realized Olivia was delivering important information. I'm sure my wife didn't write out our daughter's sentences on notebook paper and study them the way I did, with a mix of pride and concern.

"You don't sound good," my wife told me.

"I'm just tired," I said. "I've been working a lot."

"Other than the newspapers?"

"No, the newspapers are every night. It's not easy."

"How long are you going to do that?"

"As long as I have to."

I heard her sigh, and could picture her expression, the way she pursed her lips when she was frustrated. "Why haven't you ever, even once, asked about coming up to visit us?"

My jaw tightened. I could feel the blood pounding in my head. "Are you trying to get me to?"

"Don't start that," she said.

"We own a house here. This is where I live."

"I don't even know why you're saying that. What does that mean?"

"It means I have to work to pay bills, to pay the fucking mortgage."

"That's not what I meant, and you know it."

"So you don't know what I mean, and I don't know what you mean."

"I'm going to say goodbye now," she said. "Don't call me again tonight."

20

I was still rehashing that conversation when I got to the distribution station later and found a rubber-banded stack of white envelopes on my table. I asked what they were, and the woman in the purple sweatsuit said, "It's bill night. They should be in the order of your route. You just keep them next to you and slip them in right when you're about to throw the paper."

"That'll take forever," I said. "They're ruining our night so they can save the price of a stamp?"

"They're penny-pinchers," the Deadhead said. "They don't give a rat's ass about us."

"You know what?!" Carl yelled down from the loft. "I've had enough of listening to all of you bitch and moan. If you don't want to deliver the papers tonight, with the goddamn bills in them the way they need to be and the way it's your job to do, then you can just walk out the door right now. And you won't ever have to come back, because I'll replace you tomorrow with someone who'll just shut up and do the work."

Nobody said anything. It was the second time that day I'd felt like a schoolboy being scolded, and it disgusted me that I could still be made to feel that way. I bagged my papers as fast as I could, and left without saying a word.

21

I tried to sort through the bills and shove them into the papers while I drove between addresses, but it was almost impossible to mess with the papers while driving. I hated the fact that my

route was taking so long, and I replayed both the phone conversation with my wife, and Carl's challenge, over and over in
my head, savoring my anger. When I reached the boy's house,
rolled to a stop, and looked through the screen door to see a
woman holding him in one arm while she smoked a cigarette
with her free hand, I slammed the car into park and got out.
The gravel ground beneath my shoes as I walked up the drive,
but the woman turned and walked deeper into the house as if
she heard nothing. When I reached the door and knocked on
the wooden frame, two men sitting on the couch inside—they
might have been brothers—looked over in surprise. The one
closest to me, who had a dark mustache and a thin strip of
beard that followed his jawline, stood and came to the door.
He wore a plain gray T-shirt and blue jeans that were turned
up at the ankle above his bare feet, and as he came closer I
could see that his hair hung to his shoulders in the back. "Can
I help you?" he said through the screen.

"I've got a bill here," I replied, "for your newspaper." He
opened the door and I handed him the envelope.

"Who is he?" the man on the couch said.

"It's the newspaper boy, delivering the bill."

"Ask him if he wants a beer," the man on the couch said,
raising his bottle as he returned his attention to the television.
Though I was at an angle to the set, I recognized the images
of a motocross race. Motorcycle after motorcycle flew into the
air from behind a dirt hill, the riders in gear and helmets that
made them appear only slightly less mechanical than the machines they rode.

"This isn't due right now, is it?" the man at the door
asked.

"No, I just wanted to make sure you got it," I said. "A lot
of people don't notice it in the bag."

The woman I'd seen earlier stepped back into the room. "Who is it?" Her cigarette was gone, but the boy was still curled in her arms. He was in his sleeper as always, and I could see that it was gray, with a pattern of small blue cars and red trucks. His head lay on the woman's shoulder as if he were ready to go to sleep there, but his brown eyes were open, and he looked at me with a combination of curiosity and fatigue. Both he and the woman were younger than I'd thought—the woman seemed in her early twenties, and the boy murmured unintelligible babble as he ducked his head further into the point between her shoulder and neck.

"The newspaper boy's dropping off the bill," the man said.

"Does he take checks?"

"We don't have to pay, he's just delivering it."

"We have the money, though," she said. "He's standing right there. I'll get the checkbook."

The woman left the room again, and the man looked at me uncertainly before opening the door a bit wider with his foot. "All right," he said. "You might as well come in."

I stepped inside and heard the screen door bang shut behind me. The man tore the bill open and examined it. "We don't even read it," he said.

"You're collecting money all night?" the one on the couch asked.

"No, I just saw you were awake."

"Aiming for a tip, huh?" he said, and laughed as if he'd made a tremendous joke.

22

The woman returned, holding a checkbook in the hand she wasn't using to hold the boy. She tried to press it open on the back of the couch, then stopped and leaned toward us.

"Go with Daddy now," she whispered to the boy. He raised his head obediently and stretched his arms to the man at the door, who took him. The boy curled up on the man's shoulder the same way he'd been on the woman's.

"I've seen your son in the doorway sometimes when I deliver the paper," I said. "He's cute." I reached to ruffle the boy's hair then, but the man twisted away, moving the boy just beyond my reach. Both of our movements had been automatic, I think, but my hand was left in the air in front of the boy and his father until I dropped it back to my side.

The man looked harder at me. "Sometimes he has a hard time sleeping," he said, and then, studying the bill, added: "And this isn't due today."

"It's not," I said.

"What's wrong?" the woman asked.

The man on the couch slapped his leg and laughed wildly. He pointed at the television, where a number of motorcycles were tangled on the ground and riders scrambled to pull themselves from the mess. "Always the same turn," he managed between laughs, "they always fuck up the same turn."

"How much is it?" the woman asked.

"We don't have to pay," the boy's father said, looking at me as if I'd claimed otherwise.

"But he's right here," the woman said.

"Take the baby and put him in his crib." The man's voice was tense, determined. "He should be sleeping." He handed the child back to the surprised woman, who looked at me once more, and then headed from the room, patting the boy's back and whispering to him. When she was gone, the man turned to me. "What's your name?" he asked.

"Travis," I told him.

"Listen, Travis. Next time you have a bill for us, just deliver it the same as you do to everyone else. I don't care if you see our light on, and I don't care if you see my son. Just throw the paper on the fucking lawn and move on. Understand?"

"I'm sorry," I said.

"I don't give a shit if you're sorry. You don't knock on our door in the middle of the night asking for money."

I nodded and closed the screen door behind me as I let myself out, then walked up the drive to my car. I didn't look back until I put the car in gear and pulled away, and when I did, I saw the man standing in the doorway, watching me leave.

23

My hands shook so badly as I made my deliveries to the next few houses that I could barely manage to get the bills into the bags, and when I pulled back onto the highway again and headed further north, I drove past the turn I was supposed to take. It was just a small access road that led back down into the industrial area where I would deliver to a couple dozen more warehouses before being done for the day, but suddenly it was behind me, and I was still going. It was easier to drive straight and fast on the highway instead of continuing to struggle with the newspapers, whose plastic bags snapped in the breeze roaring past the open window. After a few minutes, as an experiment, I dropped one of the papers out the window of the car and turned for a moment to watch it tumble crazily along the road behind me.

The sky was starting to brighten in the east, which meant that I was way behind schedule. I knew that if I just kept going north, though, I would cross the Columbia River soon, and would be somewhere new when the sun rose. I pressed the gas to the floor, and the car strained to pick up speed. And when I tossed the stack of bills out the window, I watched in the rearview mirror as they exploded into a mass of fluttering shadows, like a flock of birds in the night.

PART II

Crooks & Cops

THE WRONG HOUSE

BY JONATHAN SELWOOD

Mount Tabor

I'm working the pry bar along the north side of Mount Tabor Park trying to scrape together enough to make a buy off the Mexicans on 82nd. Normally I cop from Voodoo Mike downtown, but I'm already into that dreadlocked cocksucker for almost a hundred.

The neighborhood is practically virgin this far up the hill, without a single security door along the whole block. I start off with a well-kept dark blue Victorian that looks like it got flipped right before the housing market went to shit. There's an old Sam Adams campaign poster still on the lawn and not one but *three* of those stupid plastic horses wired to the iron hitching ring on the curb. One of the smaller side windows is painted shut, but not latched, so I loosen it with the bar and slip in through what turns out to be a bathroom.

Inside the house, the primary décor is giant action photos of a middle-aged lesbian couple climbing, biking, and even riding an elephant in some Third World country. The place is stuck in the last millennium when it comes to electronics— they're still using a fucking VCR—but I score big with a dresser drawer full of heirloom jewelry and some antique-looking carved Buddha heads on display above the fireplace.

The sliding glass backdoor of the neighboring split-level ranch isn't locked, so I just walk right into what turns out to be medical marijuana central. Even congested and junk-sick, the place smells to me like a flatulent skunk doused in patchouli. I spend a good twenty minutes turning the place upside down, but despite finding a bunch of dope scripts and a collection of vaporizers rivaling the Third Eye, I never manage to locate the actual weed. On the plus side, the place is a fucking gold mine of game consoles. By the time I'm out the door, I can barely zip my piece-of-shit duffel closed.

As usual, the jonesing part of me wants to just hoof it straight down the hill and see what Tearoom Timmy will give me for it all, but popping these rich fucks' houses is like shooting monkeys in a barrel. It'd be sin not to rip at least one more.

Skipping a couple lots down from the last one I hit to throw off any eyeballing neighbors, I settle on a beige Craftsman with the standard black thumb landscaping of bark mulch and rhododendrons. All that separates the miniscule backyard from the park is a six-foot chain-link, so I can get a good look without actually having to trespass—the blinds are pulled, but it seems quiet enough.

Fuck it.

I hide the duffel in some blackberry thorns by the tennis courts for safe keeping, and hop the fence.

When I get to the backdoor, I notice that there's at least an eighth of an inch gap between the door and the jamb, so I slip the pry bar in easy and give it a hard pull. The rotted wood splinters like fucking matchsticks and the door just swings open.

I step quickly into the house and push the door closed behind me to get out of view, then stop and listen for sounds of life. The forced air is blowing as background noise and the fridge is humming in the kitchen, but other than that the place is dead silent. I wait a few more beats just to be sure, then head up the short staircase out of the mud room and into the kitchen.

Immediately I sense something is off.

All of the major appliances are brand new and top-of-the-line, yet sitting on the granite kitchen counter is one of those cheap-ass single-serving coffee makers with a metal carafe. The thing stands out like a pile of dog shit on a putting green. It even has a fucking Motel 6 sticker on the side.

I don't usually bother with kitchens, but I'm so thrown by the coffee maker that I find myself opening the cabinets anyway. They're all filled with roughly the right kind of stuff, but the shit's just jammed in there at random—Froot Loops next to the Liquid-Plumr, Hamburger Helper on the same shelf as a Costco-sized box of panty shields, and Bob's Red Mill Quinoa under the sink with a whole case of laundry borax. It's like the place was stocked by a fucking schizophrenic.

My brain still trying to puzzle out what's going on with the kitchen, I head down a narrow hall to the front living room, and I'm finally stopped cold. The whole fucking thing is decorated with the kind of crappy stuff they rip out of remodeled office buildings and hotel rooms and then sell discount—butt-ugly baby-blue love seat, hideous plaid couch, and a mammoth black enamel entertainment center dating from at least the late-'80s.

What the fuck?

As if in answer, I hear a woman's voice behind me.

"Freeze."

I'm so surprised that I spin around to face her before the meaning of the word sinks in. I actually see the flash of the pistol.

When I come to, I find myself sitting on the rug, with my legs splayed and my back partially propped up by the love seat. I have no clue how long I've been out.

"I have a gun! I have a gun!" the woman starts shouting as soon as she realizes that I'm awake.

"No shit," I manage to whisper.

She stops shouting and takes a step toward me. I force my eyes to focus. Generic thirty-something blonde dressed like she's about to drive her hybrid SUV to the yoga studio. Christ, if it weren't for the Ruger 9mm in her left hand, she could be in a Whole Foods commercial.

"Don't move or I swear, I'll . . . I'll kill you."

"I can't move. My legs don't work."

I look down at my lower abdomen and see the little hole in the front pocket of my hoodie. There's no blood, but somehow just looking at it cuts through all the endorphins and sends the first wave of pain rolling across my torso.

"Did I hit you?"

"What the fuck do you think?"

She takes a step back again and tries to calm herself down by doing some sort of ridiculous deep breathing/grunting exercise.

"*Huh-uuuunh . . . Huh-uuuunh . . . Huh-uuuuuunh . . .*"

I put my right hand on my thigh. There's no feeling in the limb at all—it's like I'm touching someone else's leg.

"Why the hell did you break in here?" The blonde stops hyperventilating for a moment. "I mean, are you psycho or something?"

"Lady, I need an ambulance. Did you call 911?"

"The cops? Are you crazy? You know I can't call the cops."

"It's okay." The second wave of pain hits and lingers awhile. I grit my teeth and try to reassure her. "I'm just a junkie who broke into your house. Legally, you're in the clear."

"Legally?" She lets out a semihysterical laugh and starts with the ridiculous breathing exercises again. "*Huh-uuuunh . . . Huh-uuuuuuunh . . .*" I swear to God, it's like the bitch is in labor or something.

I'm about to speak again, when the third wave of pain hits, and just stays. It feels like somebody left a hot soldering iron in my stomach. I decide to change tactics.

"Look, you *fucking cunt*, you shot me in the stomach. If you don't call 911, I'm going to fucking die, and you're going to fucking prison for the rest of your fucking life."

She finally stops with the deep breathing, hesitates a moment, and then pulls out her phone. She hits the speed dial, and to my surprise, starts talking to somebody in rapid-fire Spanish. Not the lispy shit you might learn from a college year abroad in Spain, but Mexican street slang. The conversation moves so fast that about all I can pick up is the name Esteban. This bitch isn't just fluent, she's a goddamn native speaker.

"He wants to know who you work for." She flips the phone shut and switches back to an equally native-sounding English.

"Work for? What do you mean?"

"He's sending someone. He says to keep you alive."

"Who's sending someone?"

"Esteban."

"Esteban?"

She nods.

"Who the fuck is Esteban?"

"I'm going to see if there're any bandages in the bathroom." She ignores my question. "I swear to God, if you move while I'm gone, I'll kill you."

"I told you, I can't move. I think you hit my spine."

"Good."

She leaves the room and I'm left to ponder why she speaks native Mex slang, who the hell Esteban is, and why the bitch doesn't even know what's in her own medicine cabinet. I look down again at the bullet hole in my hoodie. There's still no blood.

A minute later, she comes back with a roll of duct tape, paper towels, and a bottle of Extra Strength Tylenol.

"Lady, I'm a fucking junkie. Tylenol is not going to cut it."

"That's all there was."

"Well, maybe if you called a fucking ambulance they might have something a little stronger?"

"I told you. Esteban is sending someone. Do you want the Tylenol or not?"

"No."

"All right, I'm going to see if I can make a bandage." She puts the Ruger and Tylenol over on the coffee table out of my reach, and then kneels down next to me with the duct tape and paper towel.

"Christ . . . is that blood?" She notices my soaked jeans.

"It's piss."

"Eww!" She recoils.

"I'm fucking dying here and you're scared of a little piss?"

She does her best to regroup and folds up a piece of paper towel into a half-assed square, adding strips of duct tape to the four sides to form a makeshift bandage.

"What the hell is that?"

"It's the best I can do, is what it is." She does a few more deep breathing exercises, and then slowly lifts my hoodie and T-shirt.

The hole seems almost ludicrously small—about an inch below, and an inch to the left of my navel. My whole stomach is smeared with blood, but not a Hollywood amount. For some reason, exposing the wound to the air makes it hurt even more, and it's all I can do to keep from screaming.

"You don't have HIV or anything . . . ?" She hesitates at the sight of the blood.

"No," I lie.

She looks at the hole for a few more seconds, building courage. "Did the bullet go through?" she asks.

"How the fuck should I know?"

She reaches gently around to the small of my back to feel for a hole.

"It must still be inside you."

"Is that a good thing or a bad thing?"

She shrugs, and adds a few more strips of duct tape to the paper towel bandage.

"Okay, this is the part that's going to hurt."

She uses an extra sheet of paper towel to carefully mop up the blood around the gunshot hole, and then slaps the bandage on.

I scream.

She's so startled that she momentarily lets go.

I keep screaming.

She puts pressure on the bandage again and begins to tape it down.

I keep screaming.

She lets go.

I stop screaming. And then promptly shit myself.

"Oh gross!" She jumps back from me, covering her face with her hand to try and block the smell.

Somehow the change in bowel pressure shifts things around, and I have to start screaming again.

"Shut up!" She grabs the Ruger off the coffee table and

waves it at me for emphasis. "Shut up or I'll fucking shoot!"

I manage to stop screaming, but it's not going to last.

"Look, you fucking cunt, either finish me off or get me something for the pain."

She hesitates.

I start to scream again.

"Shut up!" She slaps a hand over my mouth.

I try to bite it.

"Look, just shut up for a minute and I'll see what I can do, okay?"

I shut up.

She speed dials the number again, and there's more rapid back-and-forth in Spanish. After a few seconds, she covers the mouthpiece with her hand.

"He says someone will be here soon."

"How soon?"

She's back on the phone for another few seconds, but then her expression changes and she covers the mouthpiece again.

"He wants to know who you work for."

"Who I work for? No one. I'm a fucking junkie."

She's back on the phone, and this time actually winces at whatever Esteban is telling her.

"He says he needs to know right now." She walks over and kneels next to me again, keeping her face turned away from the smell. "I'm sorry."

"About what?"

She winces again at what she's hearing over the phone, and then reaches out with her free hand and presses on my stomach.

"AHHHHHHHH!!!"

"Tell me." She keeps her hand there.

"AHHHHHHHH!!!"

"Tell me and I'll stop."

"Okay! Stop! Stop!"

She lets her hand up.

"Voodoo Mike." I gasp for air. "I work for fucking Voodoo Mike, all right?" The idea is completely absurd, but it's the first name that pops into my head. Besides, I owe him money.

She relays this information to Esteban, then flips the phone shut again.

"You fucking blond bitch. You fucking cunt whore cooze. I'll fucking kill you, you fucking cocksucking motherfucking—"

"I think someone's here." She runs over to look out the front window.

I hear what sounds like a truck pull into the driveway, and then a door slam. The blond bitch heads back to the coffee table for the Ruger, then sprints to the front door and opens it. A moment later, a uniformed EMT walks in.

"Esteban sent you, right?" she asks.

The EMT just nods. He couldn't be more than twenty-five, but immediately takes charge of the situation.

"How is he?"

"I . . . I tried to bandage him, but—" the blond bitch stutters.

The EMT shoves past her and comes straight over to me, putting his box of supplies down on the carpet next to where he kneels. He snaps on the latex gloves, and I tense up figuring he's going to lift my hoodie and inspect the wound, but instead he starts checking the veins on my arms and hands.

"These are fucked. Where are you shooting now?" he asks.

"My legs."

"I think the best bet is the jugular." He examines my neck for a moment, then pulls an IV bag out of the box of supplies. "This is saline. You're losing blood and need fluids to keep you from going into shock."

"You're not going to bandage it?" the blond bitch asks.

"There's no point. He needs surgery."

The guy is good and hits the jugular no problem. I can feel the cold of the saline rushing down my neck. Somehow the fluid triggers another wave of pain, and I start screaming again.

"Oh for Christ sake, shut up!" the bitch yells at me.

"He needs morphine." The EMT turns to look at her.

"Well, give him fucking morphine then!"

"I can't. They keep track of our supply."

"So what the hell do you want me to do?"

The EMT just looks at her.

I keep screaming.

"No way. Esteban would kill me." She shakes her head.

"We don't have a choice. He wants him alive, doesn't he?"

"No." She keeps shaking her head.

"Yes." The EMT nods.

"AHHHHHHH!!!" I scream.

"All right, this is all on you." The blond bitch throws up her hands and disappears down the hall.

"Where the fuck's the trolley?" I manage to stop screaming long enough to ask the EMT.

"Sorry," he says.

"What the fuck do you mean, *Sorry?*"

I'm about to start screaming again when the bitch comes back with what looks like a blob of beige packing tape.

"I'm telling you, this is all on you." She hesitates in front of the EMT. "I want no part of it."

"Fine."

He holds out his hand until she finally gives him the blob, and then uses a pair of medical shears to cut the tape away from one corner. Despite ten years of being a junkie I've never actually seen a whole kilo outside of TV news reports, so it takes me a second to comprehend what it is.

"Is that . . . Is that a fucking kilo?" I ask.

"Do you have your works on you?"

"What the fuck are you doing with a kilo?" I ask the blond bitch, but she's back to the deep breathing exercises.

"Do you have your works on you?" the EMT calmly repeats the question.

I point to my right sock.

"I'm not going to get stuck, am I?" He hesitates.

"No. It's capped."

He pulls out the works and then heads back to the kitchen with the spoon to get some water—just leaving the kilo there on the freakin' coffee table like it's nothing.

"What the hell is going on here?" I ask the bitch.

"I need you to promise me something," she leans in and whispers so the EMT can't hear in the other room. "When Esteban gets here, tell him this was all the paramedic's idea, okay?"

"Why the fuck do you have a fucking kilo of *chiva* in your house?"

The EMT comes back before she can answer and starts loading up the spoon straight from the kilo.

"What are you? A gram a day?"

"Gram and a half."

He taps a tiny bit more in.

"Hey, you're going a bit light there," I point out.

"Trust me, this shit is pure."

"It's black tar. How pure can it be?"

"Pure."

He cooks it over my lighter, then barely lets it cool before skipping the cotton ball and loading it straight into one of the horse syringes from his box.

"Jesus Christ, this is a fucking stash house, isn't it?" I ask them both.

Instead of answering, the EMT sticks the needle into a little side branch of my IV line and pushes the heroin directly into my jugular.

The shit hits me like a fucking Amtrak.

I'm not sure how long I nod, but when I come back, the pain is just a dull ache.

The EMT is gone and the blond bitch is on the phone with her back to me talking to someone in Spanish again. I spot the EMT's horse syringe on the carpet about a foot from me. With her attention focused on the phone call, I try to see if I can reach it. Everything below the waist is dead and my arms feel like boiled spaghetti, but now that the pain is gone, I'm able to shift my upper body just enough. I grab the syringe, hide it behind me, and shift back to where I was. It's not much of a weapon, but if the bitch tries pressing on my stomach again, at least I can stab her.

Outside I hear a car pull into the driveway and multiple doors slam. The bitch flips her phone shut.

I don't know what I expected Esteban to look like, but the light-skinned Mexican guy who walks into the living room strikes me more as a male model for one of those multicultural Benetton ads than a drug kingpin. The fucking guy is wearing a neon orange button-down with a baby-blue tennis sweater tied around his neck. If it wasn't for the white pit bull at his side and the keloid scar across his neck, he could pass as fucking Eurotrash.

"What happened here, Connie?" His accent isn't very strong, but it's true Mex, not Chicano.

"Esteban, he broke in . . . and I shot . . . and I shot him."

"It's okay. Give me the gun. I'll get rid of it."

She hands him the Ruger.

Without saying another word, Esteban walks over and steps on my lower abdomen. Even with the heroin, it hurts like a motherfucker. I can't imagine what the pain would be like if I were straight.

He watches my reaction.

"You're high, aren't you?"

I try not to look at him.

"That's okay, man. I've got some Narcan back at the other house. A little of that and you'll feel it plenty."

"Fuck you."

"That's funny, you know. That's just what the *mayate* said."

He yells something in Spanish down the hall, and two other Mex guys drag Voodoo Mike in. He's out cold with his hands zip-tied behind his back and a duct tape gag covering his mouth. His face is so fucked up it looks like somebody put a Rasta wig on a blob of hamburger meat. They drop him right on top of my legs, so that his head is faceup in my lap.

"Your friend here doesn't listen good." Esteban shakes his head. He says something in Spanish, and the shorter of the two Mex guys comes over. Shortie actually giggles as he bends down and pinches Mike's nose closed.

Mike comes to fighting for air, and his eyes practically pop out of his head. If it wasn't for the hamburger face, he'd look like a fucking cartoon. Esteban waves Shortie off, and Mike's eyes finally retreat back into their sockets as he starts snorting in air again.

All three of them laugh, and then crack up completely when the phone in Mike's front pocket begins playing some crappy Mariah Carey ringtone at full volume.

"Aren't you going to answer your phone, *mayate*?" Esteban asks.

Mike continues snorting, either ignoring the question or just oblivious.

"Maybe there's something wrong with his ear? No?" Esteban's brow furrows in mock concern.

"*El lapíz*." He snaps his fingers and Shortie hands him a pencil. Squatting down next to Mike, he grabs hold of his dreadlocks with one hand and whispers in his right ear. "Can you hear me now, *mayate*?"

Esteban gives me a wink, and then jams the pencil hard into Mike's ear.

The blond bitch lets out a scream and Mike starts writhing as Esteban digs around with the pencil. Shortie giggles, but the other Mex has to look away.

"Hey, Connie," Esteban calls out, "I can't find anything. You try."

"Esteban . . . I . . . Please."

"Come on." He digs in farther and Mike starts to go into convulsions. "It's fun."

"No. Please. I . . . I can't."

"Okay," Esteban sighs, and pulls the pencil out.

Mike stops convulsing. His eyes stay open, but the right one goes all wonky and looks off to the side.

Esteban stands back up and then seems to notice the kilo for the first time.

"Connie? Why is there an open brick on the coffee table?" He starts to twirl the pencil in his hand.

"That's not on me, Esteban! That paramedic you sent said—"

"What did I tell you about opening the product?"

"It wasn't me! Ask him!" She points to me.

"Him?" Esteban laughs. "You mean, the *pendejo* you shot in the stomach?"

"Tell him!" Connie begs me. Her blue eyes are wide and she's starting to go pale.

I don't say anything. All I can think about is the phone in Mike's pocket.

"Please! Just tell him it was the paramedic!" Her voice breaks into a squeal.

"*Cálmate, mujer.*" Esteban smiles, still twirling the pencil. "I think our *amigo* here just needs a little motivation."

Mike's phone makes a whooshing noise to indicate that whoever called left a voice mail, but Esteban ignores it and steps on my abdomen again.

"You don't want to help the poor *güera* over here?" he asks.

"Fuck you."

"You know I'm going to kill you, no?" He presses down harder.

I try to speak, but can't.

"Just tell me who opened the brick." He takes his foot off, and gives a squeeze of the IV bag to bring me back around. "If you do that, I'll let you load a few grams into that syringe you're hiding behind your back, and you go off to junkie heaven . . ." He reaches over with the pencil and tickles my ear. "Or, if you want, we can always play a little more of Hide the Pencil."

"Esteban . . ." Connie tries to intervene.

"Shhhh." Esteban waves her off and speaks to me. "What do you think? Do you want to die the easy way or like the fucking *mayate?*"

Connie's given up and is just staring at me.

Shortie and the other Mex guy are staring at me too.

Esteban is smiling.

Fuck it.

"It was her." I tilt my head at the blond bitch, figuring it might buy me some time.

"No! Esteban, he's—"

"*Está bien,*" Esteban reassures her. "Connie, do you really think I'm going to take a *pinche* junkie's word over yours?"

"No, but I—"

"*Está bien*, okay?"

She nods, uncertain.

"Why don't you help Jaime and Mario move the bricks out to the truck. This house isn't safe anymore."

Connie just looks at him.

"Okay?"

"Okay."

She reluctantly heads back into the hall, followed by the taller Mex, but Shortie lags behind and looks to Esteban for instructions.

Esteban hands him the Ruger and nods.

Shortie giggles as he slips the gun into his coat and trails the other two out into the hall.

"I guess we're going to need a new *güera.*" Esteban walks back over. "And you know what? I think I changed my mind. We are going to play Hide the Lapíz after all." He tickles my ear with the pencil again. "But first, I'm going to get that Narcan." He gives some sort of command in Spanish to the pit bull, and then leaves.

I listen to his footsteps going down the hall, my eyes fixed on the faint outline of a phone in Mike's front pocket. Knowing I'm only going to have one shot at this, I wait until I actually hear the backdoor open before making my move. I can barely lift my arms and my hands are so clumsy that they feel like oven mitts, but after a minute or so of struggle, I manage to pull out the phone.

There's a muffled gunshot down in the basement, followed by Shortie's giggle. The pit bull lets out a tentative growl.

"Good doggy."

I use my teeth to help flip the phone open, and then use my knuckle to dial.

Nine . . .

One . . .

Shit. I hear the creak of the backdoor and footsteps coming quickly down the hall again.

I fumble with the phone and manage to jam it in the pocket of my hoodie just before Esteban walks in.

He spots it anyway.

"I knew I forgot something." He pulls the phone out of my hoodie and checks the numbers on the screen. "Ninety-one! Oh . . . you were so close, *amigo.*" He laughs.

"Fuck you." I try to spit, but it just dribbles down my chin.

Despite the fact that it was barely audible, for some reason this final *Fuck you* seems to get to him. He bends forward as if he's gonna hit me, but stops short at the last second. The smile returns, and instead of smacking me, he laughs.

"You know, I'm going to tell you a little secret." He bends forward to whisper in my ear. "I believe you, *amigo.* You're not working for the Tijuanans. You're just some piece-of-shit junkie who broke into the wrong house, no?"

Esteban stands back up and waits for my response, but I don't give him one.

"I'm right, aren't I?" He laughs again, then pulls out the pencil again and gives it a slow twirl. "So now we get to play our little game just for pleasure, no?"

He pockets both the pencil and the phone, and then blows me a kiss before leaving.

Once Esteban's gone, everything just drains out of me.

I look down at Mike. His right eye is still all fucked up and looking the wrong way, but his left is staring at me. Almost pleading.

"Sorry, man. I tried."

Figuring I might as well speed things up, I make a feeble attempt to pull the IV out of my neck, but my arms are so heavy I can't seem to raise them above my shoulder anymore.

The pit bull growls again at my movements, and I start to wonder if there's any way I can provoke him—hell, even getting mauled by a pit bull has to be better than that fucking pencil.

"Hey, dog. Fuck you," I try to yell, but it comes out more like a whisper.

The pit bull promptly trots over and starts licking my face.

Goddamnit.

Out in the hall, I hear what must be Connie's body being dragged out, and then the backdoor slam shut. There's another giggle from Shortie outside in the driveway, and after a minute or so, the truck drives off.

The pit bull curls up next to me on the carpet, and I begin to feel lightheaded. There's something oddly comforting about just giving up, and the pain actually recedes a bit. For some reason I think about my stepmother, and how before she got cancer she used to try and grow radishes in that vacant lot next to the gas station . . .

Just as I start to nod again, I hear a snorting noise and glance back down at Mike.

His one good eye is still pleading.

"What?"

His eye starts to move. First looking at me, and then down at his jeans. He keeps doing it. Over and over.

"What the fuck is that supposed to mean?"

And then I hear it. A faint ringtone coming from Mike's other front pocket.

BABY, I'M HERE

BY Monica Drake

Legacy Good Samaritan Hospital

Rebar's first day out of the big loony bin on the hill, just checked into transitional housing, I agreed to meet him at the Marathon Taverna. I should've said no. Bad plan. But I went along with it. Over the phone, he said, "I need to get out, see people. Get back in the swing."

I said, "The only people you'll see at the Marathon are drunks. Maybe your dad if we stay late."

He said, "I need to see you, Vanessa."

And I gave in.

Before that, he'd wanted to meet up at my place. Problem was, my place was his. He owned the house. If I let him in, he'd never leave. He'd pick through my things looking for his things, any sign of him and me together, like playing husband and wife or some other sorry story. His was one of the last shacks set between warehouses in deep Northwest. Rebar'd said I could use it until he got out—out of jail, out of detox, out of the Mental Motel that was part of his sentence. Sounded like a long enough list, I hadn't expected him back anytime soon. He's not known for good behavior.

I took a bus down Twenty-first and walked along Burnside. Overhead it was a gray sky. My raincoat flapped against the wind like a dying bird, slapped my knee with each step. Traffic lined the street thick as a parking lot. More cars jammed the McDonald's. Across the way, somebody'd built a high-rise condo. The whole town was turning into a city of glass pillars.

A guy in a pickup held back at a green light. He let me cross Eighteenth. When I got to the other side I smiled and waved thanks, wiggled my fingers in the air. The man smiled too. Looking my way, he stepped on the gas and T-boned an idling Smart Car wedged in the intersection. There was the crunch of metal, a broken headlight, something swimming-pool blue that skidded over the macadam. I pretended not to notice because the thing is, that man had been sweet. I didn't want him to feel bad about his driving problem.

Inside the Marathon, I found a table and peeled off my coat, put down my pocketbook. The tavern air was murky, thick with sweat, beer, and smoke, but warmer than outside. And it was dark. Instant night, in the middle of day. Scattered popcorn on the carpet was the glow of stars. I looked for the North Star, some guiding light in that mess, like an explorer let loose on a new world. Rebar, now sober, crazy, and adjusting to antipsychotics, he was a new world. A new planet. I had no idea how to handle him.

Taki, the Greek who ran the place, dropped his rag. He said, "Ah, Vanessa, *my beauty*. What can I do for you?" He wiped his hands on his pants.

He always said *my beauty*. It didn't mean much, but I liked it, and liked him for it. I said, "I'll have a beer and Snappy Tom's, if you got it." In that bar, beer meant Budweiser. There was nothing else.

Taki said, "You're alone?"

I said, "Not alone. With you." My hair was thick and hung heavy over one eye. I shook it out of the way, but it fell back again. One of these days I'd get a real haircut.

Taki brought the drink to my table. "If I wasn't working, I'd take you someplace better than this. I'd take you to Greece. You been there?"

I hadn't been anywhere. I'd walked the same city blocks long as I could remember. An old guy at the bar rapped his glass against the wood. Taki had to get back. Other than people like me and Rebar, who went there for cheap drink, it was geezers who inhabited the Marathon Tavern. Men who lived in single rooms for rent upstairs. When I found the place, I'd lived down the street in the Tudor Arms apartments with a guy named Ray.

The door opened to let in a big slice of midday sun, traffic, and exhaust. It was Rebar, his shadow joining the dark with the rest of us. He saw my red beer. "Shaking off a hangover, Angel?"

I said, "Wish I had a hangover angel. Somebody to come rub the aches away." This time it wasn't a hangover I wanted to shake, but a life of mistakes, wrong men, places like this dive I found myself in all over again.

Rebar said, "Here I am." Like he was my angel.

His black hair stood up in front. His jeans were stained with cement mix, from the rock wall he'd been building before he got picked up. Instead of his work boots, he was wearing Sketchers, tennies right out of Payless Shoes. They were as out of place as hospital slippers on Rebar's big feet. But still he was beautiful, wiry and strong, an olive-skinned James Dean. He was comic-book thin, muscled and taut. He said, "Got a hello for me?"

I stood, let him pull me close. He lifted me off my feet, squeezed my ribs, tipped me out of my stilettos. I lay my arms over his shoulders. He'd been gone for months. Now he smelled like soap and shave cream. He smelled like a man on parole, trying to do things right. That wouldn't last. When he let go I said, "Didn't they wash your clothes in that place?" I sat, to put a tiny table between us.

He said, "Maybe. This stuff doesn't come out."

"Maybe nothing changes."

Rebar put his fingers around my wrist. "Maybe I changed." His fingers were handcuffs.

Before Rebar went in the hospital, he hadn't been sleeping. He hadn't been drinking in the last days of his crazy spell, but was talking to strangers in sounds that weren't real words. That's against some kind of law, I guess, because the cops knocked him flat on the sidewalk, tased him in the bus mall outside of Pioneer Square, did what they called "subdued." They hauled him off.

Now, between the rash of razor burn and a scar on his forehead where he hit the sidewalk, he had the face of a baby and an old man at the same time. Least he wasn't wide-eyed, wired, ready to crack someone's jaw. He didn't look electric. He said, "Feels like I been gone for years." His voice was shaky. That wasn't new. His voice was always shaky.

I said, "Just stay off the sauce."

He nodded, and squinted at that soundless TV on in the corner. "Got a bracelet." He pulled up his pant leg. I'd never seen him wear shoes without socks before. His calve was wrapped in a brown plastic band with two boxes, one on either side. "Transdermal, they call it. Scram."

"Scram?" I thought he wanted me to leave. I was more than ready. I reached for my pocketbook, pulled it to my lap.

"Secure Continuous Remote Alcohol Monitor," he said. "SCRAM. I don't think this sucker works, though. Supposed to read your alcohol level through sweat. Five percent of everything you drink comes out through the skin."

"They made you take a class in it." I could tell, by the way he talked.

"If I don't drink, they won't know I been here, right?"

"Booze leaches through the walls in this place. It's in the air." I sipped my red beer. I ran my fingers over the glass. I ran my hand, wet from the glass, over my forehead and across my neck.

Alcohol-induced psychosis. That was the theory doctors offered for Rebar's tripped-up month, like he drank more than anyone else. He sure didn't drink more than the men who lined the counter, those old sea gulls on their posts. It didn't mean anything—he was crazy. Drinking made him crazier.

I turned a clean amber ashtray over in my palm, felt the weight of it, sharp edges of beveled glass. That ashtray was solid. My plan was to quit taking things I didn't need. I didn't need anything. I'd already filled Rebar's shack with salt and pepper shakers, coffee cups, sunglasses, doormats, hood ornaments, construction barricades. I had a plastic lawn Santa to watch me all year long, keeping tabs, naughty or nice.

The ashtray was a sure thing, hard and sharp. I slipped it in my purse. Rebar rolled a cigarette. I shifted one end of the tavern's orange curtain to see the street and knocked a curled and faded *Help Wanted* sign from the window. There was no one outside except traffic, and hardly anyone in the tavern. Rebar's eyes on me, his body so close, made the place crowded.

"You need to start eating," I said. I threw a piece of pop-corn his way.

"Did you miss me?"

"I'm glad you're better."

"Yeah?" A fleck of tobacco danced on his lip. When he

reached for my fingers, I pulled my hand back. He held on. "You don't give a rip."

I pushed with my other hand against the rock of his forearm. His skin was a thin cover over muscle. "I want to drink my drink," I said.

He pulled me closer, until my ribs leaned into the side of the table. My hand grew hot; a candle burned in a red glass globe on the table below. Rebar whispered, "When I was crucified by those cops, you were the voice in my ear. You were laughing, but you were at my side." He let go of my arm and I fell back, tipped the rickety table enough to slosh red beer against the rim of my glass. Slosh wax against the inside of the candle's little world. I lifted my glass and let beer drip.

Taki put the *Help Wanted* sign back in the window. He ran a rag over the table. "Don't break anything, you hear?"

"Like my arm," I said.

Taki said, "You okay?"

I nodded. My wrist felt the residue of Rebar's strength. I tried to rub it out. His cigarette burned in the ashtray, a long ash off the end. I couldn't stand that smell, and yet I lived in a cloud of smoke. I said, "If you're going to smoke, smoke. Don't burn 'em like incense."

Rebar said, "So, when do I get my place back?"

I knew it'd come around to that. "Thought they set you up, a place to stay."

"Only till I can prove I got my own."

"You'll have it back. Just give me time to pack, wouldya?"

"You could stay," he said, and his eyes got soft in that way that made me want to head for the door.

I found lipstick and a compact in my purse. I painted my lips red. "With you? A happy home, all over again?"

He nodded, watched me.

"Not in the least likely." I clipped the lid back on the lip-stick. Dropped it in my purse and signaled Taki for another drink.

Then Tino came in the alley door and went up to the bar without looking our way. He held his jeans pocket down from the outside with one hand and pulled money out from inside the pocket with the other. He bought a six-pack of cans to go, in a bag, and one beer in a bottle to have opened. His hands didn't shake when he counted out change. When his hands didn't shake, that meant he'd been drinking already.

Tino worked as a narc for Lincoln High, catching tru-ants, once in a while patting them down for weapons. On the side, he'd confiscate drugs from kids and sell them back to the janitors. Janitors sold the same score back to kids. Tino wasn't getting rich, but kept his head out of water.

Rebar followed my look. His neck was stiff; he had to turn in his chair. Tendons came to the surface. He said, "Your boy-friend's here." He rapped a foot against the leg of the table. It might've been more of a kick, but those Sketchers softened the blow.

I caught the table, stopped it from rocking. "He's not my boyfriend."

If Rebar hadn't been there, just out of the psych ward, working hard to not drink and keep his head together, maybe I would've walked over and reached for Tino. Maybe I'd call him a boyfriend, or close enough to it.

I never did get the dating thing, where it stopped and started.

Tino saw us. He said, "Hey. What's up?" He looked tired, his eyes ringed with circles. His top lip was chapped, cracked in a brown spot of dried blood.

Rebar said, "When do I get my Dr. Martens back?"

Tino half-laughed, blew it off.

I said, "Criminey. Not the shoes again."

Rebar'd lost his Dr. Martens to Tino in a minor drug deal. Rebar made his dough in construction, old houses, but that didn't always come through. He'd been broke that day. The shoes, as a trade, were a compromise. Rebar couldn't let it go.

He said, "Serious."

Tino said, "I'm not a hawk shop, friend." He was wearing the shoes.

I said, "Rebar's fresh out of the funny farm. Trying to put a life together. Those shoes might be part of the picture."

Rebar's house was a bigger part of that picture.

Tino said, "Down here, or up on the hill?"

"I was up on the hill," Rebar said, and he said it so quiet his mouth barely moved. He shook his head, like he didn't get it himself.

Tino said, "I'm headed to Good Sam."

Rebar said, "You going nuts too?"

"Going to see Eileen." He turned a chair backward, sat on it that way, then lit a cigarette. "She had an aneurysm in her brain." He pointed to his head with the orange tip of the smoke, his thumb aimed at the ceiling. His hand was like a gun, at his own head.

I said, "No way."

Rebar said, "Who's Eileen?"

I said, "Waitress at Chang's, dyes her hair."

Tino said, "Living with Ray Madrigal."

That was the part I didn't want to say, and didn't want to hear, the reason I knew who Tino meant—Eileen and Ray. Ray, who I'd lived with, before. I pulled the ashtray out of my purse, kept it hidden by my palm, and put it back on the table.

I didn't need that ashtray. But I couldn't let go. I moved it to my purse again.

Tino said, "They cut her head open and clamped a vein or something shut. She's fine, but she's bald."

I slid a salt shaker into my purse and said, "No shit?" Ray's new girl, with hardware in her head.

The bathroom at the Marathon was down a glowing turquoise hall, like a pool drained of water, and it smelled from mildew. It was the hallway to the rooms for rent upstairs. Just out-side the women's bathroom somebody had written in black marker, MEN WHO FATHER CHILDREN LIVE HERE. I read those words every time I turned the corner. I'd memo-rized the writing—all capital letters and jagged angles. The sentence stuck with me. It seemed wrong, reversed, blaming the men for where they lived instead of what they did, maybe even asking for sympathy, or renovation on the building. MEN WHO LIVE HERE FATHER CHILDREN, it should say. MEN WHO LIVE HERE ARE BAD—but the men in the building weren't bad, only lost and lazy. Drunks. Only men nobody should have kids with in the first place. Men who fa-ther children live everywhere.

I came out of the bathroom. Tino was in the hall. We went out back, to the alley between buildings, beside the dumpster. Tino pulled a pipe from his coat pocket.

Pot smells good in the cold. There's the density of it, that soft sweetness. I'd like to find that same sweet edge in some-thing solid.

Tino passed the pipe to me. I didn't reach for it. "You shake down a freshman for that herb?" I said.

"Maybe." He was still holding smoke in his lungs. "What're you doing with Rebar?"

"Helping him out." I shrugged.

Tino said, "Watch him close. I don't want to lose more teeth."

"That was a long time ago."

"They don't come back." He smiled, to show a gap at the side near the front. His eye tooth, his dog tooth. A fist, a party. Like two years before, but it seemed forever. I put my lips to his cracked lips, kissed his gap-toothed mouth, breathed his secondhand pot smoke. I held onto the fake sheepskin of his Sears corduroy coat. Tino's skinny body blocked the wind. One time, when he was still underage, Tino'd been busted for dealing and his folks sent him off to boot camp in Idaho. He broke out, hitched home, and hid in Forest Park at night when he couldn't find a place to crash, until he hooked up with me for a while. I don't know what happened to him out there in Idaho, but now, best thing about Tino was he wouldn't leave the neighborhood. He said it himself—he'd never go anywhere he couldn't walk home from.

One of these days I'd go as far away as I wanted, and I knew he'd be there, home, when I got back. Tino was home, and he was mine.

We went back in the tavern. Rebar worked his muscled jaw. Maybe it was time for more meds, I had no clue.

Someone said my name, *Vanessa*, in the hiss of a whisper. I looked. The men lining the bar had their backs to our table. Music rattled under bad speakers. Nobody said my name. It was just noises, a cloud of tavern sounds; my name was a patchwork put together from scrap.

Tino said, "Come see Eileen. She'd like it."

My hands were light and far away with the cold. I rubbed

them together. "I don't think we should visit Eileen. I'm fine here."

Rebar said, "Jesus, Vanessa, she had brain surgery."

I said, "Hospital-land. It creeps me out. All that mortality." Then again, the bar was lined with vulture fodder.

Rebar said, "I started to like it."

Tino said, "Ray won't show up."

I said, "You going?"

Rebar shook his head.

I said, "Okay." So I'd shake off Rebar. Maybe I'd get lost on the way too. Except when I stood, Rebar stood. He said, "Swap shoes with me, man." He kicked off a Sketcher. Tino ignored him. Rebar worked his shoes back on and hustled to catch up, snagging my arm to hold me back.

The hospital halls were miles of white, somebody's idea of a sterile heaven, broken by red emergency phones and inset shrines of faded saints. Rebar put his arm over my shoulder. I hadn't shaken anybody. He stooped to bring his face closer to mine and said, "Where I was, we had big rooms and new carpets. We had coffee machines." His big feet swung out, ready to knock things down.

I heard my name again, in a whisper: *Van-ess-a, Van-ess-a* . . . It was under the swish of clothes and the wheels of the carts. Rebar's coat sleeve rustled against my ear.

Tino skipped the reception desk.

"You been here before?" Rebar asked me.

"I was born here, but never been back." The hospital was its own world, all clean, creased green uniforms. Aluminum carts, Formica. It was a different place from the world outside. In the hospital, pretty much I didn't know anybody.

Rebar, Tino, and me—we were a walking cloud of tavern

air, smoke, and beer breath. I reached a hand, laced one finger through Tino's belt loop.

Vanessa.

I heard my name in the squish of shoes on hard linoleum, and the breath of coats as they exhaled. This time, though, when I turned, it was real. It was Mrs. Petoskey, our old grade school teacher. "Vanessa." She said it.

She was in scrubs.

Rebar, Tino, and me, we stopped together. I said, "Hi."

Mrs. Petoskey said, "Good to see you. How's your mom?"

I shook my head. Brushed my hair out of the way. My mom? I didn't know. I said, "Fine."

Mrs. Petoskey smiled.

I said, "Still in the slammer." Tino laughed, flashing his gapped teeth like it was a joke, and the funny thing was, it wasn't. Mrs. Petoskey moved some tubes around on her cart.

I said, "Meth charges." Then I asked, "You don't teach school?"

Mrs. Petoskey said, "No, well, things change." And she waved a hand over her cart, pulled on a face mask, and pushed on through a set of swinging doors. "Take care." Her voice was muffled by the mask.

Tino said, "Didn't she have cancer before?"

I didn't remember, but she probably did.

Eileen was in bed, watching TV, same as everyone in every dank hole of a tavern all over town. Her head was shaved and bandaged. Her face was puffy. She'd put on makeup and it sat like paint over her drained skin.

I said, "They told me there was a dead hooker in here."

Eileen said, "Thanks a lot. Got years ahead'a me."

I said, "Isn't that how every story goes?"

I gave her a kiss on her pale forehead. I wasn't glad to see her, but that wasn't her fault. She was the only patient in a room with two beds, wearing a powder-blue hospital gown. She leaned against pillows.

"'S good to see you," she said. Her voice was slow and stuttery.

Tino pulled a can of beer from his paper bag.

Eileen asked, "How 'bout a cig-rette?" There were two *No Smoking* signs.

Tino pushed the door closed. I sat on the windowsill. Rebar leaned against the wall too close beside me. When Tino passed around the rest of the six-pack, I said, "This man's got the shoes and the booze." I wouldn't've said it without a few drinks in me already, but I wanted a little space. To set Rebar back. I ran a hand over Tino's shoulders, that bony armature of a human.

Rebar looked at the shoes, his shoes, on Tino's feet, and he took a beer.

I said, "What about your bracelet?"

"I'll try not to sweat." Rebar tipped the can. He drank like drinking was breathing, like he'd been held under water and here was his can of air.

"Rebar just got out of the other one. On the hill," Tino said.

"No kiddin'?" Eileen lit a cigarette, keeping an eye on the door. "Haven't 'moked all day."

"The alarm'll go off," I said.

"What'll dey do if dey catch me—frow me out?" This was the lisp of her stroke, her brain stutter like a car with sugar in the tank.

I sat on the empty bed. Tightened my rain coat around me in case some fire alarm sprinklers went off. "What the hell happened?"

Eileen said, "Went out for drinks after work . . . my hands started feelin' weird."

Tino said, "Must've felt pretty weird if they brought you to Emergency."

I felt my own hands, imagining my head as light, losing blood and circulation. I looked for Ray at the door, waited for the alarm to scream. I was ready to skedaddle.

"It was," Eileen said. "Cut my head open like dis." She drew an invisible *L* on the bandage, down from the top and across one side.

Rebar said, "How many channels you get?"

The dark circles under Eileen's eyes made her beautiful, like a face-lift patient or a drug addict in treatment. She was being taken care of, and that meant cared for. The blue hospital robe rested against her skin at her clavicle in a way that said fragile and yet still living, meaning strong. Who would've known light blue and bandage white could be so dreamy?

I said, "You're gorgeous."

She patted the bed beside her. I lay down, watching out for tubes and her food tray. She said, "You know, Ray doesn't talk about you at all."

"Music to my ears." I sipped my drink. Tapped the can.

Tino and Rebar watched TV like TV mattered.

She said, "I mean, he's doing it on purpose. Like if he said your name, it'd all come back . . ."

My nail polish was chipped red. I chipped it off more, letting red flakes rest on Eileen's white sheets.

She whispered, "If you wanted Ray back, you could do it."

I said, "Don't worry. I don't take anything that doesn't belong to me."

"Since when?"

"Since now, okay? He's yours." My purse was bulging with the ashtray, the salt shaker, who knows what else.

Rebar crumpled his empty can. He made it small, and put it in his coat pocket. Tino hit the remote, changed the channel.

Rebar said, "Hey, who's the asshole?"

Tino waved the remote, raised his hand. Asshole: present and accounted for.

I said, "You going to let him get away with that?" Like it mattered.

Rebar let the TV be his pacifier, eased into a new channel.

Tino changed channels again. I got up, off Eileen's bed. I put a hand on Rebar's arm, said, "Keep a level head."

Rebar said, "What're you, some kind of counselor?" He ran his fingers through my hair.

"I've got a few good tips."

He let his fingers latch on, tug, and he laughed, like a joke, but he pulled my head back and my neck gave in so easily, Rebar's face was close to mine. My hair was long, he held it, then he let go.

I was done there.

Time to go home, pack, get out of Rebar's shack in the warehouse district. I said, "You need to manage yourself." And I moved away, behind Tino, behind Eileen's bed, far from Rebar's reach. I ran one arm over Tino's shoulder and said, "Those shoes suit him better anyway. Don't they?"

It wasn't the shoes. It was everything. Rebar was a loaded gun.

"Have another beer." I tossed one of the last two to Rebar. "Calm down. I'll be back. Bathroom." I shook the nearly empty can in my hand.

Eileen said, "Use mine." She pointed to a door off the side of the room.

* * *

Eileen's bathroom was small, like a bathroom on the back of a Greyhound, only clean. Everything was made out of stainless steel and pressed board. I looked for signs of a hidden camera in the ceiling. Maybe a hospital kept watch in stray corners. What did I know? A second door on the opposite side of the toilet's small space meant a nurse or another patient could walk in, and I was afraid I'd touch something meant to stay clean. I wasn't drunk, but was on my way, and drunk was where I'd rather be.

When I stood to flush, I saw I'd peed in an aluminum pan meant to catch a urine sample. The pan hung inside the toilet bowl. I'd peed in Eileen's collection cup. For all I knew, Eileen's pee was there too. I hadn't looked first, and wouldn't touch it afterwards. Eileen's urine and mine, they'd go to the lab together.

Then I heard Ray. His hoarse voice. I heard him in the hall. He knocked on the door to Eileen's room. He yelled, "Eileen? Baby? I'm here." I didn't run the water. I listened.

Tino yelled back "Baby, we're all here."

Eileen said, "Come on in, sweets."

I listened for my own name, Vanessa, but didn't hear it now. MEN WHO FATHER CHILDREN LIVE HERE. I read the words across the bathroom's blank wall, saw those lines and jagged angles. The last time I'd seen Ray, he'd given me three hundred bucks and walked me to the Lovejoy clinic. What I didn't tell him back then was, I'd already lost his kid. He left me on the corner, bleeding in ways he didn't know anything about, with a pocketful of cash. Now he was back.

I tipped my beer can upside down over the urine collection tray, then put the can on the floor and crushed it.

On the other side of the door, Ray said, "Bushmills. Excellent stuff."

Eileen laughed, said, "Blood thinners and painkillers."

Rebar was a soft murmur at the far wall, saying things I couldn't hear.

I turned the handle on the second door. The hallway was out there. I could walk out and keep going. I had my coat. We hadn't gone so far I couldn't walk home.

I leaned into the mirror, fixed my lipstick. Rebar, on the other side of the door, said, "You think you're some kind of fucking comedian?"

Now Ray was the murmur I couldn't hear. If Rebar was drinking Bushmills, let them be Christ crucified. I wasn't going back.

The ashtray in my purse was like brass knuckles. Solid, hard, and beveled.

There was nothing in the bathroom worth anything unless I needed a plastic yellow pitcher or a roll of toilet paper. I wanted a powder-blue robe. A souvenir. A robe soft and sweet as pot smoke in cold air.

I found a place where the counter opened from the top. I opened the piece of hinged pressed board, and down below was a dark hamper. Linens. There was the peeping corner of a robe. I reached in. I'd take one.

On the other side of the wall Tino said, "Where'd Nessa go?" There was my name.

"She's here?" Ray said.

I could leave. Leave Ray, the one man I wanted to stay with. Leave Rebar, who I couldn't get away from. And then there was Tino. There was no place far away enough.

I closed my fingers around a robe in the hamper. When I lifted the cloth, there was the blooming flower of watery bloodstains. Maybe it was Eileen's blood. Inside the hamper, instead of clean pillowcases and sweet robes, there was a pile of bloodstained sheets, towels, and robes twisted and tangled. The hospital linens were thick as bodies. They were a pool of what's left after you slice open a brain, arms and legs, hearts and lungs, clamp a vein shut. They were soaked in all that life, intertwined.

I dropped the bloody robes. Washed my hands. I wasn't getting anything here.

I went back in Eileen's crowded room. I leaned against the bathroom door. "Ray," I said.

Ray looked at me. He looked me up and down, took me in with his eyes, and when he did, it was like he was stealing something. Something I didn't want to give up.

I reached for Tino. I gave him the longest, deepest kiss I could. I let his lips crack against mine, let his blood seep, so full of salt, find its way to my mouth. I ran a hand over his hair. I breathed in Tino, drank his sweat and salt and alcohol, and he gave in. He put a hand to the curve of my back, put a cold beer to the side of my neck.

Because when there's nothing else, there's comfort in skin.

I had barely pulled away before there was the crack of Rebar's fist, Tino's tooth breaking. Tino fell backwards, hit his head on a steel tray on the way down. It was that car wreck all over again, like metal on metal. Eileen screamed. She screamed, and flung an arm so fast, her IV pulled out. Blood ran from her arm where it tore. It marked the white sheets.

"Now whose the friggin' asshole!" Rebar yelled. He yelled at Tino on the floor, and at his own shoes. But then his face went white, his knuckles red. He pulled back. He'd lost it. He knew he'd lost. He knew the answer to his own question. And Tino didn't get up. I kneeled, and called his name.

I said, "Get a doctor."

Ray was too stoned to move fast.

Eileen hit the buzzer on the wall beside her bed. Tino pooled a slow leak of blood on the floor.

When the cops got there, they'd cleared the room out. Tino was in Emergency. Rebar was in a cop car, on his way back to jail, the psych ward, or Hooper Detox. I didn't know which. Eileen had gone back into testing, something about blood pressure, busted veins. Only me and Ray stood in the hallway, answering questions.

A cop asked, "What's the victim's name?"

I said, "Tino Schmino."

He said, "Tino Schmino? What's that, a joke?"

"It's for real. His folks were Pig Latin, maybe. I never could figure it out."

He said, "Listen, lady, we're not playing. If your pal doesn't come out of that sleep, somebody'll be looking at murder."

I said, "That's the name I knew him by, the name he gave me. If there's more to it, get one of your gumshoes to sort it out."

He said, "Tell me what happened."

I said, "I have no idea. We were all getting along famously. I stepped into the ladies' for powder."

Eventually they left me and Ray there, outside Eileen's room.

I said, "Tino's a good man."

Ray said, "You always have been an idealist."

"What do you mean?"

He said, "A good man? There's no such thing."

I shrugged. "It's just you and me now."

"Is that what you wanted?" He reached out, ran a cal-loused hand over my cheek.

I said, "I don't ask for anything, you know that."

"But you want something, don't you?"

Rebar'd be back in the slammer for a good long time. Tino, who could say. I leaned against the doorway. "There's one thing I want."

Ray looked at me. I reached out, brushed his hair out of his eyes, let him catch my hand and hold it.

"Come with me, Ray, back to my place." I wouldn't have to pack for a good long while, now. "The one thing I want is to not be alone, not again, not tonight."

COFFEE, BLACK

BY BILL CAMERON
Seven Corners

Twenty-five years a cop, seven working homicide, and this is what I've come to: staking out Starbucks in the middle of the night in the hope of catching a vandal in the act of bricking the windows. Welcome to retirement. I'm parked in the shadows outside the food mart at Seven Corners, a tangled confluence of streets at the southeast edge of Ladd's Addition. Starbucks is across Division, part of a corner development that includes a day spa, a pasta restaurant, and a cramped parking lot apparently designed in anticipation of the oil bust. Three nights, and the most exciting thing I've seen so far is a half-naked couple humping in the cob outside the kitchen shop on the opposite corner. I snapped a few pics, but even with the shutter wide open, it's going to take someone with more Photoshop voodoo than me to make the shots Internet ready.

Just after midnight, as I'm thinking about taking a piss behind the dumpster next to my car, I catch sight of a figure approaching down 20th. He high-steps across the parking lot, elbows flared, as if he learned his ninja moves off Cartoon Network. Jeans, black hoodie pulled tight around his face, medium height, medium build. Cigarette held behind his back, a smoldering tail light. About what I expected, some nitwit tweaked on vodka-'n-Red Bull who thinks he's striking a blow against insatiate corporatism.

I slip out of my car and rest the long lens on the roof, sight through the camera's LCD. The light isn't good, a silver-jaundiced mix of mercury vapor and sodium streetlights, sky-glow, and the gleam from the quickie mart. It's adequate. I'm not shooting art photos. I just want to capture an identifiable face.

As I snap the first pic, I hear the scrape of a shoe and turn as a broad, dark shape swoops across the roof of my car. I duck, but not fast enough. Fabric nets my face and shoulders. Hands grab me from behind, shove me hard against the car. A sound whuffs out of me, half shout, half gasp. I drop the camera and thrash, grab the cloth on my head, realize I've got the arm of a jacket. For an instant, I'm in a tug-o'-war, unable to see my opponent. Then the sleeve starts to tear and someone hisses, "Just leave it, doinkus!" The hands release me and I windmill backward onto my ass. As feet slap pavement, fleeing, I hear the sharp, brittle crash of breaking glass.

I shout, yank the jacket off my head. My assailants are gone, the camera with them. No sign of the ninja either, but across the street I see a fresh lattice of cracks in one of Starbucks' oversized windows.

My employer is an insurance company, a circumstance I see as having the moral equivalence of working for the Russian mob. They've been buying glass at least twice a month since Starbucks went in. They bought me for five nights, about the cost of one double-paned window. The camera and lens have to be worth two windows easy, maybe three. Helluva lot more than me, anyway. I'm not looking forward to explaining to the adjuster how I not only failed to stop the vandal, but also let some miscreant make off with his company's camera rig.

I drag myself to my feet and lean against my car. All I've

got to show for myself is the jacket in my hands, and it's nothing to get into a twist about. Blue, softer and darker than denim, white cotton lining, one sleeve half ripped off. I check the pockets, find a matchbox embossed with a logo—a pair of stylized legs suggestive of wisps of smoke—and a happy hour menu from the Night Light Lounge, a louche neighborhood joint two blocks down on Clinton. Stakeout blown, I figure it's the only lead I got.

The Night Light isn't my typical hangout. Smoky, dense with poseurs and reckless youth. Local art on the walls, dim light the color of old cream. I find an empty table next to the open door—a nebulous link to fresh air. Eventually a waiter approaches, drops a Bridgeport coaster on the table, and stands there. I think I'm supposed to order.

It's the kind of joint that'll sell you a Pabst Blue Ribbon for a buck and a half or a microbrew for five. I refuse to pay five bucks for a beer, but I haven't absorbed enough Southeast Portland self-conscious irony to drink shitty beer from a can. I order coffee, black, and settle back to survey the crowd.

I see a lot of piercings and even more tattoos, some more artful than others. The best peek out, mostly hidden, around the edges of straining wife-beaters—de rigueur uniform for most of the girls on hand. The music is loud, the voices louder. Cigarettes trend toward Camel straights and American Spirits. With the state-wide smoking ban due in January, everyone around me seems desperate to take advantage of indoor privileges while they can.

I lock eyes with a woman sitting alone at a table in the middle of the floor. She swirls her beer. Not a PBR. She's wearing a white camisole, Georgia O'Keeffe flower tattoo sprouting from her cleavage. Hair the color of Velveeta in a style bought off the cover of a grocery store tabloid. She's a touch thick, not quite shed of her winter fat, but she wears her flesh with oblivious self-assurance. I have no doubt a man ten years younger than me and with a flatter belly could pay her bar tab and bed her the same night, with no idea of the problems she'll cause over breakfast.

There's no sign of my coffee, and rather than wait around I heave myself to my feet and amble over. Her gaze brushes across me, and I lift the jacket for her to see. With no sign of recognition, she says, "Join me?"

"Sure, why not?" I drop into the chair across from her.

Some guy approaches the table from the direction of the back room, sees me, looks confused. "Dude—"

She cuts him off. "It's okay, Zeke."

"But he's sitting in my chair." He's wearing baggy shorts and an oversized Winterhawks jersey that conspire ineffectively to hide his bulk. Too big in every dimension to be my ninja—big enough, in fact, that if he decides to evict me I won't have much to say about it.

But she just shoos him off with one hand. "Idiot."

I have no opinion on that, but I am wondering why she gave me his seat.

She fishes through a purse next to her, hooks a pack of Parliaments. "Want one?"

I doubt she'll be impressed with, *No thanks, I quit.* Almost anywhere else, the smoker would be on the defensive, but here in the Night Light, I'm the outsider. So I pull out the box of matches with the embossed legs and offer her a light. I can't tell if her eyes linger on the matchbox, or if I just want them to. She inhales and says through smoke, "You're the cop that's been sitting outside Starbucks the last few nights."

So much for my unobtrusive stakeout. Jesus. "Not a cop anymore. I'm retired."

"Well, you're not going to catch them."

"Them?"

"The anarchists."

"Anarchists." I lean back in my chair. "You're kidding, right?"

"That's what they call themselves."

"And you know this how, exactly?"

"Everyone around here knows the anarchists."

I can't tell if she's shining me on. "Is your buddy Zeke one of them?"

That nets me a giggle. "Zeke is about as militant as a kitten." She looks over her shoulder to where her hulking boyfriend hangs off the end of the bar. He's drinking PBR. I can't quite make out his expression in the dim light, but friendly it's not. She waves at him, then turns back to me. "I think he wants his seat back."

"Tell me where to find these anarchists and he can have it."

"If you don't know about them already, maybe I shouldn't tell you."

"Now you gonna leave me blue-balled? You brought it up."

She laughs again. "Okay, Mr. Not-A-Cop. You know the Red and Black?"

A café a block or so up Division from Seven Corners. *Worker-Owned*, proclaims a sign over the door. I've driven by, but never gone inside.

"You *are* kidding."

"They have a problem with corporate coffee."

"How about you? How do you feel about corporate coffee?"

She brushes invisible ash off her tattoo. "I can't say as I've given it much thought." Zeke joins us, puts his hand on the back of the chair like he's worried I'm gonna walk off with it. I take the jacket and head out into the clear night air, curious about my new friend's game. Never did get my coffee.

The phone wakes me too early, the adjuster at Mutual Assurance. He's a big-voiced fellow named Hamilton whom I've never met in person. When I describe the events of the previous night, he says, "I apologize if I was unclear about this before, Detective Kadash—"

"It's just Mister now."

"Whatever. The point is we hired you to stop this crap."

"I thought you hired me to photograph the ne'er-do-well doing this crap."

"You didn't manage that either."

"This isn't just a little vandalism. I got mugged, for chrissakes."

"I thought you were a cop." I can almost hear his smirk. He's quiet for a moment. "Under the circumstances, I think we're going to go in another direction."

"What's that mean?"

"There's no need for you to continue the stakeout."

I guess I can't blame the guy, but I was counting on five nights. Nothing's getting cheaper except the value of my pension. "Maybe I could look into these so-called anarchists, get a line on the camera."

"That won't be necessary, *Mister* Kadash. Just invoice me for three nights."

I've never written an invoice. "I was just thinking—"

He hangs up without saying goodbye.

You'd think I'd know what I'm doing. Maybe I should take a class, learn how to do the job right if I'm going to pretend

I'm some kind of private investigator. But that wasn't in the plan when I retired. The plan was to hang out at Uncommon Cup, my friend Ruby Jane's café, and drink coffee. The only reason I originally agreed to the stakeout was because of her. RJ has been trying to get me involved in freelance investigation since I retired, but it took a coffee case and a fat paycheck to get my attention. Turns out she knows a guy who knows a girl who sleeps with the manager of the Seven Points Starbucks. Apparently my name came up at some java maven's secret society meeting. Next thing I know, I'm salivating over how much insurance money five nights sitting on my ass is worth.

I figure the least I can do is let RJ know how it worked out.

I catch her at her Hawthorne location, a few blocks east of the Bagdad. The place is three-quarters full and hopping when I arrive, the air thick with chatter and the smell of coffee. Customers cluster around tables or hunker down in the soft, well-worn couches against the walls. I order a black coffee and grab a table to wait until Ruby Jane can take a break.

When she finally joins me, her eyes are bright. She doesn't blink as she examines my own sunken orbs. Her chestnut hair is shiny and full, a round cap that seems suffused with its own light. "Rough night?"

"I look that good?"

"I've seen prettier road kill."

I don't argue. I give her a rundown of my evening: the ninja, the jacket, the stolen camera. When I get to the Night Light and the woman at the table, Ruby Jane interrupts me.

"Wait. Orange hair, mammalian, acts like she owns the joint?"

"Yeah, that's her. Who is she?"

RJ is quiet for a moment, thoughtful. "Well, in point of fact . . . the competition. Her name is Ella Leggett."

"Oh?"

"She's got a shop at the other end of Hawthorne. Not direct competition, I guess—there's no foot-traffic overlap. But, you know, another shop owner." She purses her lips. "What did she say to you?"

"Not much. She turned me on to some anarchists."

"Red and Black."

I'm not surprised she knows about them, or about Ella Leggett. Ruby Jane makes it her business to stay informed about the coffee crowd in Portland.

"She thinks they're responsible for the windows at Starbucks."

"She might be right."

"Seriously?"

Ruby Jane shrugs. "It's no secret George Bingham, the lead partner there, has been pissed ever since that Starbucks opened. He thinks it's cutting into his business."

"What do you think?"

"Well, the chains mostly appeal to a different kind of customer than indies do." She tilts her head. "Maybe I'd spin a different tale if one opened across the street, but I think they mainstream the idea of quality coffee. That helps all of us."

I recall Ella Leggett's phrase. "Corporate coffee as a gateway drug."

She grins. "Something like that."

"But the anarchists don't see it that way."

"I'm not sure George qualifies as an anarchist. He and his team are just small-timers like me trying to make it work."

"Still, you think they might take out their frustrations on Starbucks?"

"Maybe. Or maybe they're just working to stay afloat. It's something of an open secret the building owner wants them out so he can redevelop the whole block, add upper-story condos and high-end retail on street level. When you're working your ass off just to make rent, there may not be a lot left over for extracurricular vandalism."

"Chucking bricks wouldn't take a big bite out of someone's free time."

"You're the cop."

"Ex-cop. Ex-investigator too." I tell her about Hamilton letting me go. "I should have taken that kidnapped dog with the MySpace page you told me about instead."

"What are you going to do?"

Ruby Jane once described me as having the determination of a rat guarding a chicken bone. I'm not sure she meant it as a compliment, but I take what I can get. "Gonna earn out my contract."

I'm curious about Ella Leggett, but I decide to start with the Red and Black. It will probably turn out to be a dead-end; too easy, really, to blame the anarchists. But the sight of the glowering, dreadlocked fellow behind the counter, arms folded across his chest, suggests maybe I shouldn't be so hasty.

"You must be George." His stature matches my ninja, but I see no evidence of a hoodie.

"And you must be that asswipe who's working for Starbucks."

Hamilton's decision to can me is starting to look pretty good, considering how effective my attempt at a covert operation had been. I step up to the long, wooden counter. The wall behind looks like it belongs in a tavern, though on closer inspection the lined-up bottles turn out to be a variety of flavored syrups and cane sugar soft drinks. Booths run along the opposite wall. The place is half-full, the customers a mix of young hipsters and older tweedie types. Talking politics, I presume.

I want my usual—coffee, black—but I decide to test George and order a grande latte. "We call it a *medium* here." I hand him a five, leave the coins behind when he slaps my change on the countertop.

"What's your beef with Starbucks anyway?" My tone is chatty. "Besides the jargon, I mean."

He turns his attention to my latte, disinterested in enlightening an asswipe. He fills and tamps the portofilter, pulls the shot with his hand on a knob. He moves with fluid confidence, no wasted motion. The espresso dribbling into the shot glass is the color of warm caramel.

He notices me watching him. "You know what we got here?"

"Cockroaches?"

"Ambience."

I look around. Red stars on the wall, monochrome photos of Latin American men and women picking coffee beans. Radiohead posters, Che Guevara. The music is a hip-hop remix of a Ramones song.

"And you know what else?"

There's no need for me to answer. He's given this speech before.

"Free WiFi."

I stare, bemused.

"At Starbucks, you have to sign up first, use one of their cards. They want your secrets before they let you surf."

"Okay."

"You don't get it."

"Maybe if I had a laptop." Or secrets.

"Couple of times a week, I'll see a guy sitting at one the picnic tables outside." George steams milk as he declaims, rotating the frothing pitcher and checking the temp with the back of his hand. "On his comp, surfing the web. Drinking from a Starbucks cup." He shakes his head as he adds milk to the espresso in a ceramic cup.

"I can see where that would piss you off."

"Hell yeah, it pisses me off." He presents the latte with a flourish, a work of art, the surface foam an artful swirl resembling butterfly wings. "Try it."

I take a sip. It's like drinking silk, as good as any latte Ruby Jane ever served me. Not that I'll tell her that. "It's excellent."

"Exactly. That's because I give a damn. Nothing's automated here, none of that homogenous chic interior design. This is an authentic café run by actual people with genuine pride in our work. We don't charge for our WiFi, but is it too much to ask that you at least buy your coffee from us when you sit down to use it?"

"You can't possibly believe that Starbucks is sending them down here."

"They're part of a larger problem."

"So you respond by busting out their windows."

That earns me a derisive snort. "I'd just be doing what they want."

"You think Starbucks wants you to break their windows?"

"They want the Red and Black to fail. Cast us as villains, turn the neighborhood against us. We don't have a corporate behemoth propping us up during slow times. One bad month, and we could lose it all. They're counting on that."

I'm dubious. I remember what Ruby Jane said about the chains, how they cater to a different customer base. I doubt anyone at Starbucks loses any sleep over the Red and Black. They've probably got their hands full with McDonald's. But that doesn't mean there aren't others who might benefit from R&B closing. The landlord, for instance, who maybe wants the space for something other than a coffee commune.

All that remains is to ask George where he was shortly after midnight last night. I don't see the point. He's not the tearful-confession type. I finish my latte and mutter a thanks, head for the door. "Come back anytime." I'm tempted to take him up on it.

I find Hot Leggett's Café in the ground floor of a building midway up the long block between Sixteenth and Maple on Hawthorne. Great spot for foot traffic from Ladd's or the Buckman neighborhood to the north. The construction looks recent, reminds me of Ruby Jane's description of what R&B's landlord wants to do. I see evidence of a roof-top garden three stories above, espalier pears growing along the anodized balustrade at roof's edge.

Inside, almost every table is in use by the kind of middle-years affluent types that seem to always find a way to spend half the morning kvetching over lattes in the neighborhood café. The furnishings are IKEA, the music reedy instrumental fusion, the aprons an ionizing shade of green. The only surprise is the Hot Leggett logo, a stylized demitasse emitting steam shaped like a pair of legs. I dig out the matchbox—the logo's the same. I hadn't noticed the cup the night before.

I don't see Ella, but one of the baristas catches my eye. Zeke. He frowns, but finds a thin smile as I step up to the counter and surprise myself by ordering a small cappuccino.

"Dry or wet?"

RJ would approve of the question. "Dry."

He takes my three bucks and gives me back a dime. The same at Uncommon Cup would be forty cents less, but then Ruby Jane isn't paying for chi-chi recent construction and eight hundred square feet of Swedish furniture.

Unlike R&B, the espresso machine is fully automated, bean to brew. A half-minute of grinding, bubbling, and hissing, then Zeke sets a to-go cup in front of me. Guess he doesn't want me hanging around. I take a sip. It's fine.

"Where's your girlfriend?"

He looks confused a moment, then recognition hits him. "You mean my sister?"

"Ella is your sister?"

"You thought she was my *girlfriend?*" His laugh is scornful. Last night he was the idiot; this morning I am.

"Either way, is she here?"

"I haven't seen her."

"You mind if I ask you some questions?"

"I don't know anything about the broken windows."

"What about this?" I show him the matchbox and he sniffs.

"I don't know why we have those. We're nonsmoking."

"Ella's not nonsmoking."

"It's still a stupid thing to spend money on. This isn't a bowling alley."

Color dots his cheeks. He's clearly not on board with the Leggett legs matchboxes. But when I tell him where this one came from, his face goes carefully blank. "That could be any-one's."

"I'm sure."

"We give them away."

"What size do you wear anyway? Jacket-wise, I mean."

I give him a hard stare, but he meets it without expression. I hear movement and a pair of women in hand-woven cotton blouses approach the counter, their salty hair pulled back with contrived insouciance. They smell like skin cream. There are two other baristas, but Zeke says, "Excuse me. I need to help these ladies."

Chalk that one up to fumble-tongued luck. It never occurred to me to check the jacket's size. Some investigator. But it's still in my car, and upon inspection I can see it'll never contain Zeke's beefy shoulders. Probably fit Ella just fine though.

I return to Uncommon Cup. Ruby Jane is working the counter, so I show her the jacket. "Would you wear this?"

She shrugs. "Maybe, though it's a men's cut and I prefer my clothing not to hang in tatters. Why?"

"I'm still working things out. Do you mind if I use your computer?"

She directs me to her little office in the back. Within a few minutes I learn that the owner of record of Hot Leggett's Café is Leggett Partners LLC—company officers, Ella and Zeke—while the business license for the Red and Black is held by one George Called Bingham, whatever the hell kind of middle name that is. No wonder he's an anarchist. Leggett Partners owns a scattering of small businesses and mixed-use buildings around Southeast Portland, a humble empire. That gives me an idea, but it turns out R&B's building is owned by a real estate holding firm out of L.A. It will take more digging to discover what connection, if any, exists between the holding company and the crowd here in Portland. I have one more thought and check on the Starbucks landlord. Not Leggett Partners, not the L.A. company, but a branch of the

156 // PORTLAND NOIR

Schnitzner family, which seems to control half the commercial real estate in Portland. It's hard for me to think they'd give a wet fart about the Red and Black.

Up front again, I ask Ruby Jane if I can borrow her car. Too many people know mine. I can tell she enjoys the idea that her old beater Toyota might be party to a caper. She tosses me her keys and a few minutes later I'm rolling past Hot Leggett's. Zeke is still inside, working the counter. I loop through Ladd's and return to Hawthorne a couple of blocks up. There's a space on the street in front of an Ethiopian restaurant, close enough to see who comes and goes from Hot Leggett's, not so close I'm likely to be noticed. Of course, with my recent track record, I probably shouldn't get too cocky.

This stretch of Hawthorne isn't as busy as the run nearer to 39th, but in recent years as more shops and restaurants have gone in, foot traffic has increased. Hot Leggett's is getting its share, as well as the froufrou ice cream shop and the furniture boutique adjoining. A loading zone in front of the boutique allows me an unobstructed view. On the backseat, I find a two-week-old edition of the *Mercury*, Portland's hipster alt weekly, and settle in for a wait.

An hour into my vigil, the paper's snark exhausted, a white Prius stops in the loading zone. Ella jumps out and trots around to the passenger side, gesticulating toward the café. I start the car. As she climbs back into the Prius, I hear her shout, "Hurry the hell up, idiot!"

Zeke storms out of the café, carrying a nylon duffel bag in one hand and flipping Ella off with the other. He gets behind the wheel, and an instant later bounces Ella's head off her headrest as he peels out. I keep a couple of cars between us as we head down to Powell and then across the Ross Island Bridge. Traffic bunches us up through the south edge of downtown until the Sunset Highway, but they don't seem to notice me. Ten minutes later we take the Sylvan exit, make a couple of turns, then park in the lot outside an anonymous office building. Three stories of glass and stucco hunkered below an ivy-clad hill. I wait until they're inside, then head for the foyer. No sign of them, but a quick scan of the building directory gives me a pretty good idea of where they've gone.

Suite 210, Mutual Assurance of Oregon.

Mutual Assurance is a single large room, a cube farm. From the landing, I can see the front desk through glass double doors, no receptionist. A sign on the counter next to a telephone reads, *Press 1 for deliveries*. I don't plan on making a delivery, though if my guess about what's in Zeke's bag is correct, I might make a pickup.

I hesitate, then figure I got nothing to lose and push through the doors. It's hard for me to picture Ella Leggett with her orange hair and tattoo in this leaden space. The air is heavy and cold, the sounds of white-collar work deadened by the B-flat hum of fluorescent lights and acoustic ceiling tiles. At first, I don't see the siblings, but then I glimpse their heads moving among the cubicles off to my left, a third figure—a man—with them. I tack right, keeping them in sight as I mosey along the outside wall with forced nonchalance. I pass a number of occupied cubes, but no one speaks to me—well-trained to avoid questions or, heaven forbid, confrontations.

The trio stops at a cube, huddles together to confer. I watch, hands folded in front of me. A woman catches my eye from a nearby cubicle, and I stare back until she drops her gaze. Maybe she's afraid I'm there to downsize her.

After a moment Ella raises her voice, but all I can make out is a petulant squeak. Zeke throws up his hands, semaphore for *Calm the hell down.* When the three return the way they came, I scoot up the passageway between cubicles from the opposite end, stop when I see the nameplate affixed to cube wall fabric. *N. Hamilton, Adjuster.*

The camera, long lens attached, rests on the desk. My first instinct is to grab the whole rig, but then I realize there's no need for felony theft when a misdemeanor will do. I slip into the cubicle and open the back of the camera, pop out the CompactFlash card. When I step back into passage, hands in my pockets, the man I assume is Hamilton is coming toward me.

"Can I help you?" Definitely the adjuster's voice from the phone. He's an unremarkable specimen, round head, brown sidecar hair, suspicious eyes.

"Restroom?"

He looks into his cubicle, seems relieved. Like I could hide the camera in my sock. Or maybe he was afraid I took a dump on his chair. "It's out on the landing." He points with his chin. "To your left."

He has no idea who I am. Something to be said for doing business strictly by phone.

Back at Ruby Jane's, I hand her the camera card, ask her if she can download the pics.

"Easy peasy." She leads me back to her office and plugs the card into the CF jack on her computer. After a moment, a blank window appears on the monitor. Ruby Jane shakes her head.

"There's nothing there."

I sit back. It only makes sense they already downloaded the pictures.

"Don't panic." RJ snatches the card. "This is a coffee shop.

If there isn't a geek sitting out there right now, there will be before the afternoon is over. I'll find someone who can undelete whatever was on here." She leaves me there, stewing in my own techno-cluelessness.

I turn to Google, hoping to redeem myself by trolling for background info among the dot-govs. An hour later, about the time my eyes are boiling out of my head from reading too many poorly formatted web pages, RJ is back with the flash card and a CD. "There were a lot of fragmented files, but we were able to recover some photos from a couple of days ago with intact metadata and one picture from last night." She inserts the CD into her computer, and this time the window opens populated with thumbnails.

The first dozen or so are of the couple in the cob across from my stakeout. I remember when they started building these cob structures around town, oddly shaped public benches tarted up with ceramic-shard mosaics and glaze. Some guy appeared at my door one day, all breathless as he explained that I, too, could join the cob revolution and transform my front yard into a community living room. I live in the kind of neighborhood where people grow grapes and sweet corn in the parking strips, so a mud-and-straw bench with a thatched awning wouldn't draw a second glance. But when it became clear I'd be responsible for construction and materials, I told the guy to go sell crazy somewhere else.

Others don't share my reticence, including the folks who run the kitchen store across from Starbucks. And amazing to an old curmudgeon like me, people actually use the cobs—and not just my humping couple.

As I'd suspected, the photos are murky, but I can make out the guy leaning back on the cob bench, the woman straddling him. Their faces are in a shadow, but that doesn't really matter. Even in the dark the radioactive cheez framing the woman's head is unmistakable. I click through the images. In the last, the couple has turned to face the camera. On to me.

I click again and there's the ninja in front of Starbucks. Better light, better focus. Hair hidden by the hoodie, but it doesn't matter. The face is clear enough.

"What do you want me to do?" RJ asks.

"Fire up the printer. I got some calls to make."

I catch Hamilton at his desk, which saves me the trouble of shakedown via voice mail.

"What can I do for you, Kadash?" No Detective, no Mister. His tone suggests it had better be nothing, but I disappoint him. I tell him to meet me at the Night Light at 6. "Ella can tell you where it is."

"I don't know who you're talking about."

"Don't be coy." I hang up without saying goodbye.

The Night Light's main area is smoke-free until 10, so I'm not surprised to find the gang tucked away in the back room. Zeke sits in the rear of the circular booth, taking up space and refusing to make eye contact. Ella is to his left, a beer in front of her and a smoldering Parliament in her hand. Hamilton sits hunched to Zeke's right, nursing something urine-colored and on the rocks. When I arrive, Ella blows smoke my way. I slide in next to Ham.

I wonder if the coffee I ordered last night will finally appear. "Should we get appetizers?"

Hamilton isn't in the mood. "Get to the point."

I chuckle and toss the CF card onto the table, along with some printouts from Ruby Jane's inkjet. In the first, Ella's face peeks out from inside the ninja hoodie. In the others, her hair shines out from the cob like a flame.

"What kind of a perv are you anyway, taking pictures of people like that?"

If Ella expects me to blush, I've got news for her. "I'm not the one screwing in the community's living room."

She looks like she wants to argue, but Hamilton is on point. "You were supposed to be watching Starbucks."

"Is that you?" I tap the silhouette of Ella's cob partner, then drop another sheet of paper on the table before he can answer. Hamilton snatches it up. He can read, but I don't want to leave the others hanging. "Quotes from a half-dozen glass vendors to replace the window broken at Starbucks last night. You might notice a number there from Allied Commercial Glass."

"So?" Hamilton says, but Zeke is shaking his head, disgusted. I'm warming to the great oaf.

"It's a lot less than the insurance payment you authorized to Allied for that same window earlier today."

Hamilton and Ella exchange looks. I can see the wheels spinning, the hamsters scrambling. "You requested these quotes?"

I nod.

"There was probably more to the job than you realize."

What Hamilton doesn't know is I had help with the quotes. RJ's friend of a friend, the Starbucks manager, has been dealing with these broken windows for years. He knows exactly what's involved in the job.

Ella swallows beer, breathing smoke into the glass. I wonder if she'll give up cigs when the big ban kicks in next year. She doesn't strike me as one to go down easy.

"All you had to do was watch the store for five nights," she says, "and then get paid."

"Sure, help you guys cover your ass with a little sham due

diligence for Mutual Assurance management. Almost worked too, especially with you feeding me crap about a coffee war. If not for these photos, I never would have guessed you were running a low-rent insurance scam, arranging to overpay a Leggett Partners glass company to repair your own vandalism." And if the Red and Black happened to go down in the blowback, a Hot Leggett's could anchor redevelopment there quite well. I don't want to get into speculation, though, nor my suspicion that the scam is running at more than just Seven Points Starbucks. "What I am curious about is what the hell you were doing in that cob."

"She wanted to spy on you." Zeke's voice has a bitter edge. "She thought it was funny. It never occurred to her you'd turn the camera on her." He drops his chin. "You stupid bitch, I told you to stay away from this guy. But no, you and doinkus here"—he thrusts a thumb at Hamilton—"have to go draw his attention. And that retarded stunt last night . . . well, he ended up with the pictures anyway, didn't he?"

That shuts everyone up. Ella stubs out her smoke. Zeke fumes into his chest. Hamilton picks up the CF card, gazes at it with a rueful smile. "So, what do you want, detective?"

Detective. I'm back on the case.

When I was still a cop, that question wouldn't have even come up. My job was to make cases, not express personal desires. But now I'm a guy living on a barely sufficient pension, without prospects. I don't give a shit about their scam. "I'll settle a full five night's pay, and the promise you'll throw me a little work every now and then." I look Hamilton in the eye. "And I'm telling you right now, I don't write invoices."

GONE DOGGY GONE

BY JAMIE S. RICH & JOËLLE JONES

Montgomery Park

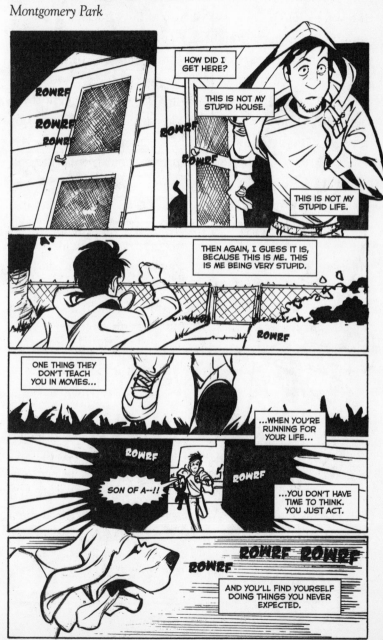

THE GUY WAS GOING TO *SHOOT* ME, HIS DOG WAS GOING TO *EAT* ME.

BUT I *STALKED* HIS FRIEND AND *BROKE* INTO THE DUDE'S HOUSE. I'D CALL THAT A CRIMINAL *STALEMATE.*

LIKE I SAID, WHEN IT'S YOUR LIFE UP FOR GRABS, YOU MAKE UNEXPECTED DECISIONS.

BESIDES, SOMETIMES, FOR CRIME TO PAY--EVEN IF IT JUST PAYS IN TRADE, AN OPPORTUNITY TO WALK AWAY CLEAN--YOU HAVE TO BECOME A PART OF IT.

YOU DON'T THINK, YOU JUST CUT YOUR LOSSES AND GO.

AND BE GLAD BLANKET DIDN'T BITE YOU IN THE ASS.

MONTGOMERY PARK

"GONE DOGGY GONE" BY JAMIE S. RICH AND JOËLLE JONES LETTERED BY JILL BEATON

VIRGO

BY JESS WALTER

Pearl District

My side of the story . . . you want my side of the story?

That's funny. The suits at the newspaper said the same thing when they fired me—that I should give my side of the story.

As I usually do, I chose to say nothing, and the next day the *Oregonian* ran its "Public Apology to our Readers" full of righteous puffery about how I *"acted maliciously and recklessly,"* how I *"broke the sacred trust between a newspaper and its readers."*

Well, here we are again . . . someone pretending to want my side of the story, as if the truth were a box that you could simply flip over when you want another version. Well, there are no sides, no box, no truth.

We both know you don't want *my side* of anything. You don't want to understand me, you don't want to know me, and you sure as hell don't want to *feel* what I felt.

This is what you really want to know: Why did he do what he did?

Fine. You want to know why I did it? I did it to let her know how much she meant to me. That's why I did it, all of it—for her.

This all began in late October. We'd had the same old fight, with the same stale grievances Tanya had been lobbing at me for three months, almost since the day I moved in: *Blah, blah, stalled relationship; blah, blah, stunted growth; blah, blah, I worry that you're a psychopath.*

I said I'd try harder, but she was in a mood: "No, Trent. I want you out of here. Now." I gathered my things. Carried four loads of clothes, shoes, CDs, action figures, and trading cards down to my car. I was about to drive away when I saw . . . him.

Mark Aikens, Tanya's missing-link ex-boyfriend, was loping up 21st like some kind of predator, like a fat coyote talking on a cell phone. She had moved to Portland for this loser, even though she made twice as much as he did. She requested a transfer from the Palo Alto software company where she worked and found a small condo in the Pearl District, but she wasn't in town six months before he'd slept with someone else and she tossed him out. Mark Aikens was a cheating shit.

He swung around a light pole and skipped up the steps of our old building. She buzzed him up. A sous chef at Il Pattio, Mark Aikens was one of those jerkoffs who acts like cooking is an art. She always said he was sensitive, a good listener. Now he was up in our old condo, listening his sensitive, cheating ass off. For two hours I sat in my car down the block while this guy . . . listened. It had grown dark outside. From the street, our condo glowed. I knew exactly which light was on—the upright living room lamp. She got it at Pottery Barn. Through our old third-floor corner window I could see shadows move across the ceiling from that light and I tried to imagine what was happening by the subtle changes in cast: *she's going to the kitchen to get him a beer; he's going to the bathroom.* How many fall nights had I snuck home early from work and looked up to see the glow from that very light? It had been my comfort. But now that light felt unbearably cold and far away, like an astronomer's faint discovery, a flicker from across the universe and the icy beginning of time.

I might have gone crazy had I stared at that light much longer. In fact, I'd just decided to ring the buzzer and run when the unimaginable happened.

The light went out.

I sat there, breathless, waiting for Mark Aikens to come down. But he didn't. My eyes shot to the bedroom window. Also dark. That meant she was . . . they were . . .

I tooled around the Pearl having conversations with her in my head, begging, yelling, until finally I crossed the bridge and drove toward my father's little duplex in Northeast. I parked on the dirt strip in front and beat on his door. I could hear him clumping around inside. My dad had lost a leg to diabetes. It took him awhile to get his prosthetic on.

When he finally answered, I said: "Tanya threw me out. She's seeing her old boyfriend. She said living with me was like living with a stalker."

"You always did make people nervous," my father said. Dad was a big sloppy man, awful at giving advice. Since my mother's death, he'd been even less helpful in these father-son moments. He sniffed the air. "Have you been drinking?"

"No," I said.

"Christ, Trent." And he invited me inside. "Why the hell not?"

Before all of this, I loved my job. And I'm not talking about the job as portrayed in my five-year-old performance evaluation, the low point of which (one flimsy charge of harassment stemming from an honest misunderstanding involving the women's restroom) the newspaper found a way to dredge up in its apology to readers. No. What I loved was the work.

As a features copy editor, I pulled national stories off the wire, proofread local copy, and wrote headlines for as many as five pages a day, but my favorite (because it was Tanya's favorite) was "Inside Living"—page two of the features section, the best-read page in the O—with syndicated features like the crossword puzzle, the word jumble, celebrity birthdays, and Tanya's favorite, the daily horoscope. That's how we'd met, in fact, four months earlier, in a coffee shop where I saw her reading her horoscope. I launched our romance with the simple statement: "I edit that page." Within a week we were dating, and a month later, in late July, when I was asked to leave my apartment because the paranoid woman across the courtyard objected to my having a telescope, Tanya said I could move in with her until I found a place.

Now, to some, I may indeed be—as the newspaper's one-sided apology to readers characterized me—*strangely quiet and intense, practically a nonpresence*, but to loyal readers like Tanya, I was something of an unsung hero.

Each morning during those three glorious months, she would pour herself a cup of coffee, toast a bagel, and browse the newspaper, spending mere seconds on each page, until she arrived at "Inside Living," her newspaper home. I couldn't wait for her to get there. She'd make a careful fold and crease, set the page down, and study it as if it contained holy secrets. And only then would she speak to me. "Eleven down: 'Film's blank Peak'?"

"Dante's."

"Are you sure you don't see the answers the day before?"

"I told you, no." Of course, I did see the answers the day before. But who could blame me for a little dishonesty? I was courting.

"Hey, it's Kirk Cameron's birthday. Guess how old he is."

"Twelve? Six hundred? Who's Kirk Cameron?"

"Come on. You edited this page yesterday. Now you're going to pretend you don't know who Kirk Cameron is?"

"That celebrity stuff comes in over the wire. I just shovel it in without reading it. You know I hate celebrities."

"I think you pretend not to like celebrities to make yourself appear smarter."

This was true. I do love celebrities.

"Hey, look," she'd say finally. "I'm having a five-star day. If I relax, the answers will all come to me."

It's painful now to recall those sweet mornings, the two of us bantering over our page of the newspaper, with no hint that it was about to end. And this is the strange part, the mystical part, some might say: on those days Tanya read that she was to have a five-star day . . . she actually had five-star days. Now, I don't believe in such mumbo-jumbo; it was likely just the power of suggestion. But I did begin to notice (in the journals in which I record such things) that Tanya was more open to my amorous advances when she got five stars. In fact, after our first month together, I began to notice that the only time Tanya seemed at all interested in being intimate, the only time she wanted to . . . you know, get busy, bump uglies, bury the dog in the yard . . . was when she got five stars on her horoscope.

Then one day in early October, when we'd stopped having sex altogether, I did it. I goosed her horoscope. Virgo was supposed to have three stars and I changed it to five.

So sue me. It didn't even work.

Obviously, though, that's where the idea came from. And yet I might have simply moved on and not launched my horoscope warfare had Tanya not fired the first shot at me by filing a no-contact order a mere two weeks after throwing me out. A no-contact order! Based on what, I wanted to know.

"Well, you do drive over there every night after work and park outside her place," my dad said as he nursed a tumbler of rum.

"Yeah, but eight hundred feet? What kind of arbitrary number is that? Shall I carry a tape measure? How do you know if you're eight hundred feet away from someone? There's a tapas place around the corner from her condo. Am I just supposed to stop eating tapas?"

"There's a Taco Bell over on M.L. King."

"Tapas, Dad. Not tacos."

Dad poured us a drink, then turned on the TV. "Look, I don't know what to tell you, Trent. You make people uncomfortable. When you were a kid I thought something was wrong with your eyelids, the way you never blinked. I used to ask your mom if maybe there wasn't some surgery we could try."

This was my father. A woman breaks my heart and his answer is to sew my eyelids shut. But I suppose he tried. I suppose we all try.

"Life just isn't fair," I said as the old widower hobbled away on his prosthetic leg to get another drink.

"Yeah, well," he replied, "I hope I'm not the asshole who told you it would be."

The very next day, November 17, Virgo got the first of thirteen straight one-star days. *"Four stars: your creativity surges. Keep an eye on the big picture,"* Virgo was supposed to read that day. I changed it to: *"One star: watch your back."* It was glorious, imagining her read that.

Horoscopes are cryptic and open-ended: *"You'll encounter an obstacle but you are up to the task. A Capricorn may help."* In fact, I could argue that what clearly began as a way to spoil my girlfriend's day became a campaign to make horoscopes more useful. And I won't pretend that I didn't like the voice, the power that changing horoscopes gave me. In the office, I kept my own counsel, going days without speaking sometimes, but with these horoscopes I could finally say the things I'd been holding inside all those years. For our new drama critic Sharon Gleason, I wrote, *"Libra. Three stars: those pants make you look fat."* For the arrogant sports columnist Mike Dunne, *"Taurus. Two stars: I hope your wife's cheating on you."* For the icy young records clerk Laura: *"Cancer. Four stars: would it kill you to smile at your coworkers?"*

Of course, there were complaints about the late-November horoscopes (thankfully, they were all routed to the "Inside Living" page editor . . . me.) In my defense, some people actually preferred the new horoscopes. Not Virgos, of course, since they were treated to day after day of stunning disappointment—*"One star: you should try to be less vindictive and disloyal . . . One star: hope your new boyfriend doesn't mind your bad breath . . . One star: you're not even good at sex."*

I'm the first to admit that I went a little far on November 24, the day I read in the crossword puzzle that the clue to 9-Across was a Jamaican spice, saw that the answer was *Jerk* and changed the clue to *Mark Aikins, e.g.* Yes, it was petty, but I was being forced to wage a war without getting within eight hundred feet of my enemy.

Yet, despite my constant barrage of single-star Virgo days and crossword puzzle salvos, I got no response from either of them. Tanya knew this was my page. She had to know I was behind her run of bad horoscopes. But I heard nothing. Some days I thought she was taunting me by not responding; other days I imagined she was so deeply mired in one-star hassles (traffic snarls and Internet outages) that she was incapable of responding.

Another possibility arose on the last day of November. I had just called in another phony customer complaint to Il Pattio ("The chicken breast was woefully undercooked, having symptoms consistent with salmonella.") and driven back to the house I now shared with my dad. That's when I found him on the kitchen floor, slumped in a corner, his artificial leg at an odd angle, fake foot still flat on the floor.

He was in what doctors called a diabetic coma—an obvious result of his nonstop drinking. "You need to take better care of him," the ER nurse said. But it wasn't until I filled out the insurance paperwork that I understood exactly how I'd failed my dad. I copied his date of birth from his driver's license: August 28, 1947. I knew his birthday, naturally, but it hadn't occurred to me until that moment.

My father was a Virgo.

In their glee to portray me as a bad employee, the suits failed to mention that on the very day my dad was fighting for his life in a hospital bed, I still reported to work. Of course, it was also that day, November 30, that my section editor responded to a complaint from the features syndicate, investigated, and called me into her office.

In the frenzy of meetings and recriminations that followed, I somehow got one last altered horoscope into the paper. Again, I don't mean to portray myself as some kind of primitive, moon-worshipping kook, but the next day, Virgos across Portland read the heartfelt plea, *Five stars: you'll get better. I'm sorry.*

Dad pulled out of his hypoglycemic coma and returned home to live dryly, me at his side. I have purged his little house of alcohol. Dad drinks a lot of tomato juice now. Since I'm not working, we play game after game of cribbage, so much that I have begun to dream of myself as one of those pegs, making my way up and down the little board. I recently shared this dream with my court-ordered therapist. She wondered aloud if the dream had to do with my father's peg leg. So I told Dad about my dream and he said that he sometimes dreams his missing leg is living in a trailer in Livingston, Montana. I'm thinking of asking him to come to counseling with me.

And Tanya? Even after the story in the *Oregonian*—from which I hoped she'd at least glean the depth of my feelings for her—I never heard a word. My probation officer and therapist have insisted, rightly I suppose, that I leave Tanya alone, but this afternoon I went to the store to get more tomato juice for Dad and I found myself down the block from her building again.

This time, however, it was different. I know it sounds crazy, but I'd begun to worry that my little prank had some-how caused her to become sick. And I take it as a positive sign that I didn't want that for her. I really didn't. I sat in my car down the street and gazed up to our third-floor corner window, just hoping to get a glimpse of her. It's winter now and the early night sky was bruised and dusky. Our old condo was dark. It crossed my mind that maybe she had moved, and I have to say, I was okay with that. I had just reached down to start my car when I saw them walking up the sidewalk, a block from the condo. Tanya looked not only healthy, but beautiful. Happy. The big, dumb, sensitive, cheating chef was holding her hand. And I was happy for her. I really was. She laughed, and above them a streetlight winked at me and slowly came on.

There was a line in the newspaper's apology that stunned me, describing what I'd done as *"a kind of public stalking."* I shook when I read that. I suppose it's what Tanya thinks of me too. Maybe everyone. That I'm crazy. And maybe I am.

But if you really want my side of the story, here it is:

Who isn't crazy sometimes? Who hasn't driven around a block hoping a certain person will come out; who hasn't haunted a certain coffee shop, or stared obsessively at an old picture; who hasn't toiled over every word in a letter, taken four hours to write a two-sentence e-mail, watched the phone praying that it will ring; who doesn't lay awake at night sick with the image of her sleeping with someone else?

I mean, Christ, seriously, what love *isn't* crazy?

And maybe it was further delusion, but as I sat in the car down the block from our old building, I was no longer wishing she'd take me back. Honestly, all I hoped was that Tanya at least thought of me when she read our page.

I really do think I'm better.

And so when I started the car to go home, and they crossed the street toward Tanya's condo, I was as surprised as anyone to feel the ache come back, an ache as deep and raw as the one I felt that night in late October when I first saw the lamp go out.

I told the other officer, the one at the scene, that I didn't remember what happened next, though that's not entirely true.

I remember the throaty sound of the racing engine. I remember the feel of cutting across traffic, of grazing something, a car, they told me later, and I remember popping up on the sidewalk and scraping the light pole and I remember bearing down on the jutting corner of the building and I remember a slight hesitation as they started to turn. But what I remember most is a spreading sense of relief that it would all be over soon, that I would never again have to see the light come on in that cold apartment.

THE RED ROOM

BY CHRIS A. BOLTON

Powell's City of Books

Jacob Black catches the kid's reflection in the window of the bookstore coffee shop and can tell right away he's the one. He knows nothing about his potential client—the brief, terse e-mail exchange only led to Powell's City of Books as the meeting place. Jacob IDing himself by the pile of books next to him: *The Big Sleep*, *The Maltese Falcon*, and *The Postman Always Rings Twice*.

The client picked the titles. Not exactly subtle.

The kid appears in the large doorway separating the Gold Room from the Coffee Room, wearing an oversized army coat with anarchy symbols and a giant messenger bag spattered with dried mud, carrying a dirt-crusted bike helmet, and whipping his head around like someone's hollering his name. Sitting at the window despite a roomful of empty tables, Jacob follows the kid's reflection in the glass and for a moment considers leaving the books and walking right the fuck out of there.

Jacob Black is used to trouble. A guy who finds clients by answering craigslist ads for obscure jobs like "cat walker" and "breast feeding for adults" deals exclusively with trouble and the sorts of people who deeply embroil themselves in it. To seek out the kind of person who knows about Jacob Black, and where to place the ad and what to put in it, requires a level of desperation that may cause cancer by close proximity. But this one—this kid in his early twenties, soft and clueless, a Reed College trust-fund brat who likes to dress up and pretend he's living in the gutter—this blend of trouble smells too strong.

The kid finds Jacob before he makes up his mind. "Are," he begins—but has to swallow, nearly chokes on it, and starts again. "Are you him?"

"I'm he," Jacob says. "Sit down, you're making the coffee nervous."

The kid perches on the next stool and tries to size Jacob up. Jacob himself would admit he isn't much to look at: a face that hasn't seen a razor since Portland last saw the sun, T-shirt and khakis that look and smell like he yanked them from the bottom of his dirty laundry pile (which is, in fact, his only laundry pile), and a disheveled head of unruly hair that used to be dark blond but has turned muddy with gray.

"So, uh, what're you exactly, like, a private detective?"

"I'm a guy who does jobs. You got one?"

The kid glances around, as though he could spot anything suspicious if it were there. "What's your rate?"

"It varies." The kid gives the coffee shop another scan and Jacob says, "Sooner or later you're gonna have to tell me what the job *is*."

The kid chews his lip, sucks it under his front teeth, chews some more. Finally he lets out the breath he's been holding. "I got something that someone wants."

"Don't be specific or anything. Just give me lots of pronouns."

He reaches into his army coat, produces a heavily wrinkled manila envelope with a small, square bulge only a few inches long. "It's a videotape. Wanna know what's on it?"

"Nope." Jacob stands, launching the kid's eyes, hands, his whole being into a frenzy of frantic motion. "You blackmailed

188 // PORTLAND NOIR

some asshole, now you want me to be your bag man? Fuck off."

"Five hundred," he whispers in desperation. "Half now, half later."

Jacob turns away, all set to walk and never look back. The kid reaches into the other side of his coat and flashes the cash. "I'm good for it."

Jacob plops back onto his stool.

The kid spits out the rest in one breath: "There's a reading upstairs, ten minutes. The guy'll be in the audience. His coat's folded up on the chair next to him, with the money under it. You sit in the next seat—take his coat, then leave yours in its place with the tape underneath." The kid reaches into his messenger bag and hands Jacob a brown Members Only jacket. "That's it. Come get your two-fifty."

Jacob thinks it over. Plays it out in his head, looks for all the flaws, every conceivable way this goes sour. He finds a dozen in under ten seconds.

The kid presses: "No risk, either—it's totally in public."

"It's a *book reading*. I'll be lucky if we aren't the only two people there."

The kid counts out 250 dollars, slaps the cash into Jacob's hands. "I'll wait for you in the Mystery section. Who's your favorite writer?"

"Michael Connelly."

"That's where I'll be. You come find me, okay?" The kid is half-sitting, half-standing, one foot solid on the floor, both eyes scrutinizing Jacob. "Okay?"

He holds the envelope out. Jacob pockets the money, thinking about his empty cupboards back home, and grabs the envelope from the kid's clammy fingers. Thinking, *This is the stupidest thing I've ever done.*

Knowing full well it isn't.

* * *

Jacob arrives a few minutes early for the event. He walks up three flights of stairs, marveling—as most do—at a four-story bookstore that encompasses an entire city block. Each room is color-coded, which either makes things easier or more confusing, depending on how readily you associate gold with genres like Sci-Fi and Romance, purple with Military History and Philosophy, and orange with Cooking and Business.

He remembers dating a woman who worked here back in the late '90s, wonders if she's still around. Her name lost to him. Probably wouldn't recognize her anymore. Pierced, tattooed, dyed Goth hair, and a fondness for industrial wear back then; now she's probably got a house, family, hybrid car, and those Mom jeans that turn a woman's ass into a denim landing strip.

Jacob enters the Pearl Room wondering what's "pearl" about it, why "pearl" and not "silver," not that there's any silver to speak of, either. A few rows of folding chairs fill the Basil Hallward Gallery next to the art books. A dais is set up beside a cart loaded with books to be signed—though, judging by the half-dozen people scattered about the seats, they won't sell many copies tonight. Jacob glances at the author's name—no one he recognizes—then pretends to be extremely interested in a 200-dollar book containing photographs of fat men in diapers.

He finds his mark instantly—a tall, muscular black man with curly hair cut close to the scalp and shoulders so broad and thick they need their own chairs. The guy sits in the back row, a high school letterman's jacket neatly folded on the seat beside him. Tight short-sleeve button-up shirt tucked into faded blue jeans. Beige hiking boots. Cell phone in a holster clipped to a leather belt.

What interests Jacob even more is the man hovering by the shelves of remaindered books. Black leather jacket, T-shirt tucked into dark blue Levi's, sunglasses resting on the back of his head. Military-style buzz cut and a thin mustache. And he's "reading" an oversized book about Gustav Dore while discreetly scanning the room.

Jacob calmly descends the stairs and strolls back to the Gold Room. As the kid looks up from a used copy of *The Closers*, startled, Jacob presses the jacket, the tape, and the cash into his arms.

"Turn around," Jacob says. "Get the hell out of here. Don't look back. This never happened."

Jacob heads through the Blue Room toward the entrance. The kid is right on his heels, completely ignoring his advice. "What're you doing? I told you, it's easy, just two minutes and—"

"And I'm dogshit. Those are *cops*, kid. At least two, maybe more. But you knew that—that's why you paid me. You are *way* out of your league. Walk away and hope they never find you."

The kid lurches ahead, blocks Jacob's path. "They pulled a Mexican out of his car and beat him."

"I don't give a shit."

"You don't wanna see what they did to his wife."

"I don't wanna see what they're gonna do to *you*. Because they'll catch you. They're police. Probably *dumb* police, since you caught them on tape—but you're even dumber, so they'll catch you."

"You know CopStalker?"

Jacob nods, *Of course*. A band of "concerned volunteers" whose goal is to hold police accountable for their actions—or that's how it started. CopStalker now mostly consists of bike messengers, anarchists, and indie media activists who need something to do while sober. They follow Portland's Finest on their bikes, documenting every traffic stop and harassment of the homeless, then post the accounts on a website whose cluttered design and abbreviated text make it nearly impossible to decipher.

Fifteen years ago, Jacob would have been one of them.

"My girlfriend shot the tape," the kid says. "She's scared shitless—jumps every time the phone rings or someone knocks. I told her I'd take care of it."

"So you blackmail cops. Brilliant."

"Not for myself," the kid says, sounding hurt. "For the victims. They're too injured to work, they barely know English, and they're terrified to leave their apartment. This is all they got."

Jacob stares into the kid's eyes, searching for a tell. The slightest hint he's being lied to. If the kid isn't giving him the truth, he'd make a killing in the World Series of Poker.

Jacob Black doesn't possess what can be called a sense of civic duty. Nor much empathy. But years ago he had a badge, and then he didn't, and the circumstances that cost him his badge suddenly feel too familiar.

He takes the bundle from the kid. "I sense the slightest fuck-up, I walk. You'll never see me again."

"Fair enough."

Jacob takes his time going back. He glances at the journals tucked into the Mezzanine, then lingers in the True Crime section of the Purple Room. Little memories bobbing to the surface like bodies in the spring thaw. When he dated the woman who worked here—*what the hell was her name?*—he'd wait for her shift to end in a different room. Can't recall if he made it to every room in the store before things ended.

Mostly they'd just fucked. Sometimes they smoked a joint in bed afterward and she told him stories about all the weird customer incidents at Powell's. Mainly junkies in the bathrooms. Though there was the time someone found a homeless guy who'd climbed up one of the twenty-foot bookcases in the Purple Room and fell asleep on top until a manager heard him snoring. And the time a crazy woman tried to abduct a six-year-old girl, so the store went into total lockdown—no one allowed in or out—while the employees combed top to bottom, front to back, until they found the girl in a restroom stall.

When he heads back up to the gallery, a paunchy, bushy-haired cowboy in snakeskin boots is reading a poem about the desert being both his mother and his lover.

The black cop has never looked more out of place. Long, muscular arms draped across the seat backs to each side, he bounces one leg impatiently—a leg almost as thick as Jacob's torso.

Jacob takes the seat next to the letterman jacket. The leg stops bouncing.

Shoulders keeps his gaze fixed on the dais, trying to appear interested, but his senses have clearly zeroed in on the man in the wrinkled T-shirt and khakis who dropped into the hot seat.

Jacob listens through another stanza. Pretends to glance at the art on the gallery walls, peripherally spotting Mustache as he crosses from the remaindered books to the info desk. A perfect spot to cut Jacob off from the stairs.

He waits. They wait.

The Poet Laureate of Somebody's Backyard declares his yearning to make love to a cactus, and Jacob makes the switch. Scoops up the letterman jacket and in the same movement drops the Members Only one in its place. He's up and away from the seats and heading for the stairs before he realizes what his hand knew at a touch—there's no money under the jacket.

Mustache comes right behind Jacob, following him to the top of the stairs, when Jacob wheels around so suddenly they almost collide. Their eyes meet, and for a moment neither is sure what the other will do.

Jacob says, "Excuse me," and steps around the cop. Walks across the floor, past the info desk with its narrow-eyed employee typing on a computer, and enters the Rare Book Room.

The ancient, balding custodian of this quiet, carpeted, precisely climate-controlled cell hunches over a book at his desk, folding Mylar over a dust jacket. He doesn't seem to register Jacob's arrival—nor, from appearances, much care about anything that doesn't have brittle old pages and hand-woven binding.

Jacob browses a hundred-year-old atlas displayed on top of a waist-high bookshelf, allowing him to watch the door as Mustache comes in. Roughly as tall as his partner and just as wide, but with a case of beer where Shoulders has a six-pack. Mustache stands directly on the opposite side of the bookcase, hardly feigning interest in the musty tome he opens.

"Boy, I'll tell you somethin," he says. "Life, huh? Whole lotta foreplay, not a lot of fuck."

Jacob glances at the book in Mustache's hands. "Mark Twain said that?"

The cop lifts his dark eyes to fix an amused gaze on Jacob—not unlike a sadistic child pepper-spraying flies. "You know you got an empty jacket, right?"

"I don't mind. It's chilly out."

"And I bet my buddy's got an empty jacket too. So. How we both gonna get what we want?"

"We could swap pants. But mine'll probably be loose in the crotch."

"Can I help either of you gentlemen?" the guardian of rare books calls out, loud enough to communicate his disdain for human voices.

"Just browsing, thanks," Mustache says. Then turns back to Jacob and says, in a softer whisper, "I know you're not him. Just some idiot took a few bucks to make a handoff. I got no beef with you."

"If you knew me, you might."

"One-time offer. Now or never." He reaches for the inside pocket of his leather jacket. Jacob tenses, and before he can recoil a brown paper bag lands on top of the bookcase. Thick, square-shaped, like a brick.

"I don't mind spendin the money. I just don't wanna give it to some shit-stain thinks he can screw me and my partner. Laugh about it with his retarded cronies on their stupid tiny bikes. That chaps my ass, man."

"Mine too. I hate those little bikes."

Jacob stares at the bag, so much thicker than the measly bundle in his pocket. His lack of civic duty coming back to him.

"The full amount," Mustache says. "Twenty grand, all yours. Just give me the punk."

Jacob's gaze returns to the dark eyes. The amusement is gone, replaced by a barely contained fury that reminds Jacob why he changed his mind.

Mustache taps the bag gently, steadily. "You don't gotta do nothin 'cept point him out. He's here in the store, right? Wouldn't be smart enough to meet somewhere else."

Jacob shrivels inside. *Now who's the dumb one?*

"Point me to him, take your money, go free and clear. No harm, no hassle. You don't ever gotta know what happened to him."

"Twenty grand, huh?"

Mustache nods confidently, his smirk returning.

"A man who'll pay twenty might go fifty."

The smirk dies. "You tryin to extort me?"

"You've already been extorted," Jacob says. "I'm just haggling."

Mustache slaps his hand over the bag, big enough to cover the entire brick. The smack it makes jars the custodian's last nerve. "If you wish to converse," he snaps, "there's a coffee shop on the ground floor."

"We're talkin books!" Mustache says. Back to Jacob: "Don't fuck with us. They'll never *find* all your pieces."

"Send Mr. Shoulders to an ATM. We can read to each other while we wait."

The bag goes back into the jacket. "Money's off the table. You had your chance, fuckface. Now you show us to him or we start breakin bones."

Evidently not intimidated by the cop's size and ferocity, the custodian of the Rare Book Room has shambled to their side and is about to utter another protest when Jacob turns to him, holding up the atlas he's been thumbing. "I'll take this one. Do you gift wrap?"

Jacob finds Shoulders standing guard outside the room, even less amused-looking than his partner. Mustache grabs Jacob's arm, steers him toward the windows by the Photography section. "I got you a present," Jacob says, handing him the atlas.

Mustache flings the book aside. "Your mistake is thinkin you're safe long as you're in public."

Shoulders adds, "It'd be *real* easy to get you someplace private."

"And *then* we'll have some goddamn fun."

"I can see you guys mean business," Jacob says. "Final offer. You keep the book, I'll take the money, and I'll go set up an introduction with my client."

Mustache and Shoulders bookend Jacob, glaring down at him from impressive heights. "You know what we are, right?" Shoulders says. "Fuck with us, you ain't safe crossin the street. Ain't safe in your home. From here on out, there's no such thing as you bein safe, ever again. Got it?"

Jacob holds out his hand expectantly. Mustache looks at Shoulders, who nods, then Mustache takes out the money and fills Jacob's palm.

Jacob goes downstairs, the cops trailing him—hanging back far enough to be inconspicuous to anyone who doesn't know what to look for. Jacob pauses on the Mezzanine entrance to the Gold Room. Then he walks over to the Green Room, the front entrance.

Glancing around, Jacob notices the cops are tense, ready to spring if he even *looks* at the front doors wrong. Jacob, never very good at improvisation, tries to work out his next step.

He lingers by the best-seller shelves, peering around with a confused expression he hopes is halfway convincing. The cops don't look convinced. They watch him with massive arms crossed in front of their huge chests, grinding their jaws.

Out of the corner of his eye Jacob steals glances toward the front doors. A constant stream of customers flows from the cashiers out onto the sidewalk, which is crowded with what appears to be a gang of suburban tourists. Mothers and their young children, mostly, perhaps wondering why anyone would make such a big deal about a bookstore.

Jacob considers his chances. He could bolt, catch the right moment, get a few people jammed between him and the cops. He *might* get away.

Then again, he might spend the rest of his life in a convalescent home.

He approaches the cops. "Not here."

"No shit. So where is he?"

"We had a backup meeting place," Jacob says, "in case either of us got nervous." The cops look skeptical as Jacob leads them back to the Mezzanine, up the stairs to the Purple Room, and then a sharp left into the Red Room.

He pretends to pretend to browse the travel guides while looking around for a client who isn't there. The cops might see right through this performance, but they'll let it play out for a few minutes before their patience finally gives out. Jacob weighing his options, hoping a few minutes is enough time . . . but for what?

Across the room, he catches sight of a memory.

The young female employee with the tattooed arms slouching at the info desk reminds Jacob of the woman he dated. She could *be* her, frozen in time. He wonders how many twenty-something kids wander into this job with temporary expectations and stagger out years later, trying to recall where they'd misplaced their youth.

Celeste. That was her name—the one she gave Jacob, at any rate.

And now he remembers the way things ended. When she'd told him she was seeing someone else now. Jacob thinking, *That's fine, it's just casual sex.* Surprised to find himself ly-

198 // PORTLAND NOIR

ing awake in a bed that felt too big. Picturing some other guy touching Celeste's tattoos in ways Jacob never would again. His hand stroking the roses twined around her calf. Lips caressing the blackbirds fluttering above the swell of her breasts. The Celtic knot on her upper arm expanding, contracting, expanding, shiny in her sweat, contracting again as she clings to his shoulders.

A lanky young man with limp black hair, who's wearing eye makeup and tight jeans that proudly display his androgyny, leans on the info desk and the employee puts her hand gently on his forearm. She beams with an unguarded warmth that no one has directed at Jacob since he was their age. In return, Lanky affects a bored expression, acting like everything else in the room is more interesting than she is.

Jacob catches the cops' eyes. Nods his head to the info desk.

Shoulders knits his brow with confusion.

Jacob nods emphatically, mimes "jacket" in his best attempt at charades, then indicates the inside pocket. Mustache eyes the studded jacket folded over Lanky's arm, and starts toward him. Shoulders hesitates another beat, clearly thinking this doesn't add up, but knowing better than to abandon his partner.

Jacob would love to stick around and see that asshole's expression as these giants hook his arms in theirs, but schadenfreude is a luxury he can't afford just now. He dashes back to the Purple Room, bounds down the stairs to the Mezzanine, runs across to the Gold Room—*never move in a straight line when you don't want to be followed*—and hurries up the aisles.

He finds the kid standing at the endcaps, right out in the open.

Jacob grabs the kid by his elbow, steers him through the

Blue Room as fast as they can hustle without looking *too* suspicious. He shoves the paper bag into the kid's hands, talking
right over his meek protests: "Get out of here. Get on your
bike and ride your scrawny ass off. Keep off major streets, ride
the wrong way down one-ways. Don't go home till you know
you weren't followed."

"Wait, I don't—"

"Tomorrow you and your girl move to another city. Don't
tell your friends, don't leave a forwarding address, and don't
come back."

"Can't we just—"

Jacob yanks the kid's arm, hard. "You got all that?"

The kid nods, and as they proceed into the Green Room,
he glances past Jacob and his eyes widen with alarm. Jacob
doesn't have to look, but he does, looks as he keeps moving
toward the front entrance, sees the cops descend the steps
from the Purple Room to the Mezzanine.

They spot him at the same instant. Both men start as if
to run, but think better of it, fast-walking past postcards and
books about Oregon. Huge legs clearing the short distance
quickly.

Jacob shoves the kid toward the front doors, putting
himself between the kid and the cops who are fast approaching. He flings himself at the info desk and the two managers
chatting behind it. He doesn't have to fake the urgency in his
voice: "My son's missing! He's only six!"

One of the managers darts for the doors—just as the kid
disappears into the night air. The other manager picks up the
phone and her voice crackles over the PA system: "White
Rabbit. We have a White Rabbit."

*"White Rabbit," Celeste had explained to him once. "Y'know,
like Alice chasing the rabbit down the hole and getting lost."*

Employees spring into action. Cashiers rush over from behind the counter to stand guard by the door, where the first manager has stopped a middle-aged woman and her son on their way out. "I'm sorry, ma'am, no one can leave just now. This should only take a few minutes."

The cops stop short. Shoulders goes for his wallet, starts to say something, but Mustache grasps him with a firm hand. Shakes his head. Wrong place, wrong time to flash a badge.

Shoulders paces a small circle, seething, utilizing every ounce of self-control to keep from punching something, someone, anything.

Mustache turns to Jacob, that sadistic gleam back in his eyes.

Jacob is too busy describing his nonexistent son—and the balding, fussy old man he'd last seen talking to the boy near the Rare Book Room—to say anything to Mustache that would get him killed.

When the manager dashes off to share the description, Jacob leans toward Mustache. "Purple Room. On the far right after you get up the stairs. Up on the top shelf, you'll find what you're looking for. And maybe a sleeping homeless guy too."

Mustache unfolds his arms, easing off his scowl a bit. "Think that's it? You just walk away scot-free?"

"The kid's gone—you'll never catch him," Jacob says, surprised to find he hopes it's true. "And I'm not worth risking your badges. Just a bag man."

Mustache scans Jacob's face like he's committing the details to memory. "Don't be too sure," he says. Then nods at his partner and they stalk away, Shoulders brushing past Jacob hard enough to knock him off balance. Jacob rights himself against the info desk, watches them take the steps to the Purple Room two at a time.

Jacob looks out the front doors and tells the manager standing guard, "Oh, there they are!" He points at the crowd of tourists milling outside—could be any of a half-dozen kids with their mothers. "Thank you so much," he says, then calls, "Honey, over here!" as he blows past the manager and out the doors.

Thinking as he goes out: *This really is the stupidest thing I've ever done.*

PART III

DESOLATION CITY

BURNSIDE FOREVER

BY JUSTIN HOCKING

Burnside Skatepark

1) Fuck Hawaii.

2) First time I see her: she's lying on a dirty-ass mattress, up in the parking lot above Burnside Skatepark, right in the place everyone goes to piss or shoot up or toss their empties or die. It's the middle of the day, 2 p.m. And she's on this mattress, sleeping with this sketchy-looking young black guy, which honestly you don't see too often down here under the bridge, and her pink g-string's hanging way out of her Dickies, which strikes me as weird too, because most homeless girls don't wear g-strings. Or not pink ones, at least. She's sleeping but I can tell she's pretty. And young. And then me and this sketchy black guy, we're staring at each other, his stare all full of emptiness and craziness and malice—all shit I stare back with in fucking spades. We're staring at each other hard, and I think to myself, *This is how wars start.*

3) Things went okay over on the islands, for the first few months at least. I did what I do: drink, surf, skate, fight. It was the first and the last things that got me in trouble. And I guess the surfing too. They called me the Lumberjack over there, and at first I think they got a kick out of me, this big haole lumberjack motherfucker out in the lineup, fighting for waves with all the locals. What you hear about Hawaii is true: they'll

punch you in the face for stealing waves; they'll do it right out in the water. But not me, not at first. They could see that I'd just been through some shit and I was over there to get away from it, just like half the other fucking Haoles on the island, but the kind of shit I'd been through was different and deeper and they could read it in my eyes and my beard and the way I'd take waves no one else would take, drop in high and late and still make it and generally just not give a fuck. Spiritual fuckers, the Hawaiians, from years of living between oceans and volcanoes. But still fuckers, nonetheless, from years of Haole lumberjack interlopers like me pissing them off, stealing their land and their waves, and the grudging respect they showed me at first wore off once I dropped in on the wrong people. Blood in the water: there was a lot of it.

4) This girl on the mattress, I don't know what it was about her. She was too pretty and dressed too well to be homeless. She had dark black hair and pale skin and turquoise eyes.

5) Awhile back I worked at a summer camp, as a cook, and the kids liked me, more than they liked some of their counselors, because I was cool to them I guess, and I skated with them and shit. And told them dirty jokes. There was this one kid, redheaded and kind of round. Some of the other kids fucked with him, called him a fag and a kook. I spent my whole day off teaching him kickflips, and after that things got easier for him.

6) So after Hawaii and I were done with each other, I came back to Portland, picked up my van—the one Amber and I bought together for surf trips—and having no immediate place to live I parked it under the Burnside Bridge and ate beef jerky and blood oranges and grapefruits that I stole from

the fruit wholesaler across the street. In the mornings I got up early to skate the park. I saw this kid do this thing in Hawaii once, before he went out into big surf. He dipped his hand in the ocean and then made the sign of the cross over his chest, all Jesus-style. So I took to doing that before paddling out, not because I believed in anything, but because it seemed right and good, and also because I'd seen Amber's uncle do it at her funeral. I do it now before I skate too, and then I skate with a clear head, the whole park to myself, the city still damp and sleeping, and it's like in Hawaii in the warm ocean water, the way it cleans you out, flushes out all the shit. Burnside can do that, but in a dirtier way.

That's the thing about me: I'm trying. I am.

7) Manny got fucked up while I was gone.

"What the fuck happened to you?" I ask. We're up in the crow's nest at Burnside, drinking beers, heckling some Californian skater in full pads and a helmet, telling him to beat it. Manny's face looks bad, real bad, with stitches around his eye and a burly dent in his forehead.

"We were downtown partying one night and we had some words with some hicks in a big lifted truck," Manny says. "Guys from Gresham, for sure. Fucking hicks, you know? So we pulled up next to them at a stoplight, and I jumped up in the bed of their truck and started bouncing that shit up and down. Startled the shit out of them! And then they just fucking took off, blew right through the red light, almost got fucking bashed by an oncoming. They drove around like maniacs, taking hard turns, just to fuck with me. I thought for sure we were going to flip over and die, man. Scariest shit ever. So finally I just jumped out and rolled about fifteen times across the asphalt. Rolled myself right into the hospital," he says, trying to laugh, but it makes me feel bad, because he's fucked up bad and there's something not right about him now, and it's not like he'd ever been totally right, but still.

8) I wake up in the middle of the night because someone's knocking on the van door. I look out and it's the girl, the one from the mattress, and she's out there shivering in the rain, and I can tell she needs something. The light is misty, chemical orange from the streetlamps up on the bridge.

"You need a blanket?" I ask, sliding the van door open.

"No," she says. "A blanket's not what I need." She looks hungry, but not for food. She takes two fingers and smacks the inside of her elbow.

"I don't have anything like that," I say.

"Please?" There's something in her eyes, something pure behind all the makeup and crust.

I invite her in out of the rain and pull a couple beers out of the cooler, even though I know that's not what she needs. Her skin's pale and strung with little beads of rain; she smells like sweat and like the sky. She shakes her hair out like a dog and I can feel the rain from her hair on my face.

"Why don't you ask your boyfriend?" I say. "Where's he?"

"I don't know."

"He leaves you here alone in the middle of the night?"

"He takes care of me," she says. "You don't know him."

I crack a beer. She sits down on the edge of the bench where I'd been sleeping, runs her hand across my pillow. She looks around my van, at my stacks of clothes and dishes and skate decks and fruit. "You live in here?" she asks.

"Right now," I say. "Just while I find a place."

"It's nice," she says.

"It's a van," I say.

"You seen where I sleep? Believe me, this is nice."

No argument there. I take a sip of beer.

"I watch you skate sometimes," she says, looking me in the eye now. "It's like you're on fire, or you want to die or something. Everyone watches out for you."

I look out the window, at the park's darkened curves and lips. I take some pride in the way I skate, in the fact that I scare people. At a place like Burnside, this says a lot.

She stands up and reaches for the beaded necklace hanging off my rearview mirror. It was something I made for Amber back when I worked at the summer camp, during arts-and-crafts time with the kids. Amber liked it for some reason, wore it all the time. It's one of the few things of hers I have left. The girl takes it off the rearview and starts to put it around her own neck. Before she can do that I grab it out of her hand.

"I think you better go now," I say.

"I'm sorry, I just wanted to try it on. It's pretty."

I open the van door for her.

"Wait," she says, "I'm sorry, I didn't mean to. Was it your ex-girlfriend's or something?"

I don't say anything.

"I'm sorry. I'll make it up to you. I'll make you feel better. I'll suck your dick if you want me to. Seriously."

Blood rushes to my head. The same way it does every time. I'd stayed up all night drinking and fucking so many times in Hawaii, but still the blood rushes to my head, because temptation does that to you, even when you remember all the mornings you woke up feeling empty and sick and regretful, so many mornings, but still, this girl's mouth is so young and full.

"What's your fucking story? Why you sleeping at Burnside

with some crackhead?" I ask, doing the concerned-citizen thing, even though I'm still considering her offer, wondering if she swallows.

And then I hear a shout from the upper parking lot, up where the mattress is, and I know who it is and that he's looking for his girl, and I imagine going out and beating the living shit out of him, but I'm tired and it's raining and I'm honestly not all that excited about going bodies with a dirty addict sleeping on a mattress at Burnside. The girl hears the shout too. She reaches out and takes my hand, pries my fingers open one by one. She buries her thumb into my palm, just enough that it feels good, and looks up at me with those eyes. Then she takes a Sharpie out of her pocket and writes in my hand.

Please don't help me, it says.

9) A text message from Manny wakes me up a few hours later, around 4 a.m. *I think I might be an angel,* it says.

10) It's hard being back in Portland, back here where it all happened. I drive past where Amber and I used to live before she got sick, our little green bungalow in Southeast, over by St. Francis Park. Some other family is living in the house now, some people with a Subaru and a swingset. They put a garden in the side yard where my mini-ramp used to be.

I park the van and walk up into the yard and peer through the front window. I can't see anyone but it looks like someone's home. I hate them, whoever they are, but at the same time I wouldn't mind if they invited me in for a sandwich.

I walk over into the garden, where everything is mostly dead, this being wintertime, except for a few onions. They have rust-colored skins with green shoots coming out the tops. They feel firm and ripe so I pick a couple. Then I turn around and there's a little blond kid standing there looking up at me. He's wearing rollerblades.

"This your garden?" I ask.

He doesn't say anything.

"It's okay," I say. "I used to live here."

But by the look on his face I can see that this only makes it worse. He turns around and tries to skate off toward the porch, as fast as he can, but he falls down and skins his knee and starts crying, and then there's a woman's face looking at us from out the window, and here I am, this big bearded fucker standing over her crying kid, with a couple of her onions in my hand, and her face disappears fast, and I want to do the same, so I make my way toward the van, and from behind me I hear someone shouting, *Hey*, a man's voice, the voice of a not particularly tough man trying to sound a little bit tough.

I start up the engine and drive off.

11) I've been on this program, eating fruit and making the sign of the cross and skating Burnside every morning early, and not too much drinking, and my head was feeling cleared out a little, but then stuff kind of started going downhill after the thing with that family and their garden. Or maybe it was the thing with the girl, I don't know.

Manny and me start drinking early at the skatepark, getting all sloppy. I take a bad slam on my elbow. I lie there for a while, looking at the underside of the bridge, all black and sooty and painted with pigeon shit, like an old cathedral. My elbow turns into a swellbow, the size of a baseball, the way it always does. And then these art school girls who Manny knows show up with some bottles of champagne, and we decide to celebrate my swellbow, and we're all drinking out of the bottle at 1 p.m. on a Tuesday, and it's good, you know, the way freedom can be good.

Then these art school girls want to hit the strip clubs, which is just fine with Manny and me, and we end up at Magic Gardens, where the ceilings are low, and one of the strippers swings her hair around all crazy and gets it stuck in the heating vent above the stage. I'm embarrassed for her a little, all naked and hanging there by the hair, but that doesn't keep me and Manny from looking and laughing. Then the bartender, this fat Asian, comes out with a pair of scissors.

"You cut that girl's hair and I'll fucking knock your teeth out," I say. "Bring me a screwdriver and I'll get it done right."

But the bartender isn't having that, so I slap the scissors out of his fat hand, and then I'm in a headlock and the bouncer and the bartender are dragging me out. They're sorry they let me go out on the sidewalk, though, because now the bartender needs some dental work, as promised.

So then we hit Mary's, where I wash my bloody knuckles in the sink while Manny looks at his crushed face in the mirror. The bathrooms at Mary's are tiny and filthy, post–lap dance come stains on the wall next to the urinal.

"Sometimes I think I should've gone ahead and died," Manny says, tracing the scar line up around his eye.

"You know what the smell of blood does to me," I say. "Right now I could kill you with one punch."

He turns away from the mirror and looks at me. "You'd do that for me?" I'm surprised to see that he's serious.

"Come on, man," I say. "You don't really want to die."

His face turns disappointed. "I'm supposed to die so I can come back as an angel." Then he walks out. Like I said, something's not right with him.

What happens next is better than Christmas morning, or

winning the lottery, or the resurrection of Jesus, or any of that miraculous shit. I finish washing my knuckles, and in through the swinging door comes that sketchy fucker from Burnside, carrying a bent spoon, eyes all red.

"Fancy meeting you here," I say, grinning. This isn't something I usually say, but using the word "fancy" here in this bathroom strikes me as fucking hilarious.

It takes a few seconds for him to recognize me, and then I can see the fear in his eyes. I smack the spoon out of his hand. He goes down on the piss-sticky floor, crawling around like a dog, looking for it.

"Just give me a couple minutes," he says. "Just let me take care of something and then we can—"

I kick him straight in the mouth.

I thought that would do the trick, but then he's up and on me, and stronger than I thought, or not stronger but more desperate maybe. I'm fighting for fun, for the girl; he's fighting for his life, for his next fix. But still, I'm not the right person to fuck with, not ever. I bear hug him, crack his forehead open with a head butt, then break the bathroom door open with his body and we spill out into the bar, me on top the entire time. Blood: there's a lot of it. I think Manny even got a few shots in, or maybe it was Manny who pulled me off him, it's hard to remember.

12) Manny figures it might not be the best idea for me to sleep at Burnside, but I don't give a fuck. Right now this place belongs to me.

Sketchy and the girl are nowhere to be found. My best guess is the hospital. I sleep sound, until there's another knock on my van.

The girl again.

She looks scared. A fresh purple bruise under her left eye.

"Is he okay?" I ask, yawning.

"No, he's not fucking okay," she says, climbing into the van. She smells like sweat again, and like something burning. Incense, maybe. Or charcoal.

"I just gave him a friendly beat down. He got what he deserved."

"It's not what you did," she says. "It's something else."

"What, the bouncers rough him up after I finished?"

She looks around nervously. "You have any more beers?"

I reach back into the cooler and grab a couple. When I turn around she kisses me hard, and I can feel that she already has her shirt half off. The way she smells does something to me, like the smell of blood does something to me. But this is different. She smells like the ocean and like fire, and the way she's all over me and hungry is like being out on a big day in Hawaii, when you bail hard and get tumbled all over the fucking place, held under a thousand gallons of seawater, churned around like a dirty sock in a washing machine. Then you finally come up for air and you know you're probably not going to drown and it feels so good to breathe that you thank God, whether or not you've ever set foot in church, and this girl all over me with her hot mouth and her soft tits is like that but better. And then it's my turn to be on top, and I keep asking to make sure I'm not hurting her, because I'm big—I make girls cry in a good way, most of the time—and the girl promises me it's in a good way, her crying, and then she begs me to come in her mouth so that I know for sure.

When it's over she lies totally still, almost like she's dead. Or catatonic. But she's breathing, and she's soft, and I kind of like her all quiet like this. I fall asleep with my hand on her stomach.

She shakes me awake. Half an hour later? Three hours? I have no fucking clue.

She has that strung-out look again, like the first time she got in my van. I ask her what's the matter, and she just sits there shivering until I touch her cheek.

"It's okay," I say. "You don't have to worry about him anymore. I'll take care of you."

She shakes her head. "I know," she says. "I trust you."

"Then what's the problem?"

"I killed him," she says.

"You what?"

"I killed him. I really did. He came back here after you beat him up and he punched me in the face, so I took his knife and killed him."

I rub my face and try to let this sink in, the fact that I just fucked a murderer.

"Okay, so you killed him. What the fuck did you do with his body?"

"That's what I need your help with," she says.

13) She leads me up the dirt path to the upper parking lot. She holds my hand the whole way. Sobbing. "He's up here," she says. "I pulled the mattress over him."

We climb further up to the spot, and sure enough, there's the mattress, all covered in bloodstains, and there's a big long lump underneath that looks a lot like a body. The girl falls to her knees and starts sobbing again. "I'm sorry," she says, looking up at me with pleading eyes. "Oh my God, I'm so sorry."

"Don't be. Fucker had it coming."

And then from out of nowhere something bashes me on

the back of the head, dropping me straight to my knees, my vision crackling with little white fireworks. Then a hard kick to my ribs that knocks the wind out of me.

I don't even have to look up, I know who it is. But I do look up, and he's got a gun and I can see that he's pretty serious about wanting to use it. I laugh. "I know a guy who'll pay you to shoot him," I say.

"You stupid motherfucker," he rasps, the gun trained right on my eye socket.

But then the girl is on his back, still crying, begging him not to.

He shoves her away and I make a move for him, but he stomps on my face. And again. And then again. Somewhere between the time I pounded on him at Mary's and now he found a pair of heavy boots.

14) I wake up on the mattress, my pulse punching from inside my head. What looked like the shape of a body at first is actually a pile of rocks and broken concrete chunks, which I highly don't recommend sleeping on. I feel around in my pockets; as expected, my van keys are gone.

15) I wake up again, maybe half an hour later, and Manny has me by the legs. His skateboard's underneath me like a little hospital gurney, and he's facing forward, pulling me by both my feet. One of my shoes is gone.

I try to open my mouth to thank him, but it hurts to talk.

He tows me from under the bridge, and out there it's a bright sunny morning, the first I've seen in Portland for a while. I'm looking straight up into the sky, from my one good eye, at the clouds and the sun and lampposts and power cables. Manny pulls me across the street, through a crosswalk, and I can see a lady in a Volvo looking out at us like, *What the fuck*, this man pulling another man like a rickshaw, both our faces wrecked, mine with fresh blood. I know Manny's taking me to the hospital, because everyone who skates Burnside knows where the nearest hospital is, and I don't have to ask about my van because if it was still here he'd be driving me. I picture Sketchy and the girl—I never did learn her name— driving south to California, the way Amber and I used to drive down there in the winter, heading toward the sun. And it's here, with Manny pulling me toward help and me picturing those two driving my van, that I start to feel how bad it hurts, everything I've been through, and I wonder if maybe the girl will wear the beaded necklace, the one I made for Amber at camp. It would look good on her, I think. It definitely would. And Manny's humming now while he pulls me, like this is no big deal, like this is what he was born to do.

HUMMINGBIRD

BY ZOE TROPE

S.E. Eighty-Second Avenue

Amy doesn't want to go to Cathie's. I don't care. "You deserve orgasms!" I tell her.

She flushes and pushes her long, sideways bangs out of her eyes. "Shut up," she says, and turns up the volume on the TV. We're watching *Ace of Cakes* on the Food Network in my parents' basement. Again.

"Luke doesn't make you come, right?"

She doesn't answer, which means yes.

I stand in front of the television. Amy crosses her thin arms and looks past me, focusing on Duff Goldman, the chef, who is up to his elbows in fondant. She can be pissy sometimes, but we've been friends since we were both straight. That was sixth grade. Then puberty hit and Amy fell in love with Samir Rajkumar, who, after two dates that involved making out at the movie theater, admitted to her, *I think I like guys*. Then the universe decided to donkey punch Amy because I told her that I was into chicks on the same day. She asked if gay was going around like the flu.

"Amy, come on. It'll be fun. I'll buy you a coffee." She ignores me and changes the channel. There's a lady on the news with pink lipstick and bad hair talking about a sexual predator on the loose.

"The suspect is a twenty-five-to-thirty-year-old white male . . ."

"Who is this guy?" Amy asks as an artist's sketch lingers on the screen.

"Some meth head who's been 'harassing women outside a local nightclub.'" I wiggle my fingers in the air, putting quotes around the second part.

"What does that mean?"

I smirk. "He's been harassing dykes outside E Room, asking if he can help them come. That's what Julia told me, anyway."

"How would she know?"

"Her friend Emma works there."

"With our luck, we'll run into some guy like that at the porn shop." Amy gestures at the screen and wrinkles her tiny, cute nose.

"Cathie's is very classy," I assure her. "It's women-owned. Minimal meth head exposure, I promise." Her green eyes move from the screen to my pleading, grinning face. "Orgasms, Amy!" I do my Martha impression, which she loves: "It's a good thing."

Amy cracks a smile, turns off the TV, and picks up her tiny purse from under the coffee table. I see her pull out her phone as she gets into my car.

"Who are you texting?"

"Luke."

"Gonna let him know that you're going to buy his competition?"

She doesn't say anything as we drive down Eighty-second, past Vietnamese restaurants and brothels with names like Honeysuckles Lingerie and The G Spot. I wonder what she's writing. *what r u doing tonight?* I pull into a strip mall with a Russian deli, a teriyaki joint, a nail salon, and a bubble tea café.

There's techno music playing in the café, which is mostly deserted except for a guy checking his e-mail and two teenage girls reading magazines in the back. Amy orders a latte. "I hate the way those bubbles feel in my mouth," she says when I order a taro root smoothie with tapioca pearls. "They're so slimy."

"Nah, they're kind of like candy," I explain.

Amy argues, "I don't think you should have to chew your drink," and adds another packet of sugar to her cup. She grabs two swizzle straws and pushes them through the hole in the lid.

We drive further south, past the community college, the Taboo porn shop, and two enormous Chinese restaurants.

I ask Amy if she came with her last boyfriend, Del, who she dated her junior year. He was tall and tan like a Ken doll. I liked him, right up until he called Samir a faggot behind his back. I did the only thing a sensible lesbian would do—I gave him a black eye. Del snitched to his parents, telling them a crazy dyke tried to kill him, and I had to spend time with my mom and a juvie youth counselor talking about why I was such "an angry young woman." I got probation. Amy broke up with Del and didn't talk to me for a month.

Amy shakes her head about Del. I suck the bubbles up from the bottom of my cup. "That blows," I say.

She stares at her phone, mid-text. "His dick was too big. It hurt."

"Okay, well, moving forward. Top 10 best things about vibrators. I'll start. They come in shapes like dolphins and beavers. Your turn." Amy will play Top 10 anything. It's my way of making her feel okay about things she doesn't want to do. One time we played Top 10 best things about abortions.

"Uh," she finishes her text and puts her phone away in her purse. "Some of them ejaculate, I've heard, which is absolutely hilarious."

"Good call. Number three, some of them light up. I even had one once that had glitter in the middle."

"Isn't that a health hazard?" Amy asks.

"Not if you wash it properly. Your turn. Four."

"They don't forget your birthday," she offers.

"Oh, bitter. I like it."

She adds quietly with a smirk, "And they can't get you pregnant, either."

I nod. "Six. They never get jealous when you sleep with someone else."

Amy rolls her eyes. "And they never choose to play Xbox over you."

"You can easily twist the base to adjust the speed."

"Number nine . . . When they get tired, you can just put in more batteries."

"Excellent point. And number ten, of course—multiple orgasms. Thank God for the Hitachi magic wand."

Amy puts down her cup mid-sip. "Wait," she says. "I thought the Bunny was the best one."

"You mean the Rabbit. And you watch too much *Sex and the City*."

"So then which one do I buy?"

"Well, that depends," I reply, "on whether you have clitoral or vaginal orgasms."

Amy bites the tiny swizzle straw in her latte, opens her mouth, and then closes it again.

I try to translate. "Neither?" I ask as we pull into the strip mall parking lot. The windows are frosted white and the neon sign above the door is written in swirly red letters with a heart dotting the i: *Cathie's*. Amy opens her door and jumps out of the car to avoid the question.

Inside, I help her decipher the wall of fake wieners. I explain the difference between jelly, cyberskin, and plastic, and the importance of noting battery sizes.

222 // PORTLAND NOIR

"See this one?" I pick up a slim white number from the wall. "This one takes double-As, so that means it's kind of like a quiet hum." I pick up a bigger one, an inch and a half in diameter, with a pink leopard pattern all over it. "This one takes C batteries. It's like having a didgeridoo against your clit." I smile and close my eyes. "Mmm. My favorite."

Amy bites her lip. "How do I know which one to pick? Should I get that thing with the hook on the end?" She picks up one that looks like a dentist's instrument—long and thin with a slight curve at the tip.

"Have you found your G spot? That's what the hook is for."

Amy cocks her head in response, her body now mirroring the shape of the vibrator in her hand. The way she holds it, it almost looks like an abstract self-portrait.

I smack myself in the forehead with the pink leopard wiener. "This is ridiculous," I say. "Do you do anything down there besides piss and put in the occasional tampon?"

Amy smirks and puts it back. "I know you think I'm an idiot, Kate, but I'm not."

"Oh yeah?"

"I'm getting more head than you right now," she says with a self-satisfied smile.

I roll my eyes. "Boy head, whatever. He doesn't give you orgasms!"

"Sometimes orgasms aren't everything," Amy explains.

"Only people who can't have orgasms say stuff like that."

Amy picks up a slim silver vibrator with a body that slowly moves in and out. The base is cupped like a spoon. The box says, *Hummingbird*. "How about this one?"

I nod. "Sure, it looks good. I think that little spoony part is for your clit."

Amy holds it firmly, decisively. "Okay. I think we're done." Her eyes dart around the store and she lowers her voice to a whisper. "See that lady over there?"

I turn to the display of butt plugs and pick up one like I'm interested. Out of the corner of my eye, I spot an older woman in her forties with bright yellow hair hanging in crispy, over-gelled waves down her back. She's wearing white shorts and her skin is brown like a hot dog. She's holding the largest bottle of lube I've ever seen. It looks like a Big Gulp cup.

I snort, Amy giggles, and then we cover our mouths with our hands. She whispers, "I hope our vags never become so sandy."

"Amen."

I notice a fat guy with a mustache reading a book in the corner. The cover says, *Guide to the Female Orgasm.* I poke Amy in the ribs and jerk my chin at him. "Do you think that's the guy?"

Amy glances at him and shakes her head. "Nah. He looks like some married man with a sad wife." She adds, "Can we please get out of here now?"

The girl at the cash register looks like she's not much older than us, with a lip ring and short pink hair. She takes Amy's vibrator out of the package, shoves batteries into it, and twists the base, which makes it hum. She disassembles it just as quickly, kind of like a soldier with a gun. The whole thing happens so fast that Amy just stands there with her mouth slightly open. Her wide eyes tell me that she's going to thoroughly disinfect her purchase before it touches her body.

Amy pays with a debit card and the lady asks for her signature.

"Why do I have to sign if it's a debit?" Amy asks.

The girl smacks her gum as she explains, "We have to

224 // PORTLAND NOIR

track all the purchases. People like to get high on meth, steal people's identities, and buy porn."

Amy doesn't know what to say to that. "Oh," she replies.

"God, I can't believe we're doing this backwards," I say to Amy. "I thought it was porn, identity theft, then meth."

Amy sighs and shakes her head. "I guess we'll get it right next time." She hooks her arm through mine. "Let's just skip the identity theft and go home to our meth."

I pat her hand. "Okay, honey."

The girl behind the counter starts to put the Hummingbird in a black plastic bag. Amy waves her hand, "I don't need a bag."

"You sure?" she asks.

"Yeah." Amy grabs the vibe and tucks it into her purse. It fits snugly.

The girl shrugs. "Have fun, ladies," she says.

We're on the road again, driving fast but aimless, zipping north on the 205 to the 84 west, racing along next to the MAX train. I refuse to roll up the windows, so we yell to hear each other over the wind and the Pretty Girls Make Graves album. I smoke three cigarettes between Cathie's and Lloyd Center, careful not to burn my long hair as it whips around in front of my face. Amy's fingers are fast on her phone. *omg i bought a vibrator!!*

I pull the car into the mall parking lot so we can ride the train for free downtown. You're not supposed to do this, but everyone does.

We get off the train in Chinatown and walk to Voodoo Doughnut so Amy can get the one with cocoa puffs on top. She says she needs some comfort after being traumatized by the wiener wall. I smile at her fake drama.

The line outside the tiny shop is understandably long and most of the people waiting for doughnuts are dressed to go out—punks in torn-up jeans and spikes, sorority girls with hard nipples pressing against their tube tops. I'm wearing jeans and a T-shirt, but Amy, in her platform sandals and halter top, looks like she could go clubbing. She's even got big sweeping strokes of purple eye shadow over each eye.

"Shit," I whisper.

"What?" Amy looks up from her phone.

I point. "It's Liz."

"Oh crap," Amy says. She knows Liz is my ex-girlfriend and that our break-up sucked, but she doesn't know that Liz dumped me after she found out I was "humping that whore from Hillsboro"—her alliteration, not mine.

Liz is easy to spot in a crowd. She looks like a Latina pin-up with dark skin, big eyes, and pouty lips. She dresses like a vintage model in big black Mary Janes, fishnets, and bright red lipstick. She keeps her black hair cut short in this sexy Louise Brooks kind of way.

I still want to fuck her.

I suddenly wish I'd worn something cool. Liz loved my soft butch look. She said it was best when I wore my long auburn hair loose with pinstripe pants and a button-up shirt.

Amy watches me staring. "Do you want to go?"

"No," I say. "There's room for two lesbos in this doughnut shop."

Liz doesn't even notice me while she orders a McMinnville cream—my favorite too, a custard-filled doughnut with maple frosting.

Some skinny dyke wearing tight jeans and Converse sneakers has her arm around Liz's waist the whole time, but I realize when they turn to leave that the girl is remarkably flat-chested and her face is blunt and chiseled under her big black glasses.

Then I see his Adam's apple.

I want to stop myself but I can't. I follow them out the door and leave Amy standing at the counter.

I yell down the street, "I didn't realize you were into dudes, Liz!"

Liz and her boyfriend turn around. She blinks once, slowly, her eyes weighed down by multiple layers of mascara, and says, "I'm not, Kate. I just like people who aren't assholes." She nods at the doughnut shop, where Amy is still inside. "Have fun with your *puta nueva*," she adds. Liz knows that Amy is only a friend, but everybody is competition to her.

Her boyfriend flips me off. Liz sashays down the street and doesn't look back.

Amy appears next to me, her mouth full of chocolate cereal and frosting. "You are a total failure at life, you know that, right?"

I shrug. Amy doesn't get it. Amy didn't make Liz come in a parked car. I still get off to the image of Liz in her tight black dress, leaning her head back with her red mouth open while I worked her clit with my fingers. And tonight I'll probably fantasize about pushing her up against the wall of that doughnut shop and reaching my hand inside her fishnet stockings. I loved the way she held the back of my neck when I fucked her, forcing my lips against hers. She gave the dirtiest kisses.

Amy licks her fingers. "Let's go to Backspace," she offers. It's one of the few late-night coffee shops downtown, which means it's always full of high school kids. I don't really want to go but, until we turn twenty-one we don't have many other options.

Amy buys a second latte and grabs a deck of cards from

another table. There's a group of boys with laptops at a big table in the back and they're all playing some computer game together. One of them leans back in his chair and sighs, "This is so fucking gay, dudes."

Amy deals gin, which means she wants to talk. We've been playing gin since we were in the Girl Scouts. We used to play a quarter per point against other troops and clean them out. She spent all her money on makeup and I bought books.

"How old is Liz, anyway?" she asks.

"Twenty-five," I say.

"So does that mean it was, like, statutory rape when you were dating?"

"Nope. Just sodomy."

"Oh." Amy looks a little disappointed, like she was hoping for a felony, but her face brightens as she lays out her hand. "Gin."

"You're a cunt," I tell her and slap my cards on the table.

She shrugs. "Homo."

"Prude."

"Dyke."

"Breeder."

Amy deals another hand and then leans across the table to whisper, "Don't be mad that you can never have me."

"Mad?" I point at her bug-bite titties. "There's nothing there to motorboat. Forget it."

Amy shakes her shoulders in an effort to make her nonexistent tits jiggle, which makes me snort. "Is that why you loved Liz?" Amy asks. "Because of her motorboat-ability?"

"And her apartment," I answer. "It was nice to have a place where I could escape."

Amy nods as she picks a discard. "I didn't see you much then."

"Yeah," I say. I feel my cheeks tinge pink. It's true. I dated Liz for nine months, right at the end of our senior year. I would live at her place on the weekends and never answer my cell phone. Amy sent me so many texts: *where r u? call me. iron chef tonight? answer yr damn phone, plz!!*

But I didn't want to deal with anyone else. I just wanted to be in Liz's apartment and see her looking disheveled in the morning. I loved the way she would roll over and smile at me with crusty raccoon eyes. "Morning, Glory," she would say. Then she'd kiss me and I'd run my hands over her bare breasts, over her back, into her panties.

"Well, too bad she was a nut job," Amy laments.

I nod and half-smile. "And now she's straight too."

Liz had moods sharp like knives. She said she was stressed with grad school and would apologize, but then she'd go into rages, break dishes, and yell at me to get out. One time she bit me so hard on my arm it left a scar. My mom asked if a dog did it.

"Some of it was good," I say. Amy looks up from her cards. "I loved going to brunch with her on Sundays. And she wrote me letters, even when we saw each other every day. Sometimes we just sat together on her porch, reading books and smoking cigarettes."

Amy nods thoughtfully. Then she gives me a big smile and I groan. "Gin," she says.

By the time we head back across the river, the train is almost empty. We sit side by side, Amy texting a mini-novella while I stare out the window. *so then i got a donut and kate was a total bitch to her ex and we played gin and i won every time and we're heading home now so maybe i'll come over later and you can meet my hummingbird?*

A guy about our age in an Old Navy T-shirt is sitting across the aisle. He's rocking his head back and forth singing "Brown Eyed Girl" to himself. *"Sha la la la la la la la la la ti da,"* he mumbles. He's got short brown hair and a hooked nose. I look at his hands because he's drumming his fingers on his leg and his hands are all fucked up and scarred and dirty. He looks familiar.

He catches me looking at him and lopes over to our seats. He goes, "Hey." He's got pale skin and he smells wet and sour, like a gutter that's been pissed in too many times. I breathe through my mouth. I look at Amy and we don't say anything.

The guy smiles like one half of his mouth is all shot up with Novocain. "Hey," he says again, and leans closer to Amy. "You're really pretty." She tenses up but doesn't move. He runs a finger along the edge of her hair, from the base of her neck down to her shoulder blade.

I swat his hand away. "Hey, man. Don't fucking touch her!"

Amy is red and frozen, not looking at either of us.

The guy straightens up and laughs. "Whatever. I'm just giving her a compliment." His Adam's apple bobs in his neck and suddenly I want to wrap my hands around his throat. Make him shut up. Make him sorry. His eyes roll around, like he's not sure where to look. He stares into Amy's lap, at her purse. "Hey," he says again, and points. "What's what?"

The Hummingbird is sticking out of her bag. He can see the cupped tip and the edge of the package, where it says, *Requires two AA batteries*, in large print. "It's a toothbrush," Amy says, and tries to push it down into her purse.

"Nah," he says. "That's a dildo." He stretches it out into two heavy syllables: Dill. Dough. He laughs again and I want to crush his windpipe. My fingernails are digging into my palms.

He touches Amy's neck. "You need some help, honey? Need a man to help you, baby doll?"

Amy cringes and I leap over her, shoving him with force. There are three other people on the train and they are all working very hard to seem like they are not looking at us.

I warn him, "Keep your fucking hands and your compliments to yourself."

"Don't touch me, you fat fucking dyke," he growls. His glassy eyes darken and he pushes me back, so I stumble into Amy, who, miraculously, is still texting. *this is so crazy!!*

I take a deep breath and feel my body hum. There's a rush of blood that starts in my feet and burns straight up my legs to my pussy. It feels like an hour passes before the train stops and the doors slowly pull apart, and in one moment I do two things—I stomp on his foot, which distracts him enough to look down for a fraction of a second, then I jam the palm of my hand upward into his face and I hear his nose pop into my fingers. Suddenly there's blood streaming down my forearm and I yell, "Run!" to Amy, who's already jumped out and is racing to the parking lot.

I run as hard as I can, pausing only once to glance over my shoulder, and I see that he's stepped off the train but he's not going to catch us. He's stumbling around with blood all over his shirt. The last thing I hear from him is a muffled cry like a broken animal.

Amy shouts for the keys and I toss them to her. She sprints ahead to the car and has the engine started before I even reach the passenger door.

We burn through signals regardless of their color and pull onto the freeway. The blood on my hand slowly dries and turns brown. Amy stares straight ahead, a death grip on the wheel, her chest heaving. Her right foot is planted to the floor. The album is still blasting from the stereo and we don't turn it down.

Stand up so I can see you
Shout out so I can hear you
Reach out so I can touch you
This is our emergency
This is our emergency

A moment turns into half an hour. I make Amy turn around at Multnomah Falls, the scenic area thirty miles east of where we started.

"I don't want to go to Idaho," I say. I try to make it funny but she doesn't respond.

Amy quietly, slowly pulls the car around. She looks left and right three times. Stops. She finally speaks: "Do you think we lost him?"

In the dark night, it's so funny, all I can do is laugh, and finally Amy laughs too, and I say, "He never even had us."

SHANGHAIED

BY GIGI LITTLE

Old Town

Eight o'clock

So, I'm walking down this seedy street in Old Town with Kit and Rhonda, silently lamenting my sorrowful existence—how rent's going up again, how I need some new clothes, how good cheese is so fucking expensive—and up ahead, on the next corner, here's this old woman begging. How's that for juxtaposition?

In other words, I'm a pathetic, whiny bitch.

She's squat like a folding chair. Hunched, head straight out from the crossbar of her shoulders. Hand out at the people walking by. And this funny look on her face, this little twisted thing with her lips, almost a smile—and, damn, look at her eyes. She's got crooked eyes. Like she's wearing crooked glasses, but she's not wearing glasses at all.

"Spare change?" she says. "Pretty jewelry?"

And that's the thing that really has me reaching into my purse. Pretty jewelry. Because Jesus, I mean, just look at her.

All right, it's not the dress—that's just some old house-dress. Yellow faded to white. Some splattery stain covering it that, when I step close enough, turns out to be what was once a pattern of flowers. But her hat. That's bright blue velvet. With one of those little feathers at the side and some torn net hanging from the brim. And her jewelry. Trying so hard to be pretty. She's covered in junky plastic—big earrings, clinking bracelets—old and broken. And what looks like—step closer—clippings of wire circled around her fingers. Necklaces made of tied-together pieces of gutter-stained string and buttons and faded sequins. Step right in front of her now, and the brooch pinned to her chest is an arthritic metal claw with no rhinestones.

She looks her crooked eyes down my face to the pearls at my neck. "Pretty jewelry?"

I've got a fistful of coins and I step up and hang it over her open hand and let go.

Her other hand comes up fast. Takes a jabbing snatch at me.

Her rough, knobby fingers around the four of mine.

The top of my head does that scared thing where it feels like someone's cracked a raw egg up there. I hang my mouth open but my brain forgets what screaming's for, and then she lets go. And now we're walking away, Kit glancing back. That touch still on my fingers. The way the squirm hangs around in your stomach after the scare's over.

Rhonda's good enough to wait until we're one step away from being out of earshot. "My friend," she says, "you are such a sap."

Nine o'clock

After a couple hours walking through the dungeons and opium dens below the streets of Portland you need a drink. It was thick hot down there, and dark. They gave us flashlights and said, *Now, direct your attention to this corner where, in eighteen-hundred-and-I-can't-remember, men were held captive in foul prison cells.*

Rhonda had the reaction I thought she'd have: "Shanghai Tunnels? Shit, that was more like the Shanghai Basement."

234 // Portland Noir

But if you enjoy good lore and don't mind close, dark spaces where the air is like breathing dirt and it's so hot you could keel over but for being constantly revived by the exquisite reek of body odor coming off the tourist next to you, it's quite a hoot.

Me, I love good lore. Lore is my favorite kind of story. Because it's not only historical, it's a lie everyone knows is a lie but tells anyway. I love that. Of course every story I tell is true. Completely true. Completely and utterly at least five-eighths of the way to being true, which is truer than any piece of lore and truer than most truths you'll hear, including the one about George Washington and the cherry tree. Look it up.

But after the tunnels and then the old woman grabbing my hand, we had to get out of Old Town. I said we could walk to the Pearl District, but Rhonda always has to call a cab. She couldn't have gotten very far anyway on those shoes of hers that are somewhere between fuck-me pumps and fuck-you pumps. She sat in the middle so she could lean in between the front seats and show her boobs to the cab driver.

And now we're at the Everett Street Bistro, Rhonda's favorite place—sitting at her favorite sidewalk table. I wanted to sit inside, and I'm trying to drown my frustrations in some sort of sugar-on-the-rim, house-infused, fruit-muddled, herb-atomized cocktail, and pommes frites with a side of béarnaise sauce.

Kit is big blue eyes over an even bluer drink. "No, seriously, Rhonda, there are tunnels running all under this city. From Old Town all the way to the Willamette River."

Kit's reciting word for word what the tour guide said. She smiles like the tour guide did. Her large, goaty teeth are a shade of blue.

"You want to know what I think?" Rhonda says, pointing a pomme frite at us. "I think they heard some old legend, found a basement, threw some old, broken shit down there, and started charging admission."

"No, seriously," says Kit and her blue teeth. "Back in the day, the bars were full of trap doors, and if you were an able-bodied man and you got yourself drunk, *bang*, down you'd go, to be chained up and shanghaied away on some pirate boat."

Again: tour guide. Except that her two drinks—closing in on three—are making Kit both more emphatic and less articulate. And I'm pretty sure the tour guide didn't say anything about pirates.

Rhonda rolls her eyes. It's ticking me off. She's rolling her eyes at the lore of our city. Which in my book is like you're dissing *my* story. I mean, this evening's entertainment was my idea. And first she's making cracks under her breath the whole tour, then she's acting like me giving some change to a woman on the street is the most obvious act of chumpdom she's ever seen. I'm going inside to find a waiter and ask if this place has a trap door I can shove her down.

Dusk is dying, and the city's washed blue to match Kit's teeth. A car drags a curtain of bright white down the street in front of us.

"You want to know what I think?" Rhonda says, but then she glances out across the road. "Hey, look who's come back for more."

Right there on the far corner. Faded dress, velvet hat, hand out at people walking by.

"I'll bet she works a circuit," Rhonda says. "I'll bet she knows exactly where to go at what time to milk the public of the most money."

I push out a laugh and try not to sound pissy defensive. "There *are* people in need in this world, you know."

"Her name's Dorothy," Rhonda says in that way she has when it's less about her knowing more than it is about you knowing less. "As in, we're not in Kansas anymore? I heard she lives at the Biltmore Apartments in Northwest." Points her chin down so she can give us the just-under-the-eyebrows look. "I also heard from an equally reliable source that she lives in a loft here in the Pearl. And owns a car."

Kit downs her drink. Her voice is just a step past not-quite-too-loud. "Well, I heard she lives in the Shanghai Tunnels."

Which is all lore—of some lame sort—and normally this would at least somewhat intrigue me, but now I look down at my hand all naked on the white tablecloth, and what the hell?

My ring.

The garnet and the amethyst are on my left hand, but the right hand, the hand she grabbed—

All right, hold on, maybe I didn't put it back on after I showered this morning. I try to remember having it on in the tunnels.

Rhonda's still going at it: "I heard she has this son who lets her beg and then takes the money and buys collectible baseball cards."

And Kit: "Well, I heard she has this son who corners people in alleys and clubs them to death with a baseball bat."

Worms in my stomach.

My favorite ring.

My grandmother's ring.

Rhonda sneering: "I heard those crooked eyes of hers can put you in a trance."

Kit slurring: "Well, I heard in reality she's the Pied Piper!"

I'm frantic eyes at the ground under my chair, at cracks in the sidewalk. The conversation moves on to how much

Rhonda hates her mother, but I can't listen, and I can't stop watching that woman.

"Mother is *always* trying to control me," Rhonda says. "All her fucking little guilt trips. You want to know what I think? It comes down to control. Everything we do, everything we feel. What's marriage? Control. Rape? Control. A mother's love? Control. Charity?" Rhonda looks at me. "Dorothy over there? What a fraud. She knows how to use guilt better than anyone I know. Yeah, the minute you locked eyes with her, you surrendered control to that old woman."

I don't answer. I've got my hand in my purse in some pathetic search all through the slink of coins at the bottom.

Dorothy swivels and sets her crooked eyes at me.

Nine-thirty

We toss crumpled-up bills out to settle the check. In my body is that perfect drone that says I've had just the right amount of too much to drink. The sun's gone down past that place where it does any good in the sky, so now everything's blue-going-to-black. It's time to hug and say, *Wow, is it really that late? We've got to do this more often.* Rhonda and Kit set off down the sidewalk. Kit big, flappy waves and blue smiles, while I'm stalling by the table. Hand in my bag like looking for keys or lipstick. Wait until they've turned the corner. Sit back down. Old, dead drink glasses and the empty pommes frites paper cone all brown and greasy.

I sit and watch the old woman.

"I hear she lives in this big Craftsman off Belmont and breeds award-winning pugs."

It's the waiter with the shaved head and the tiny braid beard. He nods big at me as if now we share a special secret. Turns. Goes off, back inside.

238 // Portland Noir

And the corner is empty.

I'm on my feet fast. A glass topples. I see she's not far. Walking in this slow shuffle like when you're a kid pretending your socks are roller skates. Grab my purse and start down the sidewalk, but it's the opposite sidewalk, and parallel means I'm not following, not really. I'm not even looking at her, just keeping her at the corner of my eye. Not-following-just-walking past the wine bar. Not-following-just-walking past the coffee house. Am I being crazy? Is my ring sitting in the dish by the bathtub? I open my hand. At the base of my finger the halo of skin is smooth and glossy.

Look up, and she's passing right in front of me.

So close, the blur of her sparks into a moment of detail: cheek like a half-deflated balloon, velvety sag of a thousand wrinkles, white whiskers, and her eye, the droop of a red rim and a flash of watery blue right at me.

Takes me a moment to catch my breath. In that moment, I could point myself in the direction of home. Instead, I wait long enough to get about fifteen feet between us. Turn, and now we're off on a little crazy-stalky tour of the city and I'm thinking she's crazy and I'm stalky, although I suppose I could be both. We see the sights. Endless shop windows, mannequins sexy with no heads. Getting darker, but the Pearl District is upscale and therefore safe, and I've got just enough rum in me to make up for my total lack of personal strength.

Whoever we pass she holds her hand out, *spare change, pretty jewelry.* Finally some couple stops to give her something. I get closer. Blond hair and lipstick, black hair and mustache up over Dorothy's head, smiling down. Both in a state of grace. They pass, glance at me as they go. I watch the hunch of her body as she shoves whatever they gave her down in some deep pocket of her dress. She starts up walking again, and now I'm right behind her. Trying to see around her arm to that pocket. She has my ring in that pocket.

And then I realize: I'm right on top of her as if I'm some mugger. I feel out of control. What's that Rhonda was saying about control? Whatever, I've got to stop this now. Powell's is right at the next block. I'll stop off there. I'll quit.

She steps into the street, and I step in after.

Sudden blaze at the side of my eyes.

A car. Right at me.

My muscles jam up, panic-stupid, and I can't move. Eyes pinned on Dorothy's back. The car jerks to a stop, bumper right at my calf, and there I am standing in the middle of the street, and in my chest is the steady pound of oh-what-the-fuck-just-happened.

Headlights flash and for a moment light up the back of Dorothy's dress. The driver shaking his hands at me. Should go forward, but I'll run right into her. Should fucking go back, but somehow I can't.

The guy shouts something muffled through the windshield. My lungs are a tight fist around an inch and a half of air. Dorothy finally steps up onto the far curb.

And I can move.

The car pulls off behind me. This time his fuck-you is loud enough to make out.

I walk on in a strange daze of comprehension. Down past the bookstore where I was never actually going to stop off, now, was I? Past closed-up restaurants, empty parking lots. Dark folding in. It's a Pied Piper dark, thick and rat black. And it's pulling me right back into Old Town. And all along I'm still asking myself what just happened, but the thing is, I know what the fuck just happened. I was pinned in the middle of the fucking street because I was not going to let that old woman out of my sight.

Ten-fifteen

Stubby, hunched buildings lumped along the sidewalk, worn-out Victorians peeling paint. Bars and abandoned storefronts. Some guy pissing on the side of a dumpster. Wine bottle in his hand—yes, this lovely, little pinot gris has a delicate bouquet with notes of urine and rotting burrito.

If I *am* to be a crazy stalker, I might as well get my method down. I set my distance at about fifteen feet, set my pace at old-lady slow. Most stalkers probably have some idea what their plan is, but I'm new to this so I just keep following. On and on through Old Town. Stalkers should wear better shoes. We walk past windows like oil-black mirrors. And I watch Dorothy's head turn. First to her reflection, then back to mine, then she swivels and she's looking right at me.

I get the egg-on-the-head thing, the kick to the gut, but my eyes grab hold of hers and don't let go. Panic turns so easy into thrill. I stare her down until she turns away.

And we're on into the part of Old Town that's also Chinatown. Chinese restaurants, some abandoned. Cheesy gift shops. A pile of trash in the darkness of a doorway or maybe someone sleeping. As Dorothy cocks a look back, I step up closer.

Ten feet. The stiffness of her body, the folding-in along her back as she walks—she's totally focused on me.

Nine feet. Stray strings of tinsel at the back of her neck.

Eight feet. The clink of her bracelets, the uneven huff of her breathing.

I let my footsteps go loud on the sidewalk to make sure she hears me.

Rhonda's right, of course. It's all about control. But now

I'm the one who has the control. Dorothy can keep walking all night, but she can't get away.

Five feet. If I reached out, my fingertips could slip right in there at the back of her collar.

Behind me is the sandpaper scuff of shoe on pavement. I glance over my shoulder. There's some man back there, walking down the sidewalk after us. I turn back to Dorothy, steady myself. Move away from her—slowly—so it looks like I'm not following.

Just walk now.

I try to calm my breathing. No need to freak out. Just because he was a little too close. But I swear he was looking right at me.

A brick wall gives way to a bank of narrow warped-glass windows. Our reflections are smears of color bobbling across, no way to separate one from two from maybe three.

And here, some sound is coming from Dorothy: a droning, rolling sound under her breath. Great—he's stalking me, I'm stalking her, she's fucking humming.

Footstep scuff right behind me. My whole body tightens.

A hand on my shoulder.

I spin, recoiling, and a scream chokes off at the back of my throat.

"Want to know what I've heard?" he says.

The guy's right over me. Shaggy black beard and stocking cap, a missing tooth as he smiles. His eyes go over my shoulder in Dorothy's direction.

"Sometimes stories are true," he says.

He reaches to his neck, pulls a set of headphones over his ears. Tinny buzz of music like the hover of a fly.

And now he's bobbing his head at me.

Crazy-omen-man likes rock and roll.

I step back. Turn, and Dorothy's gone.

I get a panic kick to my gut so hard it runs a tingle out

along my fingers. I scan desperate. Graffitied-up mailbox. Overturned shopping cart. I pound shoes to the corner. Dark, empty streets left, right, straight—no idea which way to go.

I go right. My eyes everywhere—in doorways, behind dumpsters, between parked cars. Panic turns so easy into anger—goddamn psycho headset freak—sometimes stories are true, like the one where the crazy bitch hunts down the old woman over nothing more than a ring.

Movement in the dark recess of a doorway. I lurch toward it, and there's a man crouched, shirt off. I jerk back, turn. My eyes go out across the street. To fall on the figure over there in front of that boarded-up building, pulling open that rusted metal door.

Dorothy.

My heart is going at it hard—that panic and anger thing— it's a beautiful drunk. Filling my head up like too much wine. Dorothy looks over her shoulder, and even from all the way over there, those twisted-ass eyes are right on me. Along my spine, my shoulders, the muscles tighten. She steps through the door, pulls it shut, and she's gone.

Eleven o'clock

I drag the door open.

All black in front of my face. The Old Town air is a hot breath on the back of my neck.

Don't hesitate—just go. Into the black, and it swallows me up, and I've never felt such a goddamn thrill before. I inch toward an open doorway I barely see up ahead. Doing that whole hands-out-in-front-of-you thing. Don't hear her humming or her bracelet clink. I step through this next doorway but something makes me stop. Something says *don't move.*

For a moment I just stand here in the dark. Feel the panic-anger drunk coursing lush through me. I start forward again.

My foot comes down onto nothing.

Hands out, thrashing. Clutch crazy at some metal rail. Foot finds the ledge. Stand crouched. Breathe. Hands gripping hard. The black, receding and finding shape again, settles on the smoke-thread edging of the handrail, which traces down and down.

A distant sound comes up. Dorothy's voice. A tune. A taunt.

One foot out to find a step. Next foot out. A creak under my shoe. The lower I go, the warmer it gets. Like the devil forgot heat is supposed to rise. The smell is just this side of rot. Turn at the bottom, eyes scanning the dark for her. Then I hear a sound like air forced through a tiny hole, something breathy and shrill. And a strange scuttling. Oh shit, no.

But the humming. Flat and faraway. And so I walk.

The room just goes and goes, thin and long—what, am I about to get shanghaied, are Kit's pirates lying in wait? The only light comes down from cracks between the wooden beams overhead. Corridors converge, and I listen, and I turn. Keep going deeper in. Hot sweat down my back. Ceiling just above my head. Walls close. What the hell is this place? Darker now. Nothing but fissures in the wood to let in something feeble and dim silver like moon going through water.

The whole black floor seems to crawl—oh Christ. Something brushes my heel—body jerks. I stumble forward. On and on under the streets of Portland. I've lost the way out. All I can do is hold onto Dorothy's voice and follow. Her Pied Piper song in this Pied Piper black.

Can't stop, can't breathe.

Because sometimes panic just turns into more panic, and sometimes stories are true, and sometimes you're an idiot.

My foot comes down onto something soft.

Sick squirm under my shoe.

I choke in a gasp, stagger back. For a second I've lost the floor.

Then, as my shoe comes down again—solid ground—there's a click and suddenly, light.

I'm in a chamber at the end of the line. Walls full of white Christmas lights. Hanging in swags like the piping of sweet on a birthday cake.

And all up and down and ceiling to floor: pretty jewelry.

At first I can't make it out, it's just an enormous, blurred luster. But bring it into focus, and it's gold and more gold, like an Egyptian tomb—gold all pressed into the walls—gold and silver and the crazy shimmer colors of thousands of jewels. Mosaics of rings, overlapped bracelets, winding chains, strings of pearls. I reach my hand out to touch. Stop.

Directly ahead, Dorothy in her faded housedress and blue velvet hat is hunched, face close to the wall, hands working. Her humming is so low I barely hear it. She has a little tube of glue. She presses something into the wall. Face smattered with beaded light and twinkle, and she turns and looks at me and smiles.

Crooked eyes dip down. To the diamonds in my ears, the drapes of pearls against my chest.

The glint in her hand is my ring.

I don't hear a sound from behind.

I don't hear the swift of the baseball bat before it comes down.

LILA

by Megan Kruse

Powell Boulevard

When I saw Lila for the first time it was at the Tik Tok, at a quarter past 2 in the morning. I was there because I had this terrible loneliness in me and I couldn't stand to be in my apartment, where the cars outside on Foster Road dragged their headlights over the thin walls. There was black mold on the shower curtain and the linoleum was peeling up and there was an ugly stain on the mattress. It didn't matter; I slept on the sofa anyway.

I slept on the sofa and when I couldn't sleep I sat in the Tik Tok near Powell Boulevard, watching the rows of clocks on the walls, and then Lila came in, late on a Friday night. She was tall, with rust-colored hair, and she looked like a girl I had known once, the daughter of someone who came to take care of my mother after her accident. The girl was my age and she had a puppy that she carried, with ragged, chewed-up fur, scratching its fleas and burying its head under her arm. I was eleven. I tied a red scarf around my head because I wanted to look like a soldier who had just returned from war. I dreamt the girl would hold a rag to my forehead and whisper carefully in my ear.

While her mother took care of my mother, the girl slept in the room next to mine. When she outgrew one of her dresses it was folded, washed, and put on my bed. It was blue, terry cloth, a summer dress. I wore it until I could hold it in my hands and see right through.

246 // PORTLAND NOIR

But then my mother was well enough and the woman left and took the girl with her. My mother sometimes stood and walked around, and changed her clothes, but her eyes were blank as marbles and her mouth was slack. Sometimes she sat and played the accordion but it was always the same wheezing note. She kept a fifth of whiskey in the top drawer of her dresser and when she slept on the recliner I would sip from it, lie in her bed, and imagine that girl. Her blue dress like water, like a calm and perfect sea.

Lila came into the Tik Tok that night and I watched her for a long time. She was beautiful. She folded and refolded her napkin, looked around as though she was waiting for someone. After ten minutes a tall man came in and sat at the table and I heard him call her by her name. It was a beautiful name, I thought. He sat there for a bit and they spoke quietly. Then he stood up and left.

I waited awhile and ordered a fried egg so that I could ask her if she wanted some food. Maybe she was hungry, I thought, and didn't have enough money, or maybe she couldn't decide what she wanted. I moved into her booth. She didn't look up.

"Listen," she said, "I'm not a dyke. I don't lick pussy so probably you should just go back to your eggs."

"I don't have anywhere to go," I replied. At that moment it seemed true. My apartment seemed like someplace I had resided in during a different lifetime. The job I had checking groceries was suddenly someone else's, and I felt like I had been in the Tik Tok for days, weeks, the clocks turning their slow circles, the coffee growing cold until another waitress stretched her pale arm across the table toward my cup.

Lila shrugged. She pulled a cigarette from her pack and held it between her long fingers. Her nails were bitten. "Not my fucking problem," she said. She put some money on the table, stood up, and walked out. I waited a few minutes and then I followed her, watched as she crossed the parking lot to the nearest motel, a ground-floor room marked 42, and let herself in.

From there it was easy. I didn't have any savings, but the grocery store let me cash out my retirement plan, $470, minus the taxes. I kept the apartment. The motel was closer to my work, and I liked the way it looked.

"Room 43, please," I said, and the man behind the counter took my money and handed me a key. There was a little table with cigarette burns ringing it like years of a tree, and heavy curtains that could shut out the light even in the middle of the day. The sheets were rough and when I turned against them, their scratching reminded me that I was there, that I was waiting for something. There was even a little refrigerator and I took the 72 bus to the store and bought things that I thought Lila might like—a tin of pink salmon, almonds in a pale candy shell. Above the bed was a painting of a ship tossing in a wild sea.

Every night at 7 the tall man from the Tik Tok drove up in a van and parked outside of the hotel. Lila would leave her room and climb inside. They would be gone until 3 or 4 in the morning, when I heard her unlock the door. She would set down her purse and sit on the bed; there was a click when she dropped her heels by their narrow leather straps to the floor. The water would run; I could imagine her as clearly as if the wall had fallen away—there she was in her slip, her bare feet toeing into the carpet. I slept when she slept.

It was a week before I knocked on the door. I had a fifth of whiskey and I held it out when she opened the door.

"What?" she asked.

"I was just sitting by my window," I said, "and I saw you come in." She narrowed her eyes at me. "I thought, *I should go over there and see if she wants some whiskey.*" My voice sounded shaky. "You shouldn't have to be alone," I added.

Lila looked from me to the bottle. "I *like* being alone," she said, but she opened the door anyway and grabbed the whiskey and took a long drink. In the corner was an open suitcase and inside it I could see a jumble of nylons, the egg cup of a bra. The painting above her bed showed a field, flowers, and tall grass.

She held onto the bottle and sat down on the bed. She was wearing a long-sleeved shirt that went to her knees. Her feet were bare and she looked at me. "So what's your story?" she asked. "You work out here? I've never seen you." She didn't remember me, I realized, and felt relieved. I wanted to start new. She didn't wait for me to answer. "I've been working for three years now. It's shit." She went into the bathroom and came out with the plastic cup from the bathroom sink, filled it with whiskey, and passed it to me. "But what else are you supposed to do?"

I took a drink and my throat burned. It tasted to me like the house after the accident, my mother sleeping in the living room while the television faded in and out of static.

Up close Lila was even more beautiful than I remembered. "And Mark is an asshole," she said. Mark—the tall man, I thought. "I can't believe I used to think we'd get married." She darkened a little, and turned on the television, drank half of the bottle of whiskey, then asked me to leave.

I stopped going to work at the grocery store because Lila needed me. She didn't have to say it, but I knew it was true. I didn't hand in a notice, just left my apron and name tag next to the till and went back to the motel. If the van was gone

I would knock on her door, bring her whiskey or rice paper candy from the store up the street. She didn't seem to wonder why I was there. I sat at the little table while she flipped through the channels on the television, or talked about the places she wanted to live—Paris and Greece and New York and Prague. I remembered a man I met once, someone lonely, nursing a drink in a booth at Holman's. He'd told me he might go to Prague, and now I imagined us all colliding in some narrow street, so far from home.

"Anywhere but here," she said. "Anywhere but this fucking motel."

Then one night when I knocked on the door Lila answered it right away, smiling. Her front tooth was crooked and I felt bothered that I hadn't noticed it before.

"He's gone," she said. "He'll be back at the end of the week. He's bringing some girls up from Los Angeles. Get in here." She held the door open.

I thought, I *have never seen her so beautiful.* Her eyes were bright and she leaned against me and grabbed my hand.

"Four days!" she said. "Four days of nothing to do. Fucking thank God." She sat at the little table and leaned over something, then looked up at me. "Gators," she said, and that's what they started to look like to me, white rows of teeth. She cut them with the sharp edge of a driver's license with a picture that didn't look like her.

When she was done I leaned over and she showed me how to snort them, how to follow each line with a palmful of water that dripped bitter down the back of my throat, until the room felt frantic and bright and both of us right in the center of it; fireflies, I thought, burning hot in the cup of someone's hand.

"Let's look outside," Lila suggested. She opened the curtain and the only thing I could see were our own wavering faces in the glass. I kissed her then; her mouth was dry. She pulled back. "I'm not a dyke," she said. The smell of her cigarette; I thought of my mother, waking for a second from her slow fugue when I came home with my hair cut close to my skull—*No daughter of mine is going to be a fucking dyke*, she'd said, and turned back to the wall. "I'm not," Lila said again, but then she put her mouth to mine.

We kissed for a long time and then Lila stood and went to the sink and pulled something out of the makeup bag she kept there. A knife. "Cut an X," she said. She took her shirt off and her breasts were pale and I thought about reaching out very carefully to touch them but was afraid.

She sat on the edge of the bed and put the knife in my hand. It was heavy and cold. "Just a single X," she said. "Just two crossing lines." Her skin was so white. She touched her shoulder blade. "Here . . . Ten years ago," she continued, "they say you could stand at one end of Eighty-second and watch the girls jumping in and out of cars in beautiful dresses."

I traced an X in the air above her perfect skin. I couldn't do it, I thought.

"Where did you live before here?" Lila asked. "What were you like? Did you have some beautiful life?"

The cluttered apartment; the recliner with its smell of smoke and age; my mother, in her chair, with her heavy silver accordion, pushing the bellows in and out, her eyes on the wall behind me. It was another five years before she died, and then there were eight people at the funeral, all dressed in black, like a circle of bats fluttering at each other. A necklace of them, I had thought, standing around the terrible throat of her grave.

"It *was* beautiful," I said. "I had a house with a garden. And a puppy named Soldier."

Lila sighed. "It sounds nice." She pushed her hair out of her eyes. "I thought I was in love with Mark, but then—" She looked up at me. "We could make a thousand dollars in a day, him and I, when we started. I didn't used to mind it. We were going to get a house too." She touched my arm. "An X," she said. "Do it." I squeezed the handle of the knife in my hand and pulled, twice. There were two thick red lines that swelled and spilled.

Mark came back late that night. I lay on the bed in my room next door and I could hear him through the thin wall. "What the fuck are you thinking?" he was saying. "No one will want you with that on you. What the hell is wrong with you?"

My face felt hot. What had she said, one night while she sat on the bed and flipped through a magazine, talking in long circles—*He left one girl with sixteen broken bones out by the gorge. He's served six years in prison already.*

When I heard the door slam I stood up, looked out the window until his van had pulled out of the parking lot. I counted to thirty and then knocked. There was no answer. "Lila," I called out. I pounded on the door.

She finally opened up and her suitcase was upside down, the clothes everywhere. Her left eye was half-closed and starting to bruise. She looked at me. "He took the money," she said. "And he won't let me work until my back and my eye are healed." She pulled the neckline of her T-shirt down over her shoulder and I could see what I had done, the X, red and raw.

I sat on the bed and pulled her down next to me. "So you don't need him anymore," I said. "We go somewhere else." I thought of the two of us, months from now, lit up in the summer sun. We would take the bus into the city and dance drunk in a dark bar. It would be exactly as it should be. Her bottom lip between my careful teeth, far from the string of motels, the dented van that pulled up in the dark.

"You don't get it," Lila replied. She sounded angry, the way she had sounded that first night at the Tik Tok. "You don't get it at all."

I touched her hair. "We'll be fine."

She pushed my hand away. "No one walks out on Mark. Especially not me—he'd fucking kill me."

"He can't be that bad—"

"You haven't worked for him," she snapped. Her voice was cold and she didn't look like the Lila I knew. "How would you know?"

I remembered a story my mother had told me about a woodcutter, clumsy, and his sharp axe. He kept missing the tree and his right arm went first, then the rest, left arm, right leg, left leg. Until a woman came by and looked at him, crippled and sad. *I'm sorry*, he said, *I am only half a man*. She laughed and answered, *Look*, and because she was so lovely and he was lucky, his legs grew right back to skin and bone. But his heart beat so fast it burnt right through his chest, and he died anyway, for love.

Lila stood up. "Just go," she said.

In my own room in the dark I stared at the curve of the lampshade, the square of the doorframe, shadowy slips that floated and opened their angry mouths, and I thought, *She has to love me again*. Ten years ago the little girl and her mother had left with her puppy and I had never seen her again. Her blue dress at the foot of my bed like a broken promise. *She has to*, I thought.

Mark didn't come back the next day, or the day after that.

Lila knocked on my door and she didn't seem angry anymore. I gave my key to the front desk and slept in her room, curled against her, listening to her slow breathing.

The next morning she shook me awake. "We need sixty-five dollars," she said. "We need sixty-five dollars today."

I thought about my apartment. There would be an eviction notice on the door by now. I couldn't bring her there, not to that. The grocery store would have hired someone, and I couldn't be that far away from Lila for eight hours, anyway. I had thirty-four dollars left. Not enough for another night. "Tell me what to do," I said.

The man was neither more nor less handsome than I expected. He was wearing gray sweatpants and he pulled a white envelope from the stretched waistband. He coughed. "You have the greatest legs," he said, "They're truly great."

I imagined his hands were Lila's hands, running up over my breasts. His tongue became hers. It was all for her, I thought. The envelope was tucked under the little red handbag that she had loaned me.

"The gams of a movie star," the man said. "The face of a dog, but the gams of a true old-time beauty." His pink lips like two punctured balloons, dragging over my skin.

When I opened the door to Room 42 Lila was brushing her hair. We put the money inside the lining of her little suitcase. I lay beside her that night and she smelled like honey and when I couldn't sleep I turned on the bedside lamp and the red of her hair lit up like a pyre.

Every day that week I saw someone different. After dark, I wandered through the parking lot of Area 69, stood inside by the racks of videos, the leather harnesses and handcuffs and dildos in plastic packaging, until someone asked me back to the booths. The time without Lila nagged at me, the socket left from a tooth pulled, the vague shape of what could be lost, but in an hour I could make $150, nearly three nights in Room 42. It was better this way, Lila said, than with Mark. Before she met him she would sit in the corner at Devil's Point, the strip club on 53rd, and wait for someone to pick her up. The next day she'd be able to buy a new dress or go to the movies; she could make her rent in a day and a half. Now Mark took half the money and he wouldn't let you go, she said, and he would know in a second if you'd been working on your own. He'd been locked up in Snake River after he pulled a fifteen-year-old onto the circuit, and the day after he was released he started running girls again. His probation officer was nowhere to be found. "This is better," Lila kept saying. "We keep you a secret." At night I stood in the shower until the water ran cold and then lay beside her until we both slept.

Mark came back four days later and I hid behind the shower curtain in the bathroom. "You start work again tomorrow," he said. "And you never pull that shit again. I don't ever want to see a fucking scratch on you that I didn't give you myself."

I could hear Lila, sweet and pleading. "Baby," she said, and it was silent for a while. I closed my eyes, imagined a forest, my hands up in the trees, the cool of the leaves. I tried not to think of them kissing.

After a long time Mark cleared his throat. "We go back on the road tomorrow," he said. "Have your shit packed."

Lila's voice was a murmur, something I couldn't hear, and then she said, "I need you," and panic welled up in me like a tide, a breathless gray.

She didn't need Mark, I thought. That was how things

would begin to go wrong, how they always began. My mother's accident wasn't really an accident. It was after my father had left her. For two weeks after he packed his things and took the car, she had laid on the sofa and watched daytime television, and spoke quietly, as though she was telling a secret. Then, on a Tuesday afternoon, we were walking on a busy street and she squeezed my arm. "Stay here," she said, and smiled, and walked in front of a rattling bus, and I understood that the calm had been a deceptive one, the first freeze that leaves the lake solid and the fish still swimming, fast and alarmed, a foot below ice. What kept pounding at the back of my head was that I didn't know when it had begun, that the first sign of ruin was something never recovered.

The door slammed but I stood in the shower until Lila came and pushed the curtain back. "He's gone," she said.

We had $300, slipped into the lining of Lila's suitcase. The Greyhound station was a half hour away, just off the 20 bus.

Lila wanted to go somewhere warm. "New Mexico," she said. "Or Arizona. Someplace dry as a fucking bone where we can get tan and gorgeous." She kissed my cheek. "And never again here." She gave me scissors and I cut her hair until it fell at her chin and she pulled a hat over it. "Do I look like me?" she asked. "Would you recognize me?"

I thought, *I'll always recognize you.*

I slept deeper that night than I had in what felt like years. In the dark I reached out and felt the curve of Lila's bare back, the raised scar on her shoulder blade, and then slipped into some dream that later I couldn't remember.

There was a sound like footsteps, and then a quick cold, and then in the dark I was awake and the bed was empty. The door was open. *Lila*, I thought. A sound of tires squealing and I was up out of bed. I must have been a moment too late, because there was only the empty parking lot, and the city spread out around me like a bowl of lights, a thousand smoke-gray rooms and in each one a person, waiting.

It's snowing now, but barely, gray sleet driven up over the shoulder by traffic headed toward the 205. I think of her feet, white, delicate as eggshell. I remember the first time I saw snow, how I built a snowman that looked at me with stone eyes and one fell onto the ground. I pushed rocks into his snow mouth and they disappeared. My mother said, *Love goes like water, right through your hands.* The snow closed up. I pushed a stick right through him.

I have a good route, down to Burnside and up to Johnson Creek. *The gams of a true old-time beauty.* Lila's suitcase was still in the corner. Her clothes on me look only approximate, like a memory.

The city wants to plant roses, up and down Eighty-second, to make it peaceful.

Later, my mother's accordion was sold for a song to a man who slivered the keys off and carried them away in a bag, clacking like teeth. When I dream of Lila there is a tattoo on her chest, a mask, and in the eyes of the mask I am faceup over her heart.

There are sirens outside of the Tik Tok every night and I wait. The waitress refills my coffee. Across the parking lot there is always a lit window with the curtains drawn tight across it. Inside the Tik Tok, the clocks move at once, slowly, like a song written all in the same sad note.

PEOPLE ARE STRANGE

BY KIMBERLY WARNER-COHEN

Sandy Boulevard

Whoever said Portland was a friendly city stated it from the comfortable vantage of already knowing people. Aside from the middle-aged clerk at 7-Eleven, who smiled with yellow teeth and attempted broken conversation when she walked across the busy intersection at Eighty-second and Sandy to buy cigarettes and a Big Gulp, Kara had spoken to less than ten people since she arrived four days ago. That included the woman with an eye patch behind the desk at the Cameo (closest non-chain airport motel she could find), Kara already thinking when she paid for a week in advance that it was a mistake coming here. Shouldn't have strayed from her habit of putting her finger randomly on an atlas and going.

Strangers didn't start casual conversations with her in bars, usually moved a seat over. Wasn't simply that Kara could be best described as plain, known since she could recognize her reflection that she would never be one of the blessed few who glided through life; it was the contempt in her eyes that drove them off. Being passed over was a relief, feigning interest in people's lives irritated her. Happier to sit at the end of the row in some seamy tavern where light didn't penetrate through grimy windows. Bartenders took pity and threw her an extra drink or two as the clock edged past 1:00 and other patrons sought someone other than her to share the night, or at least fifteen minutes, with.

Kara pulled the battered and stained white plastic fob with 17 printed on it in chipped gold paint from her back pocket, balancing her dinner: a fifth of Bushmills and a barely edible pizza from the dingy store across the street from the massive Safeway.

Would've eaten at the pancake house attached to the motel, where she had platter-sized portions for the past three mornings, but Kara couldn't stand the sympathetic stares from the fat, bored waitresses anymore. Same with the bar down the block, where day workers stopped in after long hours working too hard for too little money; stared her up and down before turning back to their conversations, shaking their heads. Better to stay in the room tonight, as she jiggled the wood turquoise door open that, like all the others, looked as if it'd been kicked in during an episode of *Cops*.

She could have just as easily slept at one of the chic boutique hotels downtown, with what her parents left her. Car accident when she was thirteen, Father having too many Rob Roys during one of the many charity events they attended throughout the year. Her aunt and uncle took her in after the funeral, shuffled from one affluent suburb to another.

Aunt Suzanne was barren and they doted on Kara. Decorated her bedroom as if she was five years younger (always loathed cotton candy–pink but didn't have the heart to say it when she saw their expectant smiles), sent her to the local prep school with the same Anglican pretensions as the last one, bought her gifts (clothes that were in fashion but never looked right on her, records for bands she didn't like, books she'd never read). Nothing worked. Kara would smile and politely thank them, then go in her room and throw it on top of the growing pile in the back of her closet.

Suzanne's eyebrows furrowed at Kara's disinterest in others, especially after she read the books the shrink recommended when he diagnosed Kara with an attachment disorder. Blond sons and prim daughters were dragged over with their parents and sat in uncomfortable silence as Kara openly stared at them in the den while the adults had their digestifs. When they were called in from the parlor, none disguised their relief.

Uncle Phillip hid the coroner's report between the pages of a treatise by Hobbes. Edge of the envelope stuck out, Kara found it the first time she was in the library alone. Detailed how Father's broken rib punctured his heart as he slammed into the steering wheel. Mother was nearly decapitated when a piece of windshield glass cut through her trachea as the car smashed into the tree, only thing holding her head to trunk were neck vertebrae. When Phillip realized Kara took it, he explained that they hid the details because they thought she'd be traumatized; troubled when she wasn't perturbed. Since she'd found out what her parents kept from her, Kara had no use for them.

When she was twelve, six months before they died, Kara had nightmares that woke her up every few hours. Always the same, being ripped apart by her mother and another woman whose face was shadowed. Once she was torn, her other half became a mirror image. For weeks her parents looked at each other and made sympathetic noises. Scared to dream, she would sit in the rocking chair, listening to silence until she nodded off. After one morning when she got three hours of sleep, Kara told them hysterically at breakfast she couldn't take it anymore. Father looked at Mother, who brought out the locked box from their bedroom closet that Kara wasn't supposed to know about.

Sat her in the formal living room (knew it was serious), box on the end table between them. Father tapped his foot and both began talking at the same time, tripping over each other's words until Mother touched Father on the knee, her way of shutting him up. Didn't say anything for what seemed like a long time. Why was she about to cry? Did someone die? What did that have to do with her dreams? "You had a sister."

"A twin," Father interjected.

In the time it took for her mother to pat him again, all became clear. No wonder she couldn't make friends, why no one understood her. Someone did, once, more intimately than anyone ever could. Mother only carried her, Father donated the sperm. Kara rubbed the fingers of her left hand together. "Tell me everything. Start from the beginning. She's identical, isn't she? What's her name? Where is she? You were holding back, all these years. I knew I couldn't trust you."

Mother nodded, swallowed hard, tears. "Kaya is, was, your identical twin; born first by six minutes."

The part of Kara's brain that had suppressed the memories cracked, flooded her temporal lobe. Snatches of playing with pastel wood blocks in their nursery, patty-cake, sleeping with limbs entwined. "What happened?"

"You were so adorable in your matching dresses, running through the house, always laughing. You'd only sleep in the same crib and we had to have a custom double-highchair made or you wouldn't eat. Do you remember, Steven?"

Father nodded gravely, stared at the rug.

"What *happened*, Mother?"

"It was in the park. Your nanny—"

"I had a nanny?"

"Ursula, from Sweden, very nice girl. She never forgave herself."

"How old was I . . . were we?"

"About to turn four. You were on the jungle gym and

skinned your knee. Ursula was putting the bandage on; her attention was only away for a moment."

"And?"

"And somebody took your sister." Tears made tributaries through her foundation.

Kara concentrated on her breath to keep the red in her periphery from closing in. Hate (just as much at herself for being the distraction) surging through arteries and veins instead of blood, pure white light. "Did you look for her?"

Father, allowed to speak, "Of course we did. Police, FBI, private investigators. It all happened so quickly, none of the other nannies saw anything unusual."

"Was there a note? A phone call?"

"There was never any communication. They said that it was probably a mother who'd lost her child and wanted another."

"So Kaya could still be alive?" Her tongue knew the name, slid from her lips like she said it all the time.

"We've tried so many times over the years, and nothing."

"What's in the box?"

"We shouldn't have taken it out."

"Why did you?"

"I don't know." Mascara streaked her face. "In case you didn't believe us."

"Did you think you could keep this from me forever?"

"You took it so hard at first, we didn't want you to get upset all over again." That was their way, forced forgetfulness. Soak your tears on fine linen and it won't sting as bad.

Kara wanted details, but her mother faked a crying fit and hurried (never ran) out of the room. Father doggedly followed, telling Kara they'd talk further, soon, and left her with the box. Waiting for the soon that never came, Kara would lock her bedroom door and pore over the yellowed news clippings, police and PI reports. Memorized and read again.

At the bottom, under Kaya's birth certificate and Social Security card, was a thin envelope of photos. Like Mother said, always in matching onesies, pajamas, dresses; holding hands and smiling. Searched all the hiding places she could think of, looking for more the next time they went out, but nothing. Did they care enough to burn them, or were they just shredded and tossed? Late nights running her finger over pictures of her and her mirror image.

Strange looks from Phillip and Suzanne began during the first dinner, night before the funeral, when she brought Kaya up in the middle of their coq au vin. Suzanne spit out a little of her merlot, stammered the same flimsy lines her parents did. After that, Kara caught the sideways stares, pauses as they considered how to phrase conversation, guard up. She made them nervous, Kara liked the power.

Morning of her eighteenth birthday, before the sun or the servants were up, she packed a bag, placed a note in the drawing room thanking her aunt and uncle for taking care of her, and left. Took the bus to Richmond, then Amtrak to Tampa, flight to New Orleans, short stay in Lubbock. After that they melded. At first Kara called to let them know she was all right; that dwindled as she lost herself in a sea of roads, train stations, highways. Always on the lookout for Kaya.

Decided on Portland instead of leaving it to chance this time because of a small article she read in one of those "Spotlight" columns in a free travel magazine, mentioned how many young people had been flocking to the city in the last few years. It was as good of a lead as any of the few she found. The city was still small enough to search, big enough for there to be the chance that Kaya was there; if she'd been kidnapped, maybe her home life was bad enough for her to flee.

Kara stared at the crack in the ceiling by the bathroom and took another swig. Didn't want to think anymore and lay on the polyester and particle board bed, finishing the bottle, and tumbled into a dreamless sleep, easily ignoring the fist-fight in the room below.

Sky was a lesser shade of gray the next morning and Kara dressed in dirty jeans and a brown sweater long past stretched out. The lack of sun was getting to her, didn't know how people could handle it for months at a time. Usually didn't go outside during daylight, but it was nice to know that it was there.

She weaved through kids by the bus stop in front of the 7-Eleven, either dealing or really bored, and into the too brightly lit store to get her nicotine and corn syrup breakfast. Kara passed the motel, wandered further down until she reached the strip club shaped like a huge whiskey jug, *Pirate's Cove* emblazoned on a red-and-white backlit sign, and under that, *Wet Panty Party 2nite!* Loved the anonymity of a cheap titty bar, but there were too many cars outside for the space; nowhere to hide.

Retraced her steps and turned on a side street across from Ed's House of Gems, pine and concrete glorified shack fashioned to resemble a barn, complete with the Wild West white mural and dusty windows. Thought about going in, run her eyes over the Fool's Gold or maybe some onyx and hematite, but a sour middle-aged man in a flannel shirt stretched over a belly made huge from years of cheap beer was standing by the door, glaring at nothing.

Instead turned left, down one of the residential side streets. Liked how nothing matched, everything shabby around the edges and thrown together, moss growing in between the side-walk cracks and roof shingles. Even in the chill, front lawns were teeming with green.

Kara zigzagged around corners and up avenues, streets looked identical in their individuality, until she realized she was halfway to the airport; continued past houses progressively more run-down, a mini-mart that was filthy, cement lots.

Another strip club ahead, couldn't miss the neon sign with letters burned out so it read, *Th_ La_d_ng St_ _p*; nothing be-yond that but hotels and car rentals. Much bigger than the other place, though no less decrepit, parking lot half-full. Perfect.

Kara swung open the flimsy glass doors and into the dark, stopping on the carpeted ramp to adjust her eyes. Nose hit full force with the harsh odor of baby lotion, cheap powder makeup, and desperation; same as any other strip club she went into. Main illumination were strings of lights in plastic tubing that hung on the stage, bar, crisscrossed the walls; pop-ular in the '70s and hadn't been updated since. Black plastic tables, indiscriminately placed violet plush seats.

Blue-collar guys and businessmen on layovers sat next to each other drinking Buds in front of the main stage, laying dollar bills at the edges; definitely not the A team perform-ing at this time of the day. Lots of things jiggling where they shouldn't.

Kara stood at the bar until a dim-looking guy in his early forties waddled over. "What can I getcha?"

"Stella."

"We just ran out."

"Red Stripe?"

"Don't carry it."

"Corona."

"Waiting on the delivery. Should be here later."

"What do you have?"

"Session, Bud, Bud Light, Coors Light."

Other choices nauseated her. "Session."

Surprise when she sipped it, the local beer wasn't bad. Kara sat at one of the tables and drank, half-looking at the tired peroxide blonde who had surpassed the acceptable age limit of her profession when the place was in its heyday.

Her song was finished and so was Kara's drink. She caught the eye of the waitress, who looked away, preferring to chat with the bartender. Only when she couldn't ignore Kara's waving bottle did she begrudgingly grab a fresh one.

Turned back from the small irritation and Kara's heart stopped for one, two beats. It was *her*. Body a little more toned than Kara's, hair stuffed hastily under the cheap pink wig that the lights made look cheaper. But it was *her* legs, *her* hands, *her* breasts, *her* face.

"Two-fifty."

Didn't hear the waitress until she impatiently repeated herself. Kara handed her a wrinkled bill from her pocket, palms so wet the paper was soft, no idea what denomination. The girl laid the change on the table, tapping her foot for the dollar tip Kara threw at her.

She watched herself half-heartedly twirl on the pole, backbend near the guy eating cheese fries. *She's alive.* Kara bit her bottom lip until she tasted blood to keep emotion from boiling over, muscles tensed still. Of course it would be now, here, when she least expected it. Chain-smoked through the two songs, over too soon, watched Kaya grab her clothes and tips, disappear (still naked, ass extra white in the dark) into a room behind the stage.

Kara was too lightheaded to trip up to the bar until midway through the next act. "The last girl who was on, where is she?"

266 // PORTLAND NOIR

Bartender smirked as he shook one of the taps. "Why? You want a private dance?"

"No, I want to talk to her. What's her name?"

"Tammi. I can go back there, but she ain't comin' out unless it's for a private dance."

"I want a dance."

"It'll be thirty."

"Sure, fine. Just get her."

The bartender heaved away from the bar, wishing he'd told her it cost more and split the difference with Tam. Intentionally talked to every person on his way there—anecdote to the bouncer, nudge and wink to the waitress serving chicken tenders to a guy wearing sunglasses on the other side of the stage.

Kara's hands were shaking so badly it took three tries to light one cigarette off the other. Finally, Kaya strolled out and gave Kara a disinterested once-over, looked through her. "Follow me."

She led Kara, who stared at the way Kaya's green and yellow butterfly tattoo near her shoulder blade moved as she walked, to the furthest corner of the club. Did Kara's skin sting thousands of miles away at the same moment the needle was put to Kaya's flesh? So many questions and Kara couldn't think of any that were important. Kaya peeled back a sheer black curtain with gold thread, revealing a small plastic and mirror booth with a black pleather bench.

She sat Kara down, adjusted the wig in the mirror behind the bench. "Thirty."

Instead of grabbing Kaya and telling her who she was, Kara reached into her wallet and peeled off two fives and a twenty. She had to do this right, only as much information as Kaya'd be able to handle at once, couldn't scare her off.

Maybe when Kaya started to dance, she would give Kara more than a glance, and see.

Kaya shuffled as little as possible, chest hovering six or seven inches over Kara's face as she swayed her hips and looked at herself in the mirror, yawning. Every movement was perfect and Kara was complete.

"I bet you don't even know how beautiful you are."

"Thanks."

"Did you have chicken pox when you were seven too?"

"Huh?"

"Forget that." Kara couldn't restrain, put her hand on Kaya's wrist. "Stop."

Kaya broke her bored façade and glared. "No touching."

"I'm sorry. Please, I need to talk to you."

Kaya still didn't recognize her (light in the booth was terrible), instead shrugged and sat down, picked at her cuticles. "Can I bum a smoke?"

"Yeah, sure." Kara handed them over. She even lit her cigarette the same way, protecting the flame when it wasn't necessary. "Don't you see a resemblance?"

"To what?"

"To me."

Kaya really looked at her then, but not with the expression Kara was hoping for. Instead, confusion with disgust at the edges. "You think we're related, a cousin or something?"

So many years imagining the reunion, but never pictured this. Kara played different scenarios in her mind before she went to bed until it was the only thing that could lull her to sleep. In all, Kaya recognized her instantly. She was some executive who Kara found through a magazine feature on exceptional women in business. Or homeless . . . or possibly a suburban housewife settled into some homogenous berg that Kara passed through when she took a wrong turn on the highway.

"You're my twin, don't you see it? You were kidnapped when we were young, but now things are okay because we're together now. We can leave, you never have to work here again."

Kaya ground her cigarette into the burnt carpet with the heel of her stiletto. "I don't know who you are, or what kind of sick fantasy you have, but we're not twins and I was never kidnapped."

No. Kara grabbed her sister's forearm; Kaya pulled away with force.

"Just answer me this, what do you remember before you were four?"

"I fucking told you not to touch me. You're nuts." Kaya stormed out, wadding up the money and throwing it at Kara's chest.

Stereotypical bouncer, big neck and small head, came tanking through the club, eyes on fire as he grabbed Kara roughly on the arm and pulled her up. "Time for you to go."

She knew better than to argue and stood. His grip didn't loosen when he realized Kara wasn't going to fight back, shoved her to the double doors.

"Don't come back."

In the parking lot, everything was the same. How could it be, when her world was inside out? She checked her watch. Time had stopped inside, couldn't have only been twenty minutes. On her way back to the motel, when it became so obvious, Kara wanted to slap her forehead. Stupid, did she think Kaya could let her guard down in that kind of place? She had to talk to her away from there.

Kara double-timed until she reached her rental car in the

motel's lot, straight back to the club. She parked in the back corner, eyes fixed on the entrance, scared to blink; slid down into the seat whenever the doors opened, so just the top of her head was visible. If the bouncer saw her, he'd kick her off the lot or worse, call the cops, and then Kara might never find Kaya again.

Kara knew that once she got a chance to sit Kaya down with no distraction, she'd see that they were twins (soul mates), and would be grateful for rescuing Kaya from this; never want to leave Kara's side. Everything that was hers was her sister's too. They could travel, or buy houses next to each other, a hallway built connecting the two.

Hours passed, sky evolved to a darker gray, then black. Her stomach rumbled and legs got numb, but she didn't notice.

Finally, a shift change, and Kara didn't care anymore if she was seen. Kaya was one of the last to leave, angelic in street clothes and no makeup to hide the rose in her cheeks. She fumbled with her keys, got into an old Charger. Out of the cars in the lot, Kara didn't figure that one, guessed the economical Honda or the white and red T-Bird. There was a lot to catch up on.

Kara counted to thirty after Kaya pulled out before starting the ignition. It didn't matter if cars got between, Kara could see her sister through them.

Kaya pulled into the driveway of a light green and yellow house on the dubiously named Failing Street. Not far from the motel, would've met anyway, it was meant to be. Kara parked across the street, under a wide willow, watching as her sister went in and lights turned on in succession.

Kara chain-smoked the rest of her pack before she worked up the nerve. Now or never, as she threw the last butt into the street, couldn't sit here all night. Deep breath and she walked up the porch steps. Knocked and rang the bell, did it again to be sure.

When Kaya threw the door open, Kara saw how much more breathtaking she was up close, dyed bright auburn hair (must have had it straightened). Barefoot, wearing pink yoga pants and a tank top, smoking, Kaya was more elegant than any Renaissance painting or Greek statue. Split second before she recognized Kara. "You. How the fuck did you find out where I live?"

"I followed you."

"You're crazy. I'm calling the police."

Combination of panic and the adrenaline, Kara put her hand on the door and leaned into it. "Please, hear me out."

Kaya sucked on her cigarette. "You're not going to leave me alone until I do."

Kara shook her head.

"We talk on the porch."

"Of course."

Kaya stepped into the night chill, shivering. "What do you want to tell me? Make it quick."

Kara wished for another smoke, rubbed the fingers of her left hand together. "You're my sister, my twin. You were kidnapped when we were four."

"We look nothing alike, and I wasn't snatched. My parents never hurt nobody. I think I'd remember."

"Look at my eyes, mouth, hands. Don't you see that they're the same as yours?"

Kaya shook her head, impatient. "No, they're not. I heard you out. Now, leave me alone. If you come by the strip club or here again, the cops will arrest you before you know you've been spotted." She turned to go inside.

Kara couldn't lose her now, grabbed her by the shoulder

and whipped her around to make her listen, using all the force she had to make Kaya know how important this was. Kaya slammed into the doorframe, absorbing the energy of both their weight. Corner caught Kaya on the perfect angle at the base of her skull. Crumpled like Kara had inside when Kaya rejected her.

She wasn't breathing, and Kara stood over her, very still, as she watched Kaya shiver a death shake, half-lidded eyes dull.

Kara knew she should be upset, but instead there was an overwhelming sense of relief. She'd never convince Kaya, rejection of all rejections, after spending so many years searching for her. Glad it was now, before Kara hated her. Kaya must have been brainwashed to have no memory of the kidnapping, whoever they were must have been smart.

Kara looked around. No one out for an evening stroll or looking through their front windows this late, no sound at all; even the crows were sleeping. Could've been the only beings on the planet as she dragged Kaya inside, surprised at how heavy she was.

Kaya lived alone in the house, Kara gathered from a quick tour; surprised she liked basketball, a poster of some guy mid-dunk, *Blazers* in red and black against white. Rifled through the closets for a duffel bag, something to put Kaya in, found nothing bigger than a few overnight suitcases. She kept looking over, expecting Kaya to sit up and bum a smoke, telling Kara she believed her now.

Reminded herself that she did the right thing, there was no other choice; what would she do with herself if Kaya closed the door in her face, leaving her in the cold?

Found a box of black garbage bags. She could probably fit Kaya in one of those, if she folded her into the fetal position. Once she got Kaya in the car, what then? Didn't know where to go, could be driving in circles until the sun came up looking for isolation. Her stomach tightened at the idea of getting caught. *Think outside the box.*

She flipped on the backyard light switch, all dirt with tall pine board planks for a fence. Kara tested the dirt, too hard; she'd never get more than a few feet down. Wished she had thought this through. Kara was about to leave the body in the living room and split town before they could figure out it was her, when the flood lamp shone a halo down on the answer to her problems: the huge compost heap, more than big enough to bury Kaya.

Kara found a small hand shovel under the sink, took longer than she thought it would digging a hole; manure covering her bottom half, filling her shoes so that her socks squished. Back in the house, grabbed Kaya's waxy, cold wrists and pulled; cleaned the mess she tracked in later. Managed a few inches at a time, grunting as she angled Kaya through the house; bumped her into the table, corners, oven. Kara had a blissful smile on her face for the first time, as she knew what she was meant to do.

Sun rising when she got Kaya in and covered up. Back inside, she showered and put on a pair of yoga pants and tank top (snug). Before she went to bed, she switched Kaya's license with hers. Knowing all she did about slipping in and out of personalities, this would be easy.

ABOUT THE CONTRIBUTORS

Serenity Ibsen

CHRIS A. BOLTON writes the webcomic SMASH (www. SmashComic.com), which he cocreated with his artist brother Kyle. He created, wrote, and directed the webseries "Wage Slaves" (www.myspace.com/wageslaveseries). He lives in Portland, where he works for an online bookseller of certain renown.

Jill Cameron

BILL CAMERON is the author of *Lost Dog* and *Chasing Smoke*, both Portland-based mysteries. His stories have appeared in *Spinetingler Magazine*, the *Dunes Review*, and in the anthology *Killer Year*, edited by Lee Child. *Lost Dog* was a finalist for the 2008 Rocky Award and the 2008 Spotted Owl Award. Cameron lives in Portland, where he is currently writing his third novel.

Matthew Hein

DAN DEWEESE'S stories have appeared in various journals, including *Tin House, New England Review, Washington Square,* and *Pindeldyboz*. The recipient of an Oregon Literary Fellowship and twice nominated for a Pushcart Prize, he serves as coordinator of the Writing Center at Portland State University.

Bellen Drake

MONICA DRAKE is the author of the novel *Clown Girl*. Her short stories and essays have been published in the *Northwest Review, Three Penny Review,* Nerve.com, and other places. She teaches writing at the Pacific Northwest College of Art, and has lived in Oregon since Lewis and Clark made their big trip west, more or less.

Ariel Gore

ARIEL GORE is the author of seven books, including *Atlas of the Human Heart, The Traveling Death and Resurrection Show,* and *How to Become a Famous Writer Before You're Dead*. For more information, visit arielgore.com.

Jess Rinaldi

JUSTIN HOCKING lives in Portland and is Executive Director of the Independent Publishing Resource Center (www.iprc.org). His fiction and articles have appeared in *Open City, Foulweather, Thrasher Magazine, Transworld Snowboarding, Concrete Wave Magazine, Travel Oregon,* and the *Nieve Roja Review.* He coedited the best-selling anthology *Life and Limb: Skateboarders Write from the Deep End,* and is currently at work on a memoir about surfing in New York City.

Kevin Miller

JOËLLE JONES is the Russ Manning Award–nominated artist of *Token,* a young adult graphic novel written by Alisa Kwitney. She has collaborated with author Jamie S. Rich on numerous short stories and two full comics projects—the romantic puzzler *12 Reasons Why I Love Her* and the hardboiled crime tale *You Have Killed Me*—in addition to their story in this volume.

Nisa Haron

KAREN KARBO is the author of *How to Hepburn: Lessons on Living from Kate the Great.* Her three novels have all been named *New York Times* Notable Books of the Year; *The Stuff of Life,* her memoir about her father, was a *People* Magazine Critic's Pick and winner of the Oregon Book Award. Her many essays, reviews, and articles have appeared in *Outside, Elle, Vogue, Esquire, Redbook, More, Self, Sports Illustrated for Women, Entertainment Weekly,* the *New Republic,* the *New York Times,* and Salon.com.

Jessie Dawes

MEGAN KRUSE is a fiction and nonfiction writer based out of Portland. Her work has appeared in *Oyez Review, Bellingham Review, Fiddlehead, Oregon Literary Review, Phoebe, Gertrude,* and the first volume of Vespertine Press. Kruse has been the recipient of residency grants from the Kimmel Harding Nelson Center in Nebraska and the Ragdale Foundation of Illinois, as well as an Oregon Literary Arts Fellowship.

Stephen O'Donnell

GIGI LITTLE is the author/illustrator of two decidedly un-noir children's picture books, *Wright Vs. Wrong!* and *The Magical Trunk* (both published under the name Gigi Tegge). She spent fifteen years in the circus as a professional clown and a lighting director, and she can spin a mean lasso. Now living in Northwest Portland, she's a longtime member of Tom Spanbauer's Dangerous Writing community and is currently working on a novel.

Stephanie Yao

LUCIANA LOPEZ is the pop music critic at the *Oregonian* in Portland. She has lived in Japan and Brazil, and speaks mediocre Japanese and decent Portuguese. Her writing has appeared in several journals and anthologies.

Terry Blas

JAMIE S. RICH, in addition to his graphic collaborations with Joëlle Jones, is the author of several novels, including *The Everlasting* and *Have You Seen the Horizon Lately?* (featuring a cover by Jones). His other comics work includes the series *Love the Way You Love* and *Lying Down*. Rich posts his words online at confessions123.com.

Barb Klansnic

KEVIN SAMPSELL is a small press publisher and bookstore employee living in Portland. His writing has appeared widely in newspapers, websites, and literary journals. He is the editor of *The Insomniac Reader* and the author of *Beautiful Blemish, Creamy Bullets,* and the forthcoming memoir, *The Suitcase.*

Jonathan Selwood

JONATHAN SELWOOD is the author of the dark comedy *The Pinball Theory of Apocalypse*. Like all native Oregonians, Selwood was born in California. He enjoys talking very loudly when intoxicated, composting kitchen scraps, excessively rolling his Rs when ordering burrrrrritos . . . using ellipses . . .

Rebecca Skloot

FLOYD SKLOOT has published fifteen books, most recently the memoir *The Wink of the Zenith: The Shaping of a Writer's Life*, the poetry collection *The Snow's Music*, and the novel *Patient 002*. His awards include three Pushcart Prizes and a PEN USA Literary Award; his work has appeared in *The Best American Essays, The Best American Science Writing, The Best Food Writing,* and *The Best Spiritual Writing.*

Zoe Trope

ZOE TROPE, Portland's own pseudonymous, fat, queer red-head, was born in 1986. Her high school memoir of suburban love and loathing, *Please Don't Kill the Freshman*, was published when she was seventeen years old. Since then, her writing has appeared in many newspapers, magazines, and anthologies, including *Sixteen: Stories About That Sweet and Bitter Birthday* and *Northwest Edge III: The End of Reality*. She lives, works, drinks, bakes, bikes, and writes in Portland.

Dan Pelle

JESS WALTER is the author of five books, including *The Zero*, a finalist for the 2006 National Book Award in fiction and *Citizen Vince*, winner of the 2005 Edgar Award for best novel. He has been a finalist for the *Los Angeles Times* Book Prize, the ITW Thriller Award, and the PEN USA Literary Award in both fiction and nonfiction. His books have been *New York Times*, *Washington Post*, and NPR "Best Books of the Year" and have been published in eighteen languages.

Dani Martin

KIMBERLY WARNER-COHEN is a Portland transplant and the author of *Sex, Blood and Rock 'n' Roll*. She is currently working on her next novel.

Also available from the Akashic Books Noir Series

SEATTLE NOIR
edited by Curt Colbert
280 pages, trade paperback original, $15.95

Brand-new stories by: G.M. Ford, Skye Moody, R. Barri Flowers, Thomas P. Hopp, Patricia Harrington, Bharti Kirchner, Kathleen Alcalá, Simon Wood, Brian Thornton, Lou Kemp, Curt Colbert, Robert Lopresti, Paul S. Piper, and Stephan Magcosta.

Within the stories of *Seattle Noir,* you will find: a wealthy couple whose marriage is filled with not-so-quiet desperation; a credit card scam that goes over-limit; femmes fatales and hommes fatales; a delicatessen owner whose case is less than kosher; a famous midget actor whose movie roles begin to shrink when he starts growing taller; an ex-cop who learns too much; a group of mystery writers whose fiction causes friction; a Native American shaman caught in a web of secrets and tribal allegiances; sex, lies, and slippery slopes . . . and a cast of characters that always want more, not less . . . unless . . .

SAN FRANCISCO NOIR
edited by Peter Maravelis
292 pages, trade paperback original, $15.95

Brand-new stories by: Domenic Stansberry, Barry Gifford, Eddie Muller, Robert Mailer Anderson, Michelle Tea, Peter Plate, Kate Braverman, David Corbett, Alejandro Murguía, Sin Soracco, Alvin Lu, Jon Longhi, Will Christopher Baer, Jim Nesbit, and David Henry Sterry.

"Haunting and often surprisingly poignant, these accounts of death, love, and all things pulp fiction will lead you into unexpected corners of a city known to steal people's hearts." —*7x7* magazine

LOS ANGELES NOIR
edited by Denise Hamilton
360 pages, trade paperback original, $15.95
*A *Los Angeles Times* best seller and winner of an Edgar Award.

Brand-new stories by: Michael Connelly, Janet Fitch, Susan Straight, Héctor Tobar, Patt Morrison, Robert Ferrigno, Neal Pollack, Gary Phillips, Christopher Rice, Naomi Hirahara, Jim Pascoe, Scott Phillips, Diana Wagman, Lienna Silver, Brian Ascalon Roley, Emory Holmes II, and Denise Hamilton.

"Akashic is making an argument about the universality of noir; it's sort of flattering, really, and *Los Angeles Noir,* arriving at last, is a kaleidoscopic collection filled with the ethos of noir pioneers Raymond Chandler and James M. Cain."
—*Los Angeles Times Book Review*

BROOKLYN NOIR
edited by Tim McLoughlin
350 pages, trade paperback original, $15.95
*Winner of Shamus Award, Anthony Award, Robert L. Fish Memorial Award; finalist for Edgar Award, Pushcart Prize.

Brand-new stories by: Pete Hamill, Arthur Nersesian, Ellen Miller, Nelson George, Nicole Blackman, Sidney Offit, Ken Bruen, and others.

"*Brooklyn Noir* is such a stunningly perfect combination that you can't believe you haven't read an anthology like this before. But trust me—you haven't . . . The writing is flat-out superb, filled with lines that will sing in your head for a long time to come."
—Laura Lippman, winner of the Edgar, Agatha, and Shamus awards

D.C. NOIR
edited by George Pelecanos
304 pages, trade paperback original, $15.95

Brand-new stories by: George Pelecanos, Laura Lippman, James Grady, Kenji Jasper, Jim Beane, Ruben Castaneda, Robert Wisdom, James Patton, Norman Kelley, Jennifer Howard, Jim Fusilli, Richard Currey, Lester Irby, Quintin Peterson, Robert Andrews, and David Slater.

"Fans of the [noir] genre will find solid writing, palpable tension, and surprise endings to keep them reading."
—*Washington Post*

CHICAGO NOIR
edited by Neal Pollack
252 pages, trade paperback original, $14.95

Brand-new stories by: Neal Pollack, Achy Obejas, Alexai Galaviz-Budziszewski, Adam Langer, Joe Meno, Peter Orner, Kevin Guilfoile, Bayo Ojikutu, M.K. Meyers, Todd Dills, Daniel Buckman, and others.

"*Chicago Noir* is a legitimate heir to the noble literary tradition of the greatest city in America. Nelson Algren and James Farrell would be proud."
—Stephen Elliott, author of *Happy Baby*